JOHN MARLYN

Under the Ribs of Death

With an Afterword by Neil Bissoondath

McCLELLAND & STEWART

The following dedication appeared in the original edition:

FOR RUTH
WHO KNOWS WHY

Copyright © 1957, 1964 in Canada, by McClelland & Stewart
Afterword copyright © 1990 by Neil Bissoondath

This book was first published in 1957 by McClelland & Stewart

All rights reserved. The use of any part of this publication reproduced, transmitted in any form or by any means, electronic, mechanical, photocopying, recording, or otherwise, or stored in a retrieval system, without the prior written consent of the publisher – or, in case of photocopying or other reprographic copying, a licence from the Canadian Copyright Licensing Agency – is an infringement of the copyright law.

All characters and incidents in the novel are fictional, and any resemblance to any person, living or dead, is purely coincidental.

Library and Archives Canada Cataloguing in Publication

Marlyn, John
Under the ribs of death

(New Canadian library)
Includes bibliographical references
ISBN 978-0-7710-9866-6

I. Title. II. Series.

PS8526.A67U62 1990   C813'.54   C89-095233-7
PR9199.3.M37U62 1990

We acknowledge the financial support of the Government of Canada through the Book Publishing Industry Development Program and that of the Government of Ontario through the Ontario Media Development Corporation's Ontario Book Initiative. We further acknowledge the support of the Canada Council for the Arts and the Ontario Arts Council for our publishing program.

Typesetting by M&S, Toronto
Printed and bound in Canada

McClelland & Stewart Ltd.
75 Sherbourne Street
Toronto, Ontario
M5A 2P9
www.mcclelland.com/NCL

7 8 9 10 11   11 10 09 08 07

> I was all ear,
> And took in strains that might create a soul
> Under the ribs of death.
>
> MILTON'S *Comus*

PART ONE

One

THE STREET was quiet now. His footsteps beat a lonely tattoo on the wooden sidewalk. The wind behind him ruffled his hair. Above him the lights went on, and over the face of Henry Avenue, half-hidden the moment before by soft, fraudulent shadows, there sprang into view an endless grey expanse of mouldering ruin. From the other side of the freight sheds came the rumble of the engines as they started on their nightly round of shunting box-cars to and fro.

Through the mingled odours of the neighbourhood, the pervading smell of coal gas and wood rot, there reached him suddenly the aroma of frying meat. He breathed it in hungrily and quickened his steps until he remembered that tonight there would be bologny for supper, with potato salad — yesterday's potatoes in vinegar and water with onions.

His shadow moved before him, rippling buoyantly over the uneven boards of the sidewalk. He watched it grow and a deep longing came over him. He saw himself the way he would be when he was a man, sitting in the lobby of the Hotel, bright button shoes on his feet, his hat and cane on a table nearby — rich and well fed and at ease there in one of the great leather chairs, smoking an after-dinner cigar.

Some day he would grow up and leave all this, he thought, leave it behind him forever and never look back, never remember again this dirty, foreign neighbourhood and the English gang who chased him home from school every day. He would forget how it felt to wear rummage-sale clothes and

9

be hungry all the time, and nobody would laugh at him again, not even the English, because by then he would have changed his name and would be working in an office the way the English did, and nobody would be able to tell that he had ever been a foreigner.

Sandor* crossed the street. He climbed to the bench in front of the house and peered into the front room. His father sat there in his working-clothes with his back to the light-bulb, reading; a sad grey figure with bent back and softly moving lips, his face aglow with the reflected light from the open book.

A faint scowl came over the boy's face. "Yah, books," he muttered, and dropped quietly from the bench and walked around to the side of the house, cursing as he stumbled over the rubbish that littered the back lane.

Now everything depended upon his mother. She had but to raise her voice and his father would give him a beating. He was late, his clothes were torn. He had not done his chores, and worst of all, he had been fighting again.

He crept to the open window of the kitchen and looked in. His mother was in the centre of the kitchen with the baby in her lap, humming while she swayed to and fro. It was the first time he remembered seeing her in repose. Her face was free of anxiety, her dark, luminous eyes sad in their depths. He wondered why both his parents always seemed so sad. When he looked at her again it seemed to him that he was looking at a stranger. He had not known that she was beautiful nor had he noticed that she looked so tired.

He tip-toed to the woodshed and had already begun to chop some kindling when he noticed a pile of it stacked beside the door.

"Christ-aw-mighty," he groaned. "Pa's done it awready."

He banged the door shut and walked into the kitchen, rejecting the solicitude that came into his mother's eyes.

"You been fighting," she said in a low voice . . . but not low enough.

---

*Pronounced *Shawndor* (Alexander).

There was a sudden stir in the front room. His heart sank within him as his father appeared.

The place where his lip was swollen began to throb now that he felt his father's eyes upon it. He lowered his head.

"Come with me."

As they walked into the front room his father reached for a length of cord from behind the door. "Only one thing I beat you for," he said. "Fighting. You're nearly twelve years old already — old enough to understand. Why do you fight? Does it prove something?"

He waited for an answer and then suddenly shouted, "Can you reason?"

His voice rang out. "Reason!"

He raised his arm.

Sandor closed his eyes as the cord came down across his shoulders. The pain was bearable. It was the world filled with hate and injustice and himself impotent in his humiliation that threatened his resolution not to cry. The cord came down again. He gritted his teeth.

He knew that he had only to cry out and the beating would stop. But it was a matter of pride with him not to do so. Instead he kicked and lashed out until, finally breaking loose, he ran into the kitchen and sat down on the window-sill.

Beating me for nothing, he thought, and bitterly wiped away his tears. He hasn't even got the right to beat me. He's not even my father. . . . His real father was an English lord. One day he would return and then this Joseph Hunyadi had better watch himself.

Out of the yielding stuff of memory he spun a familiar, consoling fantasy. There came back to him an image of a tall, distinguished man high above him on the deck of the ship that had brought him and his mother to Canada. Every day this man had appeared with an orange for him and a smile for his mother. He remembered the colour on his mother's cheeks and her embarrassment . . . and the mysterious death of an older brother who must also have been the son of that English lord. This Joseph Hunyadi had found out about it and killed him.

Sandor shivered, whether with fear or delight or with both he scarcely knew. There were times when Joseph Hunyadi looked at him strangely. Did he suspect? If he did . . .

He looked up and waved his mother away as she approached him with a face-cloth.

"Why do you fight?" she asked.

"I like to fight," he shouted.

She glanced into the next room. "Your father should hear you. Are you hurt?"

"No." He pulled away from her as she turned his head to the light.

"So here, take the towel and wipe your face," she said. "Now where's the messer to cut the bread?"

Sandor cupped his chin in his hand and gazed out into the back yard. Behind him his mother bustled about the kitchen. The baby began to cry. Upstairs two of the boarders were arguing. He stuck his head out of the window to listen. But they were talking Hungarian.

He wished that supper were over so that he could join the gang inside the red fence.

"Sandor." His mother pointed to the stove. "I want you should take this soup upstairs to Mr. Laszlo."

For the first time he became aware of the rich odour that filled the kitchen. Beef soup. He caught a fleeting vision of a brimming plateful of it with fine glistening bubbles of fat floating on the surface, with home-made noodles and the steaming fragrance of the vegetables — and meat, real meat that one could sink one's teeth into. It was more than he could bear.

"I won't take it," he shouted. "We eat bologny and Mr. Laszlo eats our soup. And he's not even paying."

"You're not ashamed?" his mother asked. She sighed. "Poor man. To be sick and so far from home."

"Yeah and we're not poor," he jeered. "No, we're millionaires. We like eatin' bologny every night for supper. Lookit my clothes. The English kids laugh at me in school. For over a year I been wantin' to get a bed insteada sleepin' on those chairs. An' lookit our house — not even a bedroom, no oilcloth on the floors and not even a icebox or a . . ."

His mother looked at him and nodded in the direction of the front room. He grew silent. It was not her fault. If she had her way the boarders upstairs would have left long ago, or at least started paying for their keep. But she was only a woman. In the end she always gave in to his father.

"Mr. Schwalbe has taken the kartofel salad for the others upstairs awready," she said. "Now go take the soup."

"Poor man," he snorted as he mounted the stairway. What did he have to complain about lying in his bed up there day after day and being waited on hand and foot? If anyone was to be pitied it was the family that was supporting him; and those three friends of his — eating and sleeping up there week after week, not paying a cent, and no one in the house daring to say a word because of his father who thought more of other people than he did of his own family.

His feet dragged. He would have hated them even if they were paying for their board and room. Mr. Schwalbe, who was paying, was even worse than the rest. They were all foreigners, every one of them, and as though that were not bad enough they were actually proud of their foreign, outlandish ways. Not one of them had yet made a serious effort to learn English.

He opened the door. They even smelled foreign, he thought, as he surveyed the grey sodden underwear and shirts and the coarse yellow socks hanging on the clothesline that had been suspended between the rafters.

His gaze shifted. He watched them silently, his eyes filled with hate. They were sitting in a semicircle on wickerwork trunks around Mr. Laszlo's cot, in a dim smoke-shrouded tableau, silently intent upon a photograph behind the candle above Mr. Laszlo's head. The expression on their faces annoyed him. It was as though they were glad and peaceful within themselves and unhappy only outside.

Probably wishing they were still in the old country, he thought, where the sun was always supposed to be brighter, where everyone laughed and sang all day, and where even a crust of bread tasted better. Well, why didn't they go back there, then? He placed the tray on the table and as he did so he noticed that they had covered the tablecloth with a newspaper.

"Yah, when it's too late," he muttered. Two days ago they had spilled coffee all over it. He noticed that the newspaper was a foreign one and stared at it resentfully. It was German. All he could read was the date — May 17, 1913. It reminded him, for the fourth or fifth time that day, that tomorrow was Saturday. And two days later it would be Monday, he thought. That's the kind of a world it was.

As he walked back he looked into the private cubicle of Mr. Schwalbe who was sitting there writing a letter. His red moonface glistened with sweat, his paunch rose and fell. The last time he had come waddling downstairs to pay for his room and board, he had unerringly and for the second month in a row chosen the only hour of the day when Frau Hunyadi was out of the house and Herr Hunyadi was alone in the front room. What happened then was almost beyond belief. Sitting at the kitchen table doing his homework, Sandor had overheard every word that had passed between them.

His father could truthfully say that he had not refused the money, but he had inquired with such solicitude and at such length into the state of Mr. Schwalbe's finances that the boarder, after a whining recital of his outstanding debts, had simply pocketed his money and gone upstairs whistling. That Sandor on the following evening had had to stand and humiliate himself in front of Mr. Letzman, the grocer, for a few cents' worth of ground meat — that, evidently, meant nothing to his father.

How could he be like that, Sandor wondered.

Some of the things he had done were almost unbelievable, like the time he had gone into partnership with Schwalbe and a friend of his who claimed to be a jeweller. What happened then was still not clear, but Schwalbe and this other man had taken his father to court and when the lawyers were through, Schwalbe had the shop, the money, and what was more

important, his father's watch-repairing tools. Witho
he had been unable to return to his own trade and had
take a job as a janitor.

And then one fine day who should return but Mr. Schwalbe
to weep on the Hunyadi doorstep and beat his breast with a
long tale of woe? He had remained there until the master of
the house not only forgave him, but fed him too, for the next
six months.

Sandor shook his head in sorrow and bewilderment. Then
his lips tightened. They had seen him.

"Here's Mr. Laszlo's supper," he said in German. "And
don't forget it's only for Mr. Laszlo — so don't the rest of you
go and gobble it up."

He ran down the stairs and into the kitchen. His parents
were waiting. He sat down and began to eat, not raising his
head until he became aware toward the end of the meal that
they were talking about him. He could tell by the way they
avoided his eyes.

They were speaking Hungarian, of which he remembered
scarcely enough to ask for a crust of bread. When they had
arrived in Winnipeg it was to find that for every Hungarian
there were twenty Austrians or Germans, so that over the
years the Hungarian language was heard less and less at home
and German, the second language in their mother-country,
more and more. English began to alternate with German when
Sandor was present; and it was only on rare occasions now,
or when they had something to keep from him, that they spoke
Hungarian.

As he sipped his coffee, he smiled to himself at the ease
with which he had nevertheless assessed the subject and the
overtones of their conversation. He was scarcely surprised
when his mother turned to him and inquired whether he would
like to go out with his father. "He is going to call on Mr.
Nagy," she said, "and then he is going back to work. He
thinks maybe you would like to help him."

Sandor lowered his head. It was not help his father wanted.
This was just his way of trying to make amends for the
beating.

But Mr. Nagy was the only Hungarian he knew who was an office man. To see him was one of the great and rare pleasures of Sandor's life. And the things he might hear in the building where his father worked — in the barber shop, in the billiard room, and the steam bath — intriguing, forbidden things, the mere prospect of which sent a shiver of delight through him. It was an unusual concession on his father's part to suggest that he might enter there. It was also very clever of him. The temptation was strong, but he struggled against it.

"I've still got my homework to do," he said.

It was an irreproachable reason for not going. Anything to do with learning was sacred in his father's eyes. That his father was probably reflecting at this very moment upon the fact that Sandor never did his homework on Friday night merely added piquancy to the situation.

That'll learn him how I feel when I get a licking for nothing, he thought. He raised his head. His elation collapsed at the weary look of resignation on his father's face.

"I can do my homework later," he said. "I got the whole week-end." His father had already risen. Sandor jumped to his feet. "Honest to God, Pa, I can do it later."

"So hurry awready," his mother exclaimed. "What are you waiting for? Go and get your father his cap."

She sighed as she wiped his face on her apron.

Sandor ran to the front room, found the cap and handed it to his father who was waiting for him at the door.

It was pleasantly cool outside. People sat on their doorsteps, the men quietly smoking, the women sewing or knitting, talking to their neighbours, watching the children at play. A westerly breeze stirred the manure lying on the road. All day long it had been drying in the sun, flattened by waggon wheels, shredded by sparrows. Now the wind brushed over it, with soft fingers pried it apart in little flakes and carried it to the billowy clouds of smoke gushing heavenward from the freight-yard engines, blotting out the early stars; and then settled it slowly and leisurely on the houses and heads of the people below.

From the red fence came a distant sound of laughter. That meant that Louis was in a good mood, Sandor thought. Right now he and the older fellows were probably sitting in the hide-out under the ramp smoking, and later on, if Louis had had a good haul, there would be a feast. He wished he were with them.

Above him he heard his father clearing his throat.

"Why did you fight?" he asked gruffly.

Sandor trembled.

The shame he had felt that afternoon standing in front of the class, spelling out his name for the new school nurse, while his teacher smiled and even his friends giggled and grimaced — the hatred he had felt for everybody and everything swept over him again.

"I didn't wanna fight," he cried. "I don't like fightin', but they made me." His voice grew shrill. "They call me . . ."

It rang in his ears, the way he heard it sometimes in his dreams before he wakened clammy with sweat and terror. "Hunky, Hunky — Humpy Ya Ya."

"Everywhere I go," he cried, "people laugh when they hear me say our name. They say 'how do you spell it?' The lady in the library made fun of me in fronta all the people yesterday when I took your book back and she hadda make out a new card. And the school nurse . . . everybody . . . even the postman laughs. If we changed our name I wouldn't hafta fight no more, Pa. We'd be like other people, like everybody else. But we gotta change it soon before too many people find out."

"So?" his father laughed, "and who are all these people?" And there was an indulgence in his voice that caused Sandor to take heart. The subject was an old and bitter one between them but tonight he felt that he might be able to make his father understand.

"The English," he whispered. "Pa, the only people who count are the English. Their fathers got all the best jobs. They're the only ones nobody ever calls foreigners. Nobody ever makes fun of their names or calls them 'bologny-eaters,' or laughs at the way they dress or talk. Nobody," he concluded bitterly, "'cause when you're English it's the same as bein' Canadian."

His father walked on a few steps before answering. But at his first words Sandor knew that it was hopeless. His father would never understand.

" . . . to the first point," he heard his father saying in German. "You told me the English make you fight. But not once have you told me that you tried to reason with them."

"But, Pa, for God's sake they chase me," he cried. "When they catch me they make me fight. How can I talk to them while they're punching me?" If he continued, he knew that he would start to cry.

He grew silent.

"It is not only stupid," his father said. "It is meaningless to call anyone a foreigner in this country. We are all foreigners here. And what is more I detect a prejudice against the English in what you say. This is wrong, as I have told you many times. Nationality is of no consequence. In the things of the spirit there is no such barrier."

Things of the spirit, Sandor scoffed. That's all he thinks about.

" . . . Spencer, Huxley, Darwin," his father said reverently. "If you must envy the English, let these be the Englishmen you envy and emulate."

"Yeah, and that Russian Kropotkin," Sandor thought, "and his Mutual Aid."

He loathed the very sound of their names. From their books, he suspected, had come his father's idea that success and wealth were things of no account. And suddenly he was glad that they were poor. His father's notion of sending him to University to become a benefactor and a philosopher and one of them humanitarians he was always talking about would never be realized. There would never be money enough. It was a small consolation.

As they approached Main Street, he felt his father's hand fall lightly on his shoulder. "You are ashamed of the wrong things, Sandor," he said. "It is shameful to be a money-chaser, to be dishonest, and to remain ignorant when the opportunity for learning is so great here. But to be ashamed of your name because you are Hungarian and are poor! When you grow up you will laugh to think that such things ever troubled you. . . . Do you understand, Sandor?"

"Yes, Pa."

"You will go further than I," his father continued. "Things will be easier for you. A man who is his own teacher is not complete. There must be implanted early the habits and discipline of learning. Even to think correctly must be taught. There is a logic in such things.

"And so ever higher from father to son," he went on. "My father was a peasant and his father a serf. Yes." He paused. "And I, I am a working man. But you will go to University, Sandor, and do great things. You will teach, as Kropotkin has said, that the war of each against all is not a law of nature. You will serve mankind . . ."

At this point Sandor noticed that they had reached the corner of Logan and Main. A few hundred yards down the street was the Chinese café the gang had broken into only last winter; not so long ago but that the police might still be searching for them. As he passed by it, he peered furtively from behind his father into the window.

He had nothing to be afraid of, he assured himself. He could say truthfully the rest of them had done it; that it was the older members of the gang who had broken in. It was also true, however, that he and Willi Schumacher had stood outside to keep watch. But on the other hand, he had made certain that Willi and not he had accepted the cigarettes and stuff which they had handed out through the window.

He breathed easier when they had passed the café door. In spite of himself, he could not help admiring the way Louis had arranged everything. He had planned the whole job with nothing more to go on than the fact that a new pane of glass had been set in the back window of the café. To the rest of the gang it had meant nothing at all. But Louis had immediately grasped what this might lead to. The putty in the window was still soft. That same night they had come back and removed it with a pocket knife.

Sandor nodded emphatically. Louis was a real leader.

Now and again he heard his father's voice. He was talking about the brotherhood of man. Somebody by the name of Spencer was wrong. He was a great man, but he was wrong. Not the survival of the fittest but mutual aid was the deciding factor . . .

Mutual aid, Sandor thought. He should come to school with me for only one day. The English gang would soon learn him mutual aid!

He walked on, suddenly feeling tired and depressed, until in the distance he saw the lights in Mr. Nagy's window. They brought back to mind the purpose of this call: to pay for the steamship ticket for Onkel Janos,* his mother's youngest brother. There was a picture of him in the front room; a young man, his lips upturned with laughter beneath a ferocious moustache, dressed in a sea-captain's uniform with buttons like saucers. Sandor recalled the stories his mother had told him about this uncle — stories out of which he had spun fantasies by the hour.

As far back as he could remember, he had dreamed of him, sailing on that sea which he had never been able to pronounce, to strange far-away ports. About him was an aura of treasure chests and peril and adventure.

But they were approaching Mr. Nagy's office, and beside Mr. Nagy, Onkel Janos' adventures faded away into insignificance. As they drew near, Sandor's pace quickened. His nostrils quivered. He opened the door and took a deep breath of the musty air. It was like wine. His eyes shone. He felt his heart pounding against his ribs.

The moment his father had passed by, he released the door and ran down the aisle between the bench and the long oak counter to the little gate at the end. He stood there and looked about him, entranced. Everything here, every scrap and par-

*Pronounced *Yawnosh* (John).

ticle of it, was invested with an air of enchantment. When he grew up he was going to be like Mr. Nagy. He gazed at the great oak desk strewn over with folders, the encrusted marble inkwell he remembered so well, the same great ledger with its clasped lock (what secrets did it contain?), the same dusty brown-paper parcel, and on the wall above the safe a Notary's Certificate in a green frame.

In this little office were power and prestige and wealth. If you wanted to buy or sell or rent a house, you came to Mr. Nagy. If you needed a steamship ticket, citizenship papers, an insurance policy, or you wanted to change your name, Mr. Nagy was the man to see. Police trouble, money trouble, trouble with your neighbours, you called on Mr. Nagy. If you were scared of the Health Inspector or you wanted a licence for anything, Mr. Nagy was always there. He slept in a little cubicle in the back of his office — always polite, always ready with advice, always smiling and ready to oblige. People spoke to him with respect, even people who were not Hungarians. And Sandor had heard it whispered that there was a fortune locked away in that safe.

His glance shifted to the beaverboard partition behind which lay Mr. Nagy's private office. He caught the murmur of voices, and as he strained against the gate to hear what was being said, they grew suddenly loud; there was the scraping of chairs and then Mr. Nagy's voice in German, "In a few minutes . . ."

The door opened. Sandor caught a fleeting glimpse of Mr. Kostanuik, Mr. Nagy's contractor. Then Mr. Nagy appeared, a pallid little man — with a mouth, Sandor now recalled with sudden indignation, which Mr. Schwalbe once said reminded him of a toad. That's only because he knows Pa don't like Mr. Nagy, he thought. But at the same time he was compelled to admit that there was some truth in Schwalbe's sneer that Mr. Nagy looked dusty. He had the feeling that if Mr. Nagy were ever to go out in a strong wind he would come back clean, except for his nose. There the dust seemed to have settled permanently in little nodules under the skin, making it knobby and shapeless. But that didn't matter very much since Mr.

Nagy always reminded him, when looked at from the side, of that picture of a Roman emperor in his Latin reader. Sideways, his nose looked fierce and splendid.

He smiled shyly as Mr. Nagy looked down at him, and was rewarded with a few words. "Well, well, Sandor. And how are you? Your father now trusts you to come alone? That is fine."

Sandor looked at him in bewilderment. "No — I —" he stammered, and looked behind him, and discovered his father sitting on the bench reading. "Pa," he cried, "Mr. Nagy's waiting."

"Ah, good evening, Herr Hunyadi."

They began to talk in Hungarian. Sandor shifted in an agony of suspense. He caught a word here and there, but was unable to tell whether his father was being friendly or not. He watched him counting out four dollars and laying them on the counter — that was for the ticket for Onkel Janos; another five dollars for the instalment on the house; and then two toward the debt to Mr. Schwalbe's partner.

Mr. Nagy made out the receipts. They were still talking. Sandor looked up anxiously at Mr. Nagy. He saw the smile on his face; but that told him nothing. Mr. Nagy always smiled. Finally, he could bear it no longer. "Pa, talk English," he cried shrilly. "I can't understand."

"Ho," Mr. Nagy said. "So you want to understand?" He leaned out over the gate and patted him on the head. "Wait," he said. "I have something." He winked, and reached under the counter.

Sandor had almost forgotten. After every payment, it was Mr. Nagy's custom to give him a small gift — a pencil, a tin whistle; sometimes, on rare occasions, a small bag of raspberry drops. Sandor's mouth watered. He hoped it would be raspberry drops.

To his astonishment, Mr. Nagy thrust a small Union Jack under his nose. Sandor gulped. Then suddenly his face lit up. "It's for the anniversary of Queen Victoria's birthday," he cried, grasping it and waving it excitedly. "You know sumpin', Mr. Nagy? My birthday's on the same day as Queen Victoria's. May Twenty-fourth's my birthday."

He stopped abruptly and glanced at his father out of the corner of his eyes. At that moment he wanted more than anything in the world to impress Mr. Nagy, to tell him about the school contest; the composition he had almost finished about "Victoria Day — What It Means to Me." . . . But his father, if he heard of it, would insist on helping him and would change it and write down things that would spoil his chance of winning the prize.

"We're gonna have a holiday from school," he finished lamely, and observed that the flag was beginning to tear away from the stick. He lowered it so as not to embarrass Mr. Nagy, who was smiling approvingly at him — not his business smile but a warm, special smile just for him.

And suddenly it came to Sandor that if his father had stayed in the old country his birthday would have been just a birthday and nothing more. What was May the Twenty-fourth in Hungary but just another day? Here in Canada it was a national holiday. There would be a parade with soldiers and bands. The streets would be decorated. He sighed as his father took him by the hand. He waved to Mr. Nagy as he walked out.

On the street once more he thought of the prize he would win. He knew he was going to win. He had to. Nothing could stop him.

And yet it was not for the prize alone that he had worked so hard, but in order to show the English gang what he could do. He laughed quietly to himself. They were English and yet it was his birthday that came on Queen Victoria Day. It was the kind of joke he appreciated. He chuckled to himself and lengthened his stride to match his father's.

No, it was certainly not the prize itself he was after. What good was it anyhow? A book — and on Canadian History of all things. He had therefore promised it to Mary Kostanuik. His smile widened and softened; a half-shameful, tender expression came over his face. She believed everything he told her. He remembered how she had cried the day her family had moved away from Henry Avenue.

Sandor looked up at his father uneasily. His mind drifted. He glanced absently into the window of a second-hand store.

That day he had watched the movers carrying out the Kostanuiks' furniture, little things had come back to him, warnings of the new status they had achieved, which until then he had noticed but not fully understood: Kostanuik's steady job, winter and summer, with Mr. Nagy, and the white store-bread he had seen in their house, Mary's store dresses, and the fact that Mrs. Kostanuik had over the months slowly stopped borrowing lard and sugar and things from her neighbours. And there was the new floor-lamp in their front room.

If the Kostanuiks could buy a new lamp and eat store bread and move away to a better neighbourhood, why couldn't his own family do the same? Mr. Kostanuik, before he had got this job with Mr. Nagy, had only been a carpenter — an ordinary working man — while his own father was a watchmaker. Why, then? Because his father didn't believe in getting rich, because he always tried to see how other people felt and never worried about the feelings of his own family, that was why.

Sandor came to with a start. They had arrived.

The barber shop was empty. But the peppermint-striped sheets hanging over the chairs gave it a festive air that was augmented by the clean, sweet odour of the lotions and the soap. And there was something gay in the glittering reflection of the coloured bottles in the mirrors. The private white shaving-mugs, row upon row of them, each in its tiny cubicle, proclaimed this a man's world. Beyond lay the pool room. Sandor's face brightened as they entered it. He began straining at his father's hand. He always had the feeling that something was about to happen here. It was noisy and smoky and exciting. He looked about him to see if he could catch sight of Mr. Friedel, the owner. Mr. Friedel usually gave him a package of cough drops or peppermints. Next to Mr. Nagy he liked Mr. Friedel better than any man he knew.

Through the smoke spiralling lazily upward to the green

enamel reflectors he caught a glimpse of the men who were playing. But it was their talk that fascinated him. From the looks on their faces, yellow and seared when they came within the glare of the lights, he was sure they were talking about women. He tried to stop, if only for a moment, to overhear something really gross. He hung back tugging at his father's arm and was unexpectedly rewarded by a mild obscenity — which no member of the gang would have deigned to utter — on the lips of a young man who looked directly at him as they passed. Sandor stared at him enviously. He was dressed in the height of fashion; his hair, parted in the centre, was smeared down flat and smooth against his scalp. Beneath a dove-grey waistcoat, across which hung a series of gold ornaments on his watch-chain, he wore a light-coloured shirt with armbands. His collar reached almost to his ears. But it was his shoes that wrung a sigh from Sandor's lips: glittering black patent-leather, they were, with dove-grey buttons that matched perfectly the cuffs of his tight narrow trousers.

He turned back to look at him as his father hurried him along. The next moment he was on the back stairs. The air was heavy and damp. Here, too, at the foot of the stairs, he dragged his feet. To the left was the steam bath. A month or so ago, as he was passing by, the door had opened and he had seen several naked steam-enshrouded figures in the act, so it appeared to him, of enthusiastically flagellating themselves with bundles of twigs. He made only a half-hearted attempt to hang back here, however. One night a week those members of the gang who could raise the money went to the Public Baths where they could observe all the naked men they wanted to. But what was the good of that? It was not naked men they wanted to see.

His father left him in what Sandor called his office: a dimly lit little hole walled in on three sides by packing-cases which were stuffed with soap and towels and water-stained cartons. A packing-case served as a table, an upturned box as a chair. From a row of nails hung a few damp bills and receipts and some bath tickets.

Sandor brushed aside a cockroach and sat down. He

removed an invoice from one of the nails and glanced at it absently. It was depressing down here. He wanted to get upstairs again. He rose to his feet. "Pa," he shouted, "I wanna help you. Kin I?"

"Stay where you are," his father called back. "I won't be long."

He sat down again, listening to the rattle of the furnace, thinking of the work his father had to do, the long hours he spent here from six in the morning until six at night, every day of the week, and every night after supper to return and look after the furnace and clean the bath tubs. And besides this, there was the stove in the steam bath, the floors in the pool room and the barber shop, the mirrors and the sinks.

For eleven dollars a week. . . . This was what happened to you when you worked with your hands. And all he had to do was get some paying boarders upstairs and save the money he got from them and in a year or so he would be able to buy some tools and open his own watch-repair store. But no, he had to . . .

An angry roar from the top of the stairs brought him suddenly to his feet. It was some time before he recognized the voice. It was Mr. Friedel's. There must be some mistake, he thought. Mr. Friedel wasn't like that. He couldn't be talking in such a tone to his father, who had come to Canada on the same ship with him and from the same village in Hungary. Mr. Friedel was almost a relative. He was a *landsmann.*

"Joseph! Where the hell are you?"

Sandor held his breath. He heard his father answering as he hauled a log to the furnace.

Then came the owner's voice again. "Well, damn your soul, what do you think I'm paying you for? To sit on your ass all day? Get some steam in those boilers . . ."

It went on and on. The words were like blows, only they hurt more, more than any pain that Sandor had ever known. They went deeper. They were already a part of him. Every time he looked at his father from now on they would come back. He felt a sudden, overwhelming need to take them upon himself, to shield his father from them. His father was not made to cope with such things. They were foreign to him. In his world people did not talk like that.

In helpless anguish he pounded the fist of his right hand into the palm of his left until he heard his father's voice again. It was quiet and strong, the way he had not dared to hope that it might be, with the unhurried calm dignity of his father's way of living in it.

But the owner was still at the head of the stairs, his bellow crashing through the cool, reasoned texture of his father's words. "Those boilers are good enough for me. You just get more steam up, you hear? And pretty damn fast or get the hell out."

Then silence, and Sandor, his head in his hands, crying with deep racking sobs. That's how it was, then. It was not the first time his father had been spoken to this way. He could tell.

His father, who was wise and knew four languages and read deep books, who loved all men and whose only thought was to help others, yelled at and ordered around like a dog! He worked so hard in this dirty, stinking hole that sometimes when he came home at night he could not even straighten his back. And what was it for? So they could eat bologny and onions and dress in rummage-sale clothes. That's how it was. If you were rich, nobody would yell at you. Nobody yelled at the owner or Mr. Nagy. Why couldn't his father understand that?

The furnace door clanged. Sandor heard footsteps approaching, and his father came in. He looked old and tired. His back was bowed; his hands hung at his sides. Sandor's lips trembled and a sob broke from his throat.

"Pa," he began. But the word choked him.

"Pa," he said, under his breath.

His father held out his hand. They walked silently up the stairs, through the pool room and barber shop, and out into the street.

Two

THE SKY was bright, the air cool and clear. From over the edge of the Mancheski roof the sun appeared, turning to molten gold the miasmic puddles in a lane off Henry Avenue, gilding with brief splendour the ash heaps and the mounds of refuse that lay in the yard.

Morning had come and, with the sun, life stirred and quickened in the houses, and in the puddles and garbage heaps wriggled and rejoiced.

Men appeared with lunch pails. The smoke of the first freight-yard engine darkened the distant sky.

A shaft of sunlight entered the kitchen window. It struck the pillow of Sandor Hunyadi sleeping there on his makeshift bed of chairs. Ever since the Mancheski chimney had collapsed, the sun had been wakening him. He turned, shifting cautiously; on restless nights the two middle chairs sometimes slid out from under him.

In half sleep he burrowed deeper into the enormous goose-feather quilt that covered the chairs. In the hallway, a stair tread creaked. The coffee pot simmered quietly. A mouse squeaked behind the baseboard under the sink.

He had not done his homework last night. Miss Thatcher would . . .

Suddenly he leaped out of bed. Today was Victoria Day. He slipped into his clothes, poured himself some coffee, cut himself a piece of bread, and with his mouth still full ran out into the lane and on up to Logan Avenue to the centre of town.

Two hours later as he walked up Main Street toward Portage under the waving flags, jostling his way through the crowds, past store windows gay with red, white and blue streamers and shields and pictures of the old Queen draped in Union Jacks, there grew within him the belief, nursed to half-playful yet earnest conviction, that all of this — the people on the streets, the decorations, the proclamation of the holiday, the closed stores and the parade that was to come — all this was for him, in honour of his birthday. This was his day.

He knew that it was not so and admitted it. But on the edge of awareness, in a recess which Queen Victoria had never entered, it was Sandor Hunyadi's birthday and a public holiday. It made him feel that people were glad he had been born. Flag in hand he pressed on, looking up into the faces of the men and women about him, throwing up his heels, with an exultant sense of well-being, of oneness with the world around him and everyone in it.

If only he could tell them, he thought. How surprised they would be to learn that this boy whom they passed with scarcely a glance was something of a celebrity — and not only because it was his birthday. Yesterday afternoon at school, Miss Thatcher had called him to the front of the room and there to the astonishment of the whole class had announced that Sandor Hunyadi (possibly the worst student in the school and certainly the worst in her class) had won first prize for his essay on Victoria Day.

But that was not all. Accompanied by no less a person than the principal, he had made a triumphal tour of every classroom in the school to recite his composition. His new status was brought home to him during recess. Small boys jumped out of his way without being pushed; boys he had never spoken to came up to him to clap him on the back and congratulate him and to look at the book. Best of all, however, was his meeting with Mary Kostanuik in the school hallway under the stairs, where nobody could see them. He found her crying because she thought he had forgotten her. And why should he forget? Because he was famous.

Sandor's heart gave a great leap at the memory of it. He nodded to himself as he crossed Portage Avenue. What she had said was nothing more than the truth. He was known to every student in the school. It was also true that this day of triumph was not completely unalloyed. The English gang had threatened him with a beating such as he had never received for daring, as one of them expressed it, even to show his hunky face in their class-room. At four o'clock they had chased him almost nine blocks out of his way. And when he finally got home, it was to discover that Willi Schumacher, coming belatedly to offer congratulations, had informed his parents about what had happened at school that day. He had also given them a fairly accurate idea of the sentiments expressed in the composition. Sandor shivered. He had never seen his father so angry. All evening he had listened to a furious . . . But no. He shook his head. He would not think of it. Not on his birthday. He would not spoil it. Besides, there was nothing new, either in the quarrel with his father or in the trouble with the English gang. He thrust it from him and by the time he had reached the next block he had almost forgotten it in anticipating the pleasure that awaited him at Mary's party. He had never seen the inside of her house, nor had he ever been to a real party. Her description of the things they would have to eat made him suddenly light-headed with hunger. He swallowed, and at that moment caught sight of a small boy in a blue-white sailor suit crying as he dragged an enormous silk flag behind him. Sandor eyed him thoughtfully. He was obviously from the south end of town.

"Where's your Ma?" Sandor asked.

"I don't know," the boy wailed. "My name ith George Aikinth and I live on . . ." Sandor grabbed at the flag. The boy shrieked. He clung to it tenaciously. Sandor swung and caught him on the ear. A look of outrage and incredulity spread over the boy's face. The blow silenced him. This was unfortunate. If he had continued to scream he might have emerged from the encounter with his pockets unrifled. Sandor ran through them expertly. He extracted two coppers, a pearl-handled knife, a bundle of bird pictures and a coloured handkerchief.

As he thrust them into his pocket the boy began to shriek. Sandor gave him another cuff and ran. Two blocks away, shoving and pushing his way through the crowd that lined the road, he reached the curb and sat down.

A mounted policeman rode by. In the distance he heard the first faint wail of the bagpipes. He jumped to his feet and began waving his silk flag. Mr. Nagy's had long since been torn to shreds. Ah . . . there they were; with a bronzed giant at their head. And behind him, their skirts swirling, with cheeks blown large and ruddy, the band. The music swelled. The crowd cheered. Sandor hopped from leg to leg, yelling at the top of his voice. The bagpipes were directly in front of him now, the music splendidly shrill and wild, seizing him on a tumultuous wave that bore him aloft, to soar triumphantly in harmony with himself and the world at his feet.

As far as he could see were marching men with banners and distant bands. And on either side, to the very horizon, stretched the cheering crowds. All over Canada in every little village and town and in every city they cheered him, and the oneness of birthday and holiday was affirmed. As long as he lived, they would be celebrated together. This was his, he thought fiercely, his alone, and no one could ever take it from him.

The music wavered, grew dim and was gone. He felt cold. But now a company of soldiers appeared, and another band. Sandor raised his flag again and yelled until he was hoarse. When it was over, he was exhausted. He removed the staples from the flag and folded it carefully in his blouse pocket.

Humming "Men of Harlech" under his breath, he made his way back to Logan Avenue. A few yards from the Salter Street bridge he walked into a store, bought himself a one-cent stick of liquorice and asked for the time.

A moment later he was running up the street in the direction of the park. Half a block before he reached it, a feeling of uneasiness came over him — not because of any difficulty he expected in getting the flowers, but because they didn't seem to be quite the right kind of gift.

Mary had told him that all the guests were bringing something. But she had mentioned it so casually that he had been ashamed to ask what he was expected to bring. There was no use asking his parents — what did they know about parties? In his plight he had turned to Willi Schumacher. Willi had gone to his brother, a shoe salesman on Selkirk Avenue. He, if anyone, was sure to know.

In due time, Willi had returned. Flowers were the thing. The only time he remembered people taking flowers to anyone, Sandor reflected, was when they were sick or dead. Still, Willi's brother ought to know what he was talking about. The stories of his exploits with women were beyond belief; the things he had seen and done to women while fitting them with shoes had so filled the gang with envy that it had become the ambition of even the least member to make the selling of shoes his life's occupation when he was a man.

Sandor's confidence in his judgment grew as he recalled this. He looked around him, peered over the hedge which surrounded the park, and crawled through to the nearest flower bed. He selected those with the longest stems, pulling them up by the roots; they would probably last longer that way, he reasoned. When he had as many as he could hold in one hand, he crawled out, looked up and down the street, and then leaped to his feet and ran. He was in the heart of enemy territory here. Most of the English gang lived in this neighbourhood. He moved cautiously. Danger lurked on every street corner, in the open lots covered with weeds, behind every stack of cord-wood in the wood-yards. He kept to the centre of the road until he reached the bridge.

There, breathing easier, he began to arrange the flowers, transferring them one by one from his right hand to his left and shaking off the earth that clung to their roots.

He had passed the steps that led down to Higgins Avenue when he became conscious of the sound of running footsteps ahead of him. He looked up. They were all carrying little flags in their hands; the sound of his nickname was on their lips — "Ya, Ya, Hunky, Hunky, Humpy Ya Ya."

"Not today!" he murmured under his breath. "Geez, not today."

He stared at them, unable to move, as they came running toward him. It was always that way. There was always the desire to run and to remain, the feeling which he could never admit to himself — that he almost wanted them to catch him because when he was caught he was with them and one of them, even though they beat him. There was always the feeling, when he was being chased by them, that he was running away from the very thing he wanted most.

As he stood there, he remembered their warning. If they caught him today they would beat him unmercifully.

They had stopped calling him by that name. He turned to run back to the steps and instantly he heard it again, loathsome and shrill and filling him with the terror of his dreams. His steps faltered. He looked back. The hope that some day, in some miraculous way, they would stop hating him and accept him as one of themselves — the hope he had secretly nurtured so long — now suddenly died as it always did.

"Christ-aw-mighty!" he screamed. "I'll show you." He climbed up the railing of the bridge and looked down. He had only to let himself go now, to lean forward — to do nothing at all — and he would shut the sound of that name out of his mind forever. He would be rid of them and all his troubles would come to an end.

The cindered track looked soft and grey and as friendly as the blanket on his bed. He saw himself falling gently upon it and the thought came to him that nobody would have to bring him any flowers, because he already had them in his hand. And then as though from an immense height he observed himself lying there silent and still with a faint mocking smile on his face, his right hand crossed over his chest with the flowers over his heart. And the English gang would look down and see what they had done and feel sorry, but it would be too late. And George Martin, who always hung back when they chased him and only called him by that name so as not to be thrown out of the gang, he would cry for him and turn on the others for driving Sandor Hunyadi to his death.

And at school everyone would be in mourning and the teachers and pupils would attend his funeral to weep at his grave while the principal read to them again Sandor Hunyadi's prize-winning essay. Yes . . . while at home his father, whose hair had turned grey overnight, would sit alone in the dark front room knowing in his heart that he could have saved the life of his son. He would be sorry now. But it would be too late. And every year on his son's birthday . . .

With a start he remembered that it was his birthday. He looked back and was surprised to find that they were still so far away. They had stopped to see what he would do. When he looked down at the track again his stomach suddenly heaved and there was the sour taste of liquorice in his mouth.

He wiped away his tears, climbed down from the railings and ran back to the stairs. On the second landing, he heard them coming after him. He reached the freight-yards, dropped down on his hands and knees and crawled under the couplings of the first box-cars, ran diagonally across an empty space of track to a day coach, walked quietly through it, and made his way under another two box-cars. His breath was hot and laboured. He had torn one of his stockings. There was a hole in the knee of his Sunday pants. But that didn't matter, he told himself. He was safe, and it was still his birthday and he was still going to the party. Nothing, absolutely nothing, was going to spoil this day for him.

He hurried on toward Jarvis Avenue. There was a horse trough there where he could wash the rust off his hands and the cinders and the grime from the flowers.

When he had done this he continued on his way. A few minutes later he was knocking on the front door of Mary Kostanuik's home.

A stout woman in a flaming red dress opened it. She stood directly before him, so close that on looking up he saw only her forehead above the trough of her ponderous breasts. He stepped back and her face appeared; from the little red mouth a smile was fading. He heard the damp creaking of her corsets. Her bosom heaved and her face vanished again, and when it reappeared he found himself staring straight into her eyes which glared down at him with such hostility that his lips began to tremble. He had expected her to welcome him with open arms. She had always been fond of him. When she lived on Henry Avenue he had spent almost as much time in her home as in his own. He recalled the time his mother had been sick. For three weeks Mrs. Kostanuik had looked after her and had done the washing and baking and cooking, besides attending to him and the baby. And that weekend when the Kostanuiks were cleaning the bedbugs out of their house they had come to live with his family. They had been good neighbours, and on Henry Avenue that meant something more than just living next door without quarrelling.

He sensed that she was still staring at him. To cover his embarrassment he held up the flowers.

"I brung some flowers, Mrs. Kostanuik," he said. "Mary tole me everybody was supposed to bring sumpin'."

She smiled then, but in a way he had never seen anyone smile before — only with her mouth. It made him feel suddenly ashamed without knowing why.

His arm grew tired holding the flowers above his head, and as she continued to stare at them a feeling of panic came over him. If she refused to accept them it meant he could not join the party. And now more than ever he wanted to go. Through the half-open door came the sound of an exciting murmur and the smell of food. He raised the flowers still higher. She took them from him.

"Wait," she said, and turned and was gone. The word she had spoken hung in the tremulous silence not at all like an invitation, he thought, but more like a threat; as though she had gone into the house to prepare some punishment for him.

He stared at the door in bewilderment. What had happened to her? On Henry Avenue she would have taken the flowers and kissed him for bringing them. What was wrong, then? It was not the flowers, for she had accepted them, however unwillingly. Maybe it was something he had said. But no. She had glared at him the moment she had set eyes upon him. The truth was that she didn't want him to come. But why? . . . Well, the hell with her. Mary wanted him to come. She had pleaded with him to accept. It was her party, and what Mary wanted she usually got. Suddenly he grinned. He picked thoughtfully at a paint blister under the mail-box. They were most likely quarrelling over him right now. His grin widened as he remembered the effect of Mary's small rages upon her parents. He found another blister.

The door creaked. He turned and there she was, smiling and holding out her hand to him, all in white but for a pale pink ribbon at her waist, and another tied in a bow in her blonde hair. She stood there, her head tilted to one side, looking at him out of the corner of her eyes. The arm she held out to him was bare and pink and round, and at the sight of it he remembered an afternoon when it had been raining outside and the two of them were standing at the window watching and listening, tired of playing office, and she with her head tilted in just this way, asking him to tell her again the story of his pirate uncle. He had suggested instead that they play a new game — doctor and nurse. In the boarder's room, pretending to treat her for some weird ailment, he had undressed and examined her. All that he was able to remember, however, was his disappointment. Beyond this, try as he might, he could remember nothing.

He stared at her arm, and dimly saw her lying pink and chubby on a blanket, kicking her feet in the air. He must have tickled her for suddenly the sound of her laughter came back to him.

The very thing he wanted so urgently to recall; that eluded him. The mystery and the tormenting wonder, of which he was still so abysmally ignorant, would somehow be cleared up, he thought, if only he could recapture what he had seen on that afternoon.

He wondered if she had ever thought of it; but she had probably been too young. . . .

He took a deep breath. "I brung you some flowers," he began.

"They're just lovely," she exclaimed, "and I'm so glad you could come." She took his hand and led him into the house. "It's going to be a wonderful party," she said. "My cousin is here. I told him all about the prize you won at school and everything."

But Sandor scarcely heard her. He had been transported into a new world. The hall through which he was passing had floors as smooth and polished as glass, painted to look like oak, and on the walls the burlap had been divided into squares, and every square looked like a solid block of marble . . . and the doors had little windows in them, the wooden parts painted to look like the floor. Above the marbled burlap, wallpaper with great clusters of lush red roses. . . . They passed beneath a mirror in a heavy gilded frame with red rosebuds in the corners. Everything was clean and rich-looking. He glanced at Mary with a new respect and with sudden envy. But it was the floors that fascinated him. They were clean enough to eat on. He was so engrossed in them that he scarcely noticed where she was leading him.

When he looked up he discovered that he was in a room filled with women and children. He felt their eyes upon him and the instant disapproval of the women who sat facing him in a long straight line against the far wall, examining him with the same expression coming over their features that he had seen on Mrs. Kostanuik's face — a collective grimace which the older children around him seemed immediately to understand. He sensed that they were drawing away from him and as he glanced at them, the boys dressed in dark shorts and clean fresh blouses with bright new shoes, he saw himself as they saw him, as something darkly alien in their midst and yet disturbingly familiar. A glimmer of understanding came to him. He felt that he knew now why Mrs. Kostanuik hated him and had never invited his mother to visit her, and why all these women continued to glare at him. He was something out of their past. All of them had come from Henry Avenue. He was everything they wanted to forget.

But that these women, foreigners every one of them, with probably not ten words of English among them and for whom he had nothing but contempt, whose husbands were mere bricklayers and plasterers and sewer-diggers who happened to have steady jobs — that such people should look down on him filled him with rage. If they had been English, he told himself, it might have been excusable. but who were they, to stare at him like that? He had, after all, been invited. His gift had been accepted. It was Mary's party, and he had as much right to be here as they had — even more. It was not Mary who had invited them; it was her mother.

The room had grown silent. It was empty now of the excitement in which he had longed to participate. He lowered his eyes. There was something loathsome in the thought that his presence had destroyed it. For the first time that day he remembered the gang, lying in the cool weeds, inside the red fence. That was where he belonged, he thought.

He felt someone tugging at his hand. It was Mary. Suddenly he hated her. She must have known how it would be. She might have warned him — or better still, not invited him at all.

"I'm goin' home," he whispered. "I shouldn't've come."

"You're not going home, so there," she said. "You're going to stay and have a good time at my party."

He followed her into the hall to a small closet under the stairs. When he switched the light on, she bent down and from one of the shelves took out a box containing shoe-brushes and tin of polish.

"Now, you brush your shoes," she whispered, "you bad boy, you! I'm going to get Mamma's sewing-basket and then I'll come right back." She opened the door and was gone.

Maybe it'll be all right, he thought, as he set to work. Maybe when she's fixed my clothes and my shoes are clean it'll . . .

"Anyway," he said, "I'm not gonna go until I've et." Dropping to one knee he began to polish his shoes. He had barely finished when the door opened and closed. Mary stood before him with a small basket, holding her fingers to her lips.

"Mamma's in the front hall looking for me," she whispered.

He saw the laughter in her eyes, the bubbling-over irrepressibly into a silver peal that held him fascinated. She laughed quietly, her hands at her sides, her eyes closed.

Neither his parents nor any of his acquaintances had ever laughed like this. He continued to stare down at the crown of her head long after she had threaded the needle and begun to sew his stocking. She was sewing it to his underwear. He could feel it tightening.

"Your mother didn't want me to come, did she?" he asked.

"Don't you say that," she cried. "I told Mamma if you didn't come I wouldn't have no party."

"I hope it'll be all right," he said nervously.

"I told Mamma that you're going to sit at the head table," she continued. "Mamma has to sit on one side of me and Georgie on the other side, because he's my cousin."

She worked for a while in silence, growing intent upon her task, and suddenly to his astonishment announced that she had finished. She had barely started, he thought, and looked down to see what she had done, and turned away appalled. His pants had been pleated. His stocking looked as though it had grown an enormous wart.

She smiled at him expectantly.

"That's — that's swell," he said hoarsely. "Thanks, a million."

She flushed with pleasure. "Now we're all ready for the party," she cried, and turning to him with her fingers pressed to her lips, she opened the door and led him into the hallway.

At the far end of the living-room, Sandor saw her mother. In the same instant she caught sight of him. She rushed forward, grabbed Mary's arm and dragged her off to the kitchen.

No one seemed to have noticed. And no one paid any further attention to him. He walked slowly into the dining-room and suddenly he stopped.

Two large tables, end to end, and a smaller one — covered with more cakes, sandwiches, cookies, pies and fruit than he had ever seen in his life. He eyed them greedily and edged over so that he could rush for them when the time came. It was highly unlikely, he thought, in view of what had just happened, that he would be allowed to sit there. As he manoeuvred into position, he became conscious that he was being watched. Out of the corner of his eyes, he saw a tall, dark boy a few years older than he standing beside him.

Sandor moved back. The boy followed. He was joined by another of about Sandor's own height. They whispered and came toward him. He withdrew into the living-room. They separated as they approached him. He was glad that he had his back to the wall; they were on either side of him now.

"You guys lookin' for trouble?" he asked in a low voice.

"Mary told me all about you," the taller boy said. "An orator! You look more like you should be collectin' bottles and rags."

He plucked at Sandor's blouse. "That the best clothes you got?" They laughed.

"I guess you're figurin' on settin' at that table and gobblin' up everything you can lay your hands on," the tall boy continued. "I'll tell you somethin'. You're gonna sit with the babies — right there at that small table. My auntie told me so."

"You don't deserve to eat anyhow," the second boy exclaimed. "You didn't bring nuthin'. Flowers! I saw watcha brung. A buncha flowers. I betcha you stole 'em."

"You're a liar," Sandor said. "An' wot did you bring anyway?"

"What does anybody bring to a party?" The tall boy glanced at his nails. "I brought the cake that's sittin' in the centre of the table — the pink one."

"An' I brung salmon sandwiches."

Sandor looked at them silently. They were telling the truth. But why — for Chris'sake why hadn't she told him? All she had to say was to bring something to eat. Did she think he was so poor he couldn't even afford a cake or a few fish sandwiches? And the flowers. If it hadn't been for those damn flowers he wouldn't have torn his clothes while he was crossing the tracks. And he had risked being pinched for them.

"Anybody can bring sandwiches and stuff like that," he said. "At real parties you bring flowers or . . ."

He sensed rather than saw the glance thrown by the older boy at his companion, and prepared for what was to come by pressing back against the wall. But their next move caught him unprepared.

With one accord, each of them suddenly placed a foot upon his instep. The taller boy gave him a shove. Sandor surged toward the younger, who shoved him back again. He rocked back and forth between them like a weighted dummy, expecting that any moment the real blow would fall. But nothing happened. On Henry Avenue when you played this sort of game with an outsider, you played for keeps. This was kid's stuff. He smiled as they pushed him back and forth.

The older boy saw this and began punching him: the younger one followed suit. They had, however, Sandor observed, made the fatal error of allowing him the use of his hands. As he fell toward the taller one he brought his fist back. With all the momentum of his body and the swing of his arm he punched him in the stomach.

The boy grunted and turned grey. He doubled up and fell. His companion fled. Sandor walked slowly to the kitchen. He would explain to Mary what had happened. He caught the edge of the door, swung it back, and looked in. The kitchen was filled with women. Mary was sitting in a corner.

He walked back to the living-room. He was so hungry that the mere thought of it was painful. He had told his mother that he was going to a party, and if he left now, by the time he got home supper would be over. He sat down listlessly and waited. It was some time before he became aware that the house had grown strangely quiet. A group of younger children were sitting in a semicircle under the archway, staring at him with large, round, inquisitive eyes. On the far side of the dining-room he saw Mary's cousin lying in a stuffed chair; a crowd of women hovered over him, making sympathetic and indignant noises. In the centre he caught a glimpse of Mary patting her cousin's forehead on which someone had placed a wet cloth.

She likes him better'n she does me, he thought, and snorted with disgust. That cry-baby, bawling and making all that trouble because of a little punch in the belly! And what was he crying about anyhow? Did he think he could go around punching people and not get hurt?

He noticed that the children who had been sitting in the archway were getting up and one by one walking back into the other room; all but a few stubborn ones who sat there in wide-eyed silence looking at him until their mothers came and, with one fearful eye on him and the other full of maternal solicitude, snatched them up and fled.

He crossed his legs stubbornly. Some day, he thought, he would show them. Some day he would own a house that would make this one look like a shack. The time would come when he would throw a party and the people he invited wouldn't have to bring their own food, either. That was a dirty trick — inviting you to come and eat your own food. The people who came to his party would be told to bring nothing, nothing at all.

When he looked up again he discovered that they were no longer staring at him. He rose to his feet and walked into the next room. They were all milling around the tables. He joined the older children in the corner of the room and wondered where Mary was. She had probably forgotten him by now. . . . But it didn't matter. Nothing mattered any more. As soon as he had eaten, he would get the hell out of here. Mary would probably not even miss him. She had her cousin.

The older children were being seated now. He moved forward and suddenly he saw her cousin coming toward him. He was smiling and holding out his hand. Sandor hesitated, drew back and then extended his own. The next instant he knew that he had swallowed the bait. The other boy was kneeling behind him. There was no need to turn around. He knew it, but it was too late. The hand he sought to clasp evaded his and shoved forward. It was infuriatingly childish; the kind of trick that on Henry Avenue only the youngest punks would think of playing on anyone.

For a moment he remained precariously balanced on his heels, his hand clutching the air. Then he fell.

He heard a splintering crash. Someone was swearing. It did his heart good to hear the familiar words again. They rattled on with a soul-satisfying crackle. Two of the guys are just having an argument, he thought. In a few minutes Louis would come along and break it up.

But the words rattled on and on until at last he grew tired of hearing them and looked up and discovered that he was staring into the horrified eyes of a very fat woman. He smiled at her good-naturedly. His head began to ache. Within arm's-length he saw the boy who had pushed him. "You son of a bitch," he roared, and struggled to his feet. The boy vanished. In his place stood Mrs. Kostanuik.

"Not my liddle walnut table!" she screamed. Her mouth remained open, a black anguished hole. She wrung her hands. Two tears trickled through the folds of flesh below her eyes. "Not my new liddle table," she moaned. "My new liddle table!"

Sandor began to edge away from her. She blinked at him, and before he could evade her she had reached out and grabbed him by the ear. "Out of my house," she screamed. "Out, out, out!"

Some of the younger children began to cry. Sandor yelled. The pain was agonizing. His ear felt as though she were trying to tear it out by the roots. He struggled until someone took hold of his other ear. They dragged him out of the dining-room. He grew silent. Then suddenly he felt that his left ear had been torn off.

"No. Not that way — the back door," he heard Mrs. Kostanuik say. "The neighbours shouldn't see."

He was in the kitchen. Then the door was flung open and he was alone on the back steps, staring into the garbage pail. His flowers were there under the salmon tins, the eggshells and the banana peels. After a while he walked around to the front of the house. He saw Mary, her face pressed to an upstairs window. She raised her hand and waved it feebly.

He began to run and continued running until he reached the trough on Jarvis Avenue. He remembered the holes in his stockings, and his pants that she had sewn together. He ripped them open, slowly and methodically, and then continued on his way across the tracks.

The red fence was not far off, just on the other side of the freight sheds. He crawled in, and a tearful smile came over his face. Louis, Buggsy and Hank were lying there in the weeds, smoking.

"Hello, Sandy," Louis called out. "Watcha been doin' with yourself? Come on — dere's still some eats left."

"Sit here," Hank said.

He sat down. His nostrils flared as he sucked in the rank, astringent odour of the weeds and the sweet, familiar smell of the coal-gas drifting in from the freight-yards.

There were a few canned plums, some chocolate biscuits, and half a tin of sardines. He ate ravenously. Then Louis, who was feeling good, gave him nearly a whole package of Millbanks to keep for himself.

"A birt'day present," Louis said.

"Ya," Buggsy said, "happy birt'day, Sandy."

He lit up, settled himself on his back in the weeds, and watched the engine smoke drifting soft and cloudlike against the darkening blue sky and listened to Buggsy tell of what the gang had done that day. And suddenly he felt a lump in his throat. He loved them. This was where he belonged. He had reached home.

Three

SANDOR threw his schoolbag into the woodshed and crept silently out of the yard and out into the street. His heart singing within him, he ran past the red fence and the stables to the empty lot behind the soap company where the gang was meeting. They were going swimming tonight and after that, if there was time, exploring across the river in Elmwood. Long hours lay before him, filled with the prospect of strange things to do and see.

A block away he saw Hank waving to him impatiently. They were all there, even Willi and young Olaf and Stan — everybody except Louis, who was working tonight.

"Come on," Hank said, and clapped Sandor on the back. "'At's everybody. Let's get goin', eh guys?"

They started out, the young punks in the rear, unable to suppress their excitement, shouting and yelling and running around until Frenchy brought them to order with a clout on the ear.

"Sandy, come here." Buggsy drew him aside and unbuttoned his blouse. "Got sumpin' to show you," he said.

Sandor gazed at a magnificent black tendril that had sprouted on Buggsy's chest. Only one, but it proved that Buggsy was becoming a man. His own chest was still as shamefully bare as a girl's.

"Geez — 'at's really sumpin'," he said, and caught Hank winking at him and flushed with pleasure at this intimation that Hank did not consider him just a young punk any more, but was accepting him as a regular guy.

They crossed Main and turned up Higgins. The Red River and the Louise Bridge were straight ahead. Buggsy, who had been complaining of the heat, removed his shirt. Frenchy followed suit.

As they passed by the Hotel they looked up into the windows of the lobby. The gang, and the adventures that lay ahead, faded from Sandor's mind. It seemed to him that he always saw the same men sitting there, distinguished-looking men in dark, quiet clothes, successful and satisfied. He always thought of them as retired office men, sitting there as though they had become judges whose sole aim in life now was to select from among the thousands of passers-by the men who one day would succeed them. Whenever they spoke to one another he felt that they were talking about him. He knew this was only make-believe, and yet he always held himself erect and smiled at them as he walked by. The sight of them always set his mind moving in the direction of Mr. Nagy and his own future. Today he felt that the men up there, who had long had their eyes upon him, were reproaching him because he was with the gang. He ought to be preparing himself. . . . But how? He was good at arithmetic. What else would he need in an office?

But that was not what they meant, and he knew it. They were referring to the sort of things the gang did that might lead to trouble with the police. How would it look, after he had become an office man, if people heard that he had once been arrested, or even put in jail?

He had considered this before. He wanted to avoid trouble with the police. All right. But some of the things the gang did led precisely to this kind of trouble. And when he was with the gang he had to do what they did or be thrown out. But this was too monstrous even to consider.

As long as you stayed with the gang you could get all the smokes you wanted; and there were the feeds at night. But it was more than this — much more. Inside the red fence you could say you wished you were a man already and nobody would laugh at you. With the gang you only had to say a word and you were understood. You came into the red fence after school and took a deep breath and somebody cursed your teacher for you.

He was sure of himself when he was with the gang, because everybody was the same there. They were Italian and French and Hungarian, German, Swedish, Russian and even English — young Stan was English — but they were the same in the things that counted. They were dressed the same; they all wanted to get away from Henry Avenue; they talked the same language even though their parents did not.

The gang had been good to him. He recalled how often Hank and Frenchy had offered to help him fight the English

Inside the red fence you could just be yourself, he thought. In there you learned how to be a man, and to be thrown out was so terrible it was unthinkable.

He had fallen behind. He hurried on, found a place beside Frenchy, and grinned at him affectionately.

It was a long way to the river. They arrived hot and tired.

Usually he was one of the first to get into the water. Today he was last. He undressed slowly behind the willows with the feeling he could not shake off that They were still watching; that They knew what had passed through his mind and were angry with him — and not only angry but sad — because They had planned such great things for him.

In the water he swam about apathetically beside Willi Schumacher, watching the others splashing around and having a good time.

Afterwards, sitting on the bank, he looked across at Buggsy's chest, and Frenchy's and Hank's, with a yearning so intense to be a man already that it brought tears to his eyes. He wiped them away and saw Hank beckoning to him. Hank was more manly when he was naked than anybody else in the gang, including Louis.

"Sit down," Hank said, and waved to Willi Schumacher to remove himself.

"You gettin' tu be a reg'lar guy," Hank said. "I guess it's time I tole yu sumpin'. It's a secret."

It was unnecessary to say more.

"'At hair the guys got," Hank whispered. "'At hair didn't grow natcheral."

Sandor's eyes widened. "Then — how?" he cried. He had long suspected that the older fellows were using something. Now, at last, he was going to find out. At last the terrible fear that there might be something wrong with him was going to be stilled.

"You know 'em weeds 'at grow in the red fence?" Hank asked. "'At's wot we use. All you gotta do is take and rub their juice on you."

Sandor shivered. "Weeds?"

"Tell me sumpin'," Hank said. "Wot grows faster'n weeds, eh? Nuthin'. Nuthin' grows faster'n weeds. An' you wannit tu come up fast, don'tcha?"

This made sense. Nothing did grow faster than weeds. And what made weeds grow like that but the juice inside of them? And if you rubbed that juice on you . . .

"Geez!" He clutched Hank's arm. "Tell me wot you done."

"I jus' rubbed it all over me," Hank said. "Except not here, see. I figure growin' hair takes a lotta strength outa a guy. An' someday we're gonna need alla strength we can get down here, eh, Sandy?"

A happy, salacious grin spread over their faces.

"How long you figure it'll take?" Sandor asked.

"You gotta do it every night," Hank said. "'At's wot I did. An' inna month it started cummin' up. Three of 'em together. Not just one like Buggsy. Three atta time! Now lookit me — all 'at hair," he said softly, and brushed his hand tenderly over it.

"Not bad, eh, Sandy?" he asked.

Sandor looked up. He heard the wind rustling through the willows. There was laughter in the small waves that came on sparkling feet to shore. There was a vague stirring in his loins, so faint he was not quite certain he had felt it.

"Thanks," he said. "Geez, thanks a million, Hank. You're a reg'lar guy."

"Ah, 'at's all right." Hank rose to his feet. "Okay, guys, let's go, eh?" he said.

A few minutes later they were on the bridge, Sandor out in front blithely whistling "Men of Harlech," his favourite tune.

They came to the end of the roadway, turned a corner, and suddenly there were no houses, only an overgrown path that led from the sidewalk into what seemed to them an immense forest. The silence was unsettling. They huddled together, looking apprehensively about them as they took to the trail.

They came to a clearing, but before they reached it, they stopped. Something was moving out there . . . something big.

"It's only a cow," Willi Schumacher cried. They crept forward. It was a long way off. They stared at it. Sandor knew it was a cow. He had seen pictures.

"'At's not a cow!" Hank burst into loud laughter. "It's got horns."

"Cows got horns," Willi insisted. "I'll show you it's a cow." To their horror he walked over and began to pat it. "Come on," he called. "Look, she's tied to this tree."

One by one they joined him, to prowl around cautiously prodding and poking.

"So 'at's where milk comes from," Hank snorted. "Well, all I kin say is I'm glad I never drunk any. Lookit 'at dirt!"

"Why does she need so many of 'em tits for?" Buggsy asked, kneeling down beside Willi. "Wouldn't one be enough?"

"They're for calves," Willi said. "'At's where . . ."

Buggsy drew back with an exclamation of profound disgust. "You mean they get their milk same place as we do? Geez, you guys hear that?"

"They don't take care of her very good," Sandor said. "Lookit all 'em bones stickin' out."

"Ah, wot the hell!" Hank yawned. "Who cares? Let's go, You guys comin'?"

They followed him back to the centre of the clearing, cursing as they stumbled over the ridges in the ground. There were not only ridges, Sandor noticed, but also little mounds around the weeds.

"Might as well have a smoke before we go," Hank said.

They lit up and watched Willi Schumacher feeding the cow.

"Funny kinda weeds aroun' here, eh?" Frenchy said, "growin' in straight lines like 'at."

"Yeah."

They smoked for a while in silence.

"Cripes-aw-mighty!" Buggsy leaped to his feet. "'Em ain't weeds, 'em's carrots!"

In a moment they were tearing around the field, pulling up carrots and onions and radishes.

Sandor broke the tip off a carrot, took one bite of the remainder, and was about to reach for another when he stopped. There was a man out there moving across the field, a man in a blue coat with brass buttons, running toward them.

" . . . bring some salt . . ." he heard Frenchy saying, and spun around.

"Cops," he yelled and pointed and ran.

"A fireman," Hank cried.

Nothing more was said. They scattered as if they had been blown apart. The trouble, Sandor thought, was that they would have to converge on the trail. He looked back. The fireman knew that too. He was trying to head them off. Sandor ran on. He was losing ground, but he could run no faster. He glanced back again. Hank was over to his left and on the far side, Frenchy, both of them cut off but too far for the fireman to catch. Willi Schumacher and young Olaf and Stan were crawling into the underbrush. But Buggsy was in trouble. With a groan Sandor remembered that Buggsy was wearing his father's shoes.

Sandor reached the trail. On the sidewalk he knew that he could run no farther. His knees were shaking. He was sobbing for breath.

He staggered down the street to the nearest house and hid behind a hedge, gulping for air to still the fire in his chest.

Two blocks away, Hank appeared, then Frenchy. They stopped and looked back.

A few minutes later, Buggsy came into sight, the fireman so close behind he had only to reach out to grab him. Instead he paused for an instant, balanced himself, and with a tremendous kick, lifted Buggsy in the air. Buggsy dropped, covered his face with one hand, his crotch with the other, and remained still. The fireman looked up and down the street, and walked quickly away.

Buggsy was sitting up when they reached him. They hovered about him solicitously. Sandor and Frenchy helped him on with his blouse. Hank lit a cigarette for him. Willi, who had appeared from nowhere, helped him pull his stockings up.

Buggsy grinned. "On'y thing I was scared of . . . I thought he was gonna kick me again."

"Ah, the bastar'," Frenchy exclaimed.

"These goddamned shoes," Buggsy said and rose to his feet and dropped headlong into the ditch on the edge of the sidewalk. He lay still.

"He's dead," young Olaf screamed.

Sandor gave him a cuff on the ear.

"For Chris'sake," Hank yelled. "Wotta you guys lookin' at? Gimme a hand here."

They jumped down, raised him to the sidewalk, and stared at him. Sandor wondered if they were as frightened as he was. It was not because they weren't scared or didn't care that they looked like that, he thought. When you looked closer you saw how Frenchy's lips were trembling and Hank's face tight to show no feeling. In the gang you couldn't show that you were scared, or cry when you were hurt. . . .

Buggsy was raising himself on his elbow. He took a puff of his cigarette and grinned at them.

Hank leaped to his feet. "God damn it, Buggsy! If this is a joke," he yelled, "I'm gonna bash you."

"I jus' can't stand up," Buggsy said. "'At's all. . . . 'At son of a bitch kicked me where I fell onna track last year."

"You hurt?" Hank asked him.

"I'll be awright. It'll be the same as las' time — okay in a coupla hours."

"Guess we'll have to carry you, then," Hank said. "Me and Frenchy'll start."

They carried him, spelling each other until they reached the bridge. On the other side, they returned to their place in the willows. Here, when they had rested and had grown tired again in the water, they lay back and smoked and began to re-shape the adventure of the day into a form more acceptable to gang legend.

It was late when they rose. On the street the glow in which they had enveloped themselves fell from them. They were suddenly hungry and tired and in no mood for pretence.

Buggsy, after his swim, was able to walk about, but very slowly.

"'At son of a long-legged bastar'," Hank said. "It hadda be a fireman — Ah — the hell. A guy gets in trouble even when he aint' lookin' for it."

"We gonna have more trouble wen Louis finds out," Frenchy said. "You know Louis."

"Yeah."

"You guys dunno the half of it," Buggsy groaned. "I jus' remembered. I'm suppose to stan' guard tonight."

"'At's okay, I'll go," Frenchy said.

Hank brushed this aside. "You went Wednesday."

"I'm goin'," Frenchy said.

Sandor listened to them in bewilderment. Only a few minutes ago, lying there in the willows, he had felt at one with them. But there were times when he failed completely to understand them. It was all right to stand guard for Louis when you had to. He had done it himself. But there was always a risk. Didn't they know that? Or didn't they care? Was it the extra few packages of cigarettes and chocolates that made them so eager to accompany him? Or was it something else — something he had never felt?

They were no longer arguing: they had decided to draw.

Buggsy had two matches in his hand. "Short man, eh?" he asked.

"Jus' a minute." Hank turned to Sandor. "I guess you wanna be cut in, eh, Sandy?"

Sandor nodded. He remembered again how frightened he

had been that night, his fears growing with every sound, and every minute filled with the strain of knowing that, no matter what happened, he must stand fast because his friends had stood there before him.

"You won," Hank said, and clapped him on the shoulder.

He had lost as he had known he would. Not that it made any difference, he told himself. His turn would have come next Friday anyhow. And nothing had happened last time in spite of his fears. It was just that it had come so suddenly. It was the way Hank said. You never knew when you were going to get in trouble and that was all anybody could say.

The return home was uneventful.

Later that night, alone inside the red fence waiting for Louis, Sandor sat quietly in the weeds trying to reassure himself that he had nothing to worry about. The rest of the guys had been taking turns standing guard for nearly four months now. And anyhow, it was safer than breaking into stores and restaurants. The best thing to do was not think about it at all.

He lit a cigarette. Suddenly his face brightened. He set to work gathering the tallest weeds he could find, crushing them, rubbing the thick astringent sap on his chest, his arms and face. Then he ran up and down the yard to dry himself. He felt tired and lay down. No. There was no use worrying, he told himself. Louis knew what he was doing. You could depend on Louis.

The way Louis had solved the problem of keeping the gang in cigarettes and candy was the way a real leader planned things. Safe and simple. All he had done was to get himself a job delivering groceries for old Swanson. At the end of the first month, his relations with the grocer had reached the point where the old man was searching him — at Louis' insistence — every time he left the store. The fact that Louis was throwing packages of cigarettes, cartons of chocolate bars, biscuits and canned goods into the rubbish box, escaped the grocer's notice. Frequently he helped Louis to carry the box outside. Louis rarely laughed or smiled, but this amused him.

Yeah, a real leader, Sandor thought, and looked up and there was Louis crawling through the fence, misshapen and almost lost in one of his brother's coats.

"Wot I oughta do," Louis said, "is jus' walk out on you crazy bastar's — or take an' knock the hell outa yu. 'At's wot happens wen I'm not around'. Tomorrow you guys gonna see wot I do tu Hank. . . . Maybe I oughta give Frenchy a goin' over too, tu learn him . . ."

"But they couldn't help it," Sandor cried. "Honesta God, Louis!"

"I'm not blamin' you," Louis said. "Here. Let's go." He opened his hand and a length of broomstick slid out of his sleeve.

"I'm glad you 'membered tu wear your coat," he said.

Sandor thrust the stick into the right sleeve of his jacket.

"An' here's da bag." Louis handed him a small weighted paper bag.

"It feels heavier," Sandor said.

"I put some more ball-bearin's in it," Louis replied.

They crawled out of the red fence and walked silently down Henry Avenue and on under the bridge to Logan.

"Awright," Louis said. "Now wait here like las' time."

When he had crossed the street, Sandor followed.

Swanson's grocery was on the corner. Sandor stationed himself in the yard, between the coal bin and the back stairs. From the position he now occupied he was able to observe the street, the lane, and the steps of the back porch.

He lowered the palm of his right hand. The stick slid down. He gripped it tightly. From his left pocket he pulled out the bag of pepper.

Louis was already bending over the rubbish box in the moonlight, a dark dwarf in the jacket that came almost to his knees. He worked quickly and silently, throwing small cartons and tins into a flour sack.

Sandor listened to the pounding of his heart. His right hand grew wet and cold. A few blocks away there was a solitary footstep on the pavement . . . in the distance a street car. When the car passed, the silence rang in his ears. But nothing had happened last time, he reassured himself. And nothing would happen now.

Above him something rustled. He moved out to investigate. Only the curtains on the window ledge. He returned to his post and heard it again. It was not the curtains. It came from inside the store.

For a moment he stood there as though transfixed. His mouth opened to call out a warning, but no words came. He saw the porch door open slowly. He saw Swanson appear in a nightgown, his pants in one hand, his glasses in the other, peering and blinking in the shadowed yard. He raised his glasses to his face.

Sandor drew back. Out of the corner of his eyes he saw Louis straighten up. The pepper bag was torn from his grasp. The next instant it crashed into the old man's face. It hit him squarely in the centre of the forehead. His glasses and his pants dropped as he clawed at his eyes. He lurched down the steps, staggered, and fell.

Sandor began to laugh and forced back a sob. But when Louis motioned to him, he ran forward and tightening his hold on the stick, brought it crashing down on the old man's shin-bone, in precisely the spot that Louis had shown him, while they were practising. He saw the pain spreading over Swanson's face. It brought tears to his eyes. The old man sneezed and opened his mouth to yell, and tried to get up.

Sandor began to cry. He swung and hit him again. Then Louis was beside him, shoving the remains of the pepper bag into the old man's mouth. He looked across at Sandor with blazing eyes; the next moment he was up the steps, and in one bound into the store.

Sandor wiped his tears away. Swanson had stopped whimpering. He had pulled the bag from his mouth and was trying to get to his feet again. Sandor struck him. A wave of pity came over him. He hit him again. He had to. He wanted to tell him that he had to. Maybe the old man would under-stand. The stick rose and fell. The old man finally grew still.

As though in a nightmare Sandor saw Louis beside him, pulling the old man's nightgown up over his head and knotting it.

This done he sprang to his feet, picked up the flour sack, and walked leisurely out of the yard. Sandor followed him.

"You done good," Louis said, as they crossed Logan Avenue. "You didn't forget nuthin'."

Sandor's legs wobbled. He clung to Louis, who pulled him into the shadow of a pole. "I tell ya sumpin'," Louis said. "I never tot you had it in ya, Sandy. Every minute I tot you'd forget wot I tole you an' say sumpin'. If you'da said a word we'da been gonners. He'da known right away who we was." He laughed. "Christ, wot a stupid ole bastar' he is, comin' out like dat. An' I still got my job."

He slapped Sandor on the back. "You done swell, Sandy. Honesta gawd." Sandor remained silent. Never again as long as he lived would he do a thing like this. He swore it to himself. Even if they called him yellow or kicked him out of the gang.

"We gotta keep movin'," Louis said.

They started back, carrying the flour sack between them. The street was deserted. They walked on until they reached the red fence. They crawled in and sat down in front of the hide-out under the ramp. Louis opened the flour sack and drew out half a dozen packages of cigarettes, a box of biscuits, three tins of fruit, and a box of chocolates. "Ya hungry?" he asked.

Sandor shook his head.

"Ya think there's any chance of them finding out who done it?" Sandor asked.

Louis stopped eating. "Naw."

"They got ways," Sandor persisted. "I been readin' 'bout things like that. Cops never give up even if it takes years .... Wot was 'at?"

"On'y horses. Wot the hell's the matter wid you? Ya scared?"

Sandor held up his hand. They dropped flat in the weeds.

A dull hollow sound reverberated through the black hole under the ramp.

Sandor shivered. His blouse was sticky with sweat. This was how it would be from now on; to be frightened every time he heard a noise behind him, afraid that at any hour of the day the cops might pick him up, coming home from school to find them waiting for him, or called to the principal's office maybe — the way Buggsy's older brother had been called down, to find the office full of cops.

He looked up as Louis nudged him.

It was only Peg-a-leg, the railway guard, making his rounds, humming to himself as he hobbled down the ramp, his lantern bobbing up and down with the rise and fall of his wooden leg.

Louis was already sitting up. "I tell you wot, Sandy," he said. "You're a reg'lar guy."

He reached in his pocket and drew out a fistful of bills and began to count them. Sandor's eyes bulged with terror. He had forgotten until now that Louis had been in the store. The enormity of what they had done burst fully upon him. Pinching cigarettes and candies and things was one thing, but stealing money . . .

Louis plunged his hand into his pocket again, spilling out the remaining bills and what to Sandor seemed a fabulous amount of silver. He grabbed Louis by the arm. "The cash register! Cripes-aw-mighty! You left your fingerprints on the cash register. 'Atsa first thing the cops'll look for."

Louis looked at him for a long time, studying him intently. "You know sumpin', Sandy," he said thoughtfully. "You got brains." And there was something in Louis' look and in the tone of his voice that drew Sandor to him in spite of himself.

"I'll show you how I did," Louis continued. "Watch."

He wriggled his arm until the sleeve of his jacket dropped over his finger-tips.

"Like I tole you," Louis said. "You're a reg'lar guy." He reached for the bills and finished counting them.

"They's fifty-nine bucks here," he said. "I'm gonna give you fifteen bucks, Sandy." He peeled off three fives.

A host of desirable objects swam before Sandor's eyes. Fifteen dollars! He could get a bicycle — fifteen dollars would make a good down payment. And with a bicycle he could get a job. Or he could just save it, put it away in a safe place and know it was there, and every once in a while go and look at it. Or spend it, slowly. It would last almost a year.

But then, like a dark cloud closing in upon this dazzling prospect, the thought occurred to him that if he took the money it would make him an accomplice. If he refused, he could be brought up only for stealing smokes and candies. Was that why Louis had offered it to him?

Louis was staring at him with an incredulity that was turning to anger. "Wot in hell's the matter wid you?" he snorted. "You crazy or sumpin'?"

He shoved the money back in his pocket. "You scared, aintcha?" Suddenly he reached out and grabbed Sandor by the throat. "If ya squeal . . ."

Sandor shook him off. "I won't squeal, an' you know it. How the hell kin I squeal? On'y you had no business takin' that money. I thought ya was gonna get the smokes an' stuff. Stealin' money's different."

"Sunday-school stuff," Louis jeered. "Ya been listenin' to ole howlin' Jesus."

Sandor flushed. "I ain't been ta Sunday School nearly a year. I on'y went 'cause my mother made me go."

"An' you're yalla," Louis sneered. "Yalla."

"I jus' don't wanna go to jail," Sandor cried. "It's awright for you. You got nuthin' ta lose. But I got plans. Some day I'm gonna work . . ."

"Aw, for Chris'sake," Louis broke in, "can 'at stuff. Work!" he scoffed. "My ole man worked all his life and wot'd it get him? I'll tell you wot. A house 'at ain't even got glass windows. . . . My sister hasta carry him around. All his insides messed up. 'At's wot workin' all your life gets you."

He paused. Sandor turned away abruptly. Louis was crying.

"An' anudder t'ing," Louis said. "I heard wot you said to Buggsy. Tellin' him I ain't gotta right kinda brains for school. I oughta kill you for that, you son of a bitch. I got . . ."

"I never said that, Louis. Honesta God. I said . . ."

"Yeah, yeah. I got brains awright. I'm smart. Some day I'm gonna show the whole buncha you. You t'ink I quit school 'cause I was too dumb. I quit school 'cause my ass was hangin' outa my pants, 'at's why. My sister couldn't even cut down the old man's. He's only got one . . ." He wiped his nose on his coat sleeve and drew on his cigarette. "On'y way tu get rich is grab wot you can," he said. "I'm smart, I am. Not like my ole man. I'll get mine awright, you'll see."

Sandor felt sorry for him as he compared his life to Louis'. Then slowly his sorrow gave way to a faint elation that grew and grew until no sorrow was left. He rose to his feet.

Louis had lit another cigarette. "You wanna money?" he asked. Sandor shook his head.

"Okay den, you're out. I ever see you in here again, I'll kill ya. An' don't go shoutin' your mouth off 'bout tonight — you know wot I mean."

Sandor backed away. The moment he was out of the red fence he began running down Higgins Avenue on the wild grass that fringed the roadway. He could run silently there. A few minutes later he reached home.

He slipped off his clothes, straightened the chairs under the quilt, and got into bed.

Nothing'll happen, he told himself. Swanson hadn't seen them. And even if Louis were arrested and squealed, it wouldn't matter. The fact that he had not only turned down his share of the money but had quit the gang — wouldn't the Judge take that into account?

He nodded thoughtfully. The Judge would certainly give him credit for that — credit that was deserved. No one had ever quit the gang before, and not one member would have refused that money.

He closed his eyes. Tomorrow he would start looking for an after-school job, any kind of a job, even if he had to go to

Sunday School and ask Mr. Crawford to find him one. He saw himself walking down the street toward the store in which he worked. But Louis was there ahead of him waiting with a flour sack under his arm. Sandor groaned and opened his eyes and stared up at the ceiling.

Four

SANDOR shuffled slowly down the lane, his hands in his pockets, half-heartedly kicking a tin can before him. At Logan Avenue he turned back home, wandered aimlessly about the kitchen and the front room, and stood for a while above his brother's crib, envying him his gurgling absorption in a wooden spoon. Outside, on the front steps, his mother sat talking to a neighbour who was expecting another baby.

He returned to the back yard, rolled the chopping-block out of the woodshed and, seating himself upon it, drew a figure in the dust with a piece of kindling; the crude outline of a woman appeared which grew so monstrous and unlikely as he proceeded that he finally blotted it out and stared miserably across at the tenement on the other side of the lane, and for perhaps the thousandth time in the past three weeks wondered what he was going to do with himself. Supper was over. His homework was done. There was enough kindling in the woodshed to last his mother a month. It was still early — only eight o'clock.

He sighed and walked upstairs to the toilet, to the three loose floorboards beside the chimney. Raising them, he took out a large cigar-box filled with miscellaneous treasures; the handle of a spoon, filed into the shape of a skeleton key, a stick with a pin fastened to the end of it, several pieces of resin, a belt buckle, and finally a piece of brass tubing.

He peered through it and began to smile. Sometimes on Saturdays when there was nothing to do the gang would go down under the foot of the bridge to where there were good, big knot-holes in the sidewalk over their heads. Then Willi or young Stan or Olaf would go up on the bridge and stop some woman and ask her how to get to such and such a street. And all the while she would be standing over a knot-hole and the guys below would be taking turns seeing sights through their brass peep-tubes.

Sandor closed his eyes. A lustful shiver spread through his body. Ah, the things they had seen . . . the lovely sights. His eyes remained closed. A minute or two passed. His brow began to furrow. What had they seen? He could remember nothing. Maybe that was because it had happened so long ago. He recalled the extravagant claims he had made, and the enthusiasm of the gang as they vied with one another as to who had seen the best sights. But how could they have seen anything? It had always been too dark. The truth was that they had seen nothing. His disillusion suddenly burst from him in a loud groan. The whole thing had just been a kid's game.

He turned back to the box and rummaged idly through it, trying to recapture the untroubled early days of his life with the gang. Finally he closed the lid, returned it to its hiding-place, and went back downstairs.

If only he had somebody to talk to, or something to do. He had tried to persuade Willi Schumacher to quit the gang, but what had he been able to offer him? Nothing.

He had tried to find a job; the first person he had gone to see was Mr. Nagy. But Mr. Nagy had merely given him a few raspberry drops and a pat on the head and sent him on his way. He had applied at every grocery store within walking-distance. In desperation, he had finally returned to Sunday School and appealed to Mr. Crawford, the Superintendent.

But that was nearly three weeks ago, and although he had attended Sunday School regularly and Mr. Crawford had promised to do what he could, nothing had come of it except that Mr. Crawford had called one day and prayed over his mother.

He trudged wearily into the kitchen and out into the lane again. Right now the guys in the red fence were probably laughing at him — and no wonder. He had been a fool to refuse that money and get himself kicked out of the gang. Louis was still working for Swanson, and the guys in the gang were still having their feasts and getting all the smokes they wanted.

It was growing dark. He continued down the lane and tried to convince himself that he had done the right thing. He had refused to jeopardize his future. Only a strong character . . .

"Aw, the hell," he cried. "Wot am I gonna do?"

Tomorrow would be even worse; it was Saturday.

He picked up a handful of stones and threw them at a dog with whom he had been feuding almost as far back as he could remember. Then he returned to the woodshed, took off his blouse, and for the second time that night smeared himself with the thin, watery fluid of the weeds that grew in the lane. His chest was still bare.

He crawled up to the roof of the woodshed and began to roll himself a cigarette out of toilet paper and dried leaves. His misery was complete. At school he was in the middle of examinations and, too deeply involved in his afflictions to watch himself, had fallen into the hands of the English gang — twice within the past week.

The summer holidays would free him of this torment. But the mere thought of the long empty days that lay ahead was like a nightmare.

He knew only too well what awaited him. The last time he had gone to Sunday School it was no longer with the hope that he might persuade Mr. Crawford to find him a job; he had gone because he could no longer endure being alone. That was what things had come to. The only good thing that had happened to him since he had left the gang was that his father had either not noticed or had chosen to disregard the fact that he had been fighting.

He lit his cigarette. It came apart in a shower of sparks and charred paper. He looked at its remains for a long time, then he jumped down from the shack and walked resolutely into the kitchen. He reached for the broom and began to brush his stockings and his pants. He polished his shoes and, since Mr.

Crawford liked boys to be not only neat but also clean, he washed his hands and face. He would give Mr. Crawford one more chance.

But when he arrived at the church and stood facing the iron-studded door that led to the basement, he wondered what he was going to say. Mr. Crawford was queer. If you talked too much, he would quite likely tell you to put your faith in God. If you just mentioned your troubles quietly, he would give you a sermon on the blessings you had already received.

Next to Mr. Nagy, he was the most important man in the neighbourhood. He visited the poor and the sick, and when they were really poor, he helped them to get on relief. He knew where to find help for girls who were going to have babies. He arranged rummage-sales. At Christmastime, accompanied by English ladies, he went around distributing clothes and candies and food.

Sandor shook his head. When Mr. Nagy helped you, you paid him, and that was fitting and the way things should be. You could understand that, but Mr. Crawford did all this for nothing! What did he get out of it? Nothing except thanks, and sometimes not even that. What did he do it for?

Sandor opened the door. He had never been able to understand this man and he was afraid of him. He decided nevertheless to come out bluntly and insist on an answer — yes or no. If it was no, he knew what he was going to do.

The basement was in darkness but for the light streaming through the doorway of the office in the corner. Sandor knocked and entered.

Mr. Crawford, immensely tall and cadaverous, stood facing him. "Why, it's Sandor Hoomphadi," he boomed.

The sound echoed and reverberated like a distant hurrah through the empty basement. Sandor hung back nervously.

"Hullo, Mr. Crawford. I jus' come to see you."

The severe, angular face broke into a smile that immediately vanished. "Did you, my boy? Did you now?"

He moved to the table in a few, quick, spasmodic strides that immediately set his pants flopping, his coat-tails flying.

There was something about him that always reminded Sandor of bleached bones, of dry bread and old cheese, something about the full-fleshed red lips set in that pale mournful face that always made him shiver.

"Now then," Mr. Crawford intoned, seating himself behind the table. "What . . . ?" He jerked his head to one side, placed his thumb under his chin, his forefinger along his cheek, and slowly raised his brows.

Sandor cleared his throat. "I cum to see you 'bout that job, Mr. Crawford." But Mr. Crawford was already on his feet, ransacking the drawer of the table.

He finally found what he was looking for — a dirty little corner of an envelope. "Mrs. Creighton," he said to himself. "To be sure."

He looked up. "Are you free this Saturday?" he asked. Sandor gulped. It couldn't be, he thought stupidly. It couldn't be the JOB — not like this — not falling in his lap without begging for it or wheedling, with no arguments or tricks or threats. Things didn't happen like that — at least not to him. He stared at the little triangle of paper in Mr. Crawford's hand.

"A job," he shouted. "You found me a job, Mr. Crawford. I wanna thank you. Honest to . . . Thanks a million, Mr. Crawford. I'll never forget wot you done for me. You saved my life, that's wot you done. I'll never forget you."

Mr. Crawford smiled briefly, but with a strange kindness lighting up his eyes that abashed Sandor and abruptly silenced him.

"Saturday morning," Mr. Crawford repeated. "Here is the address. Mrs. Creighton will pay you fifty cents a week and your car fare." He paused. "Your duties will be simple. All you have to do is look after the lawn."

"'At's steady work, eh, Mr. Crawford?"

"Providing you do a satisfactory job." Mr. Crawford rose to his feet. He bent over and looked down sternly. "I'm depending on you, Sandor. If Mrs. Creighton should find any reason for complaint, it will be a reflection on my judgment. Do you understand?"

Sandor nodded. He wanted to be alone to think about it, to relish and nurse this elation and keep it alive, to gloat over it privately.

My first job, he mused, and assured Mr. Crawford that he would conduct himself like a perfect gentleman . . . the way Mr. Crawford had learned him. He thanked him again effusively, and made for the door.

"Sandor!"

Sandor turned.

"Haven't you forgotten something?"

Sandor looked up at him and bowed his head.

Mr. Crawford sighed. "Dear Lord," he began. "Bless this, Thy servant's humble effort to guide this boy to the paths of righteousness. Accept the thanks of this poor youth who in gratitude for Thy bountiful gifts comes to Thee . . ."

Sandor heard no more. Wrapped in the glow of that fifty cents a week — two whole dollars a month — he dreamed. Once he looked up and felt Mr. Crawford's bony knuckle on his skull. And once, catching a fragment of the deeply toned invocation on his behalf, he wondered again why Mr. Crawford went to all this trouble for people. Then he drifted back to that imagined neighbourhood in the South End where the rich English lived. Tomorrow he would actually be seeing it for the first time.

With a loud Amen, Mr. Crawford finally let him go. Sandor looked at him. Some day, he thought, when he was an office man, like Mr. Nagy, he would look back and remember this moment. He felt sorry now that he had always sneered at Mr. Crawford and made fun of him. In a burst of overwhelming gratitude, of remorse and triumph, he called to him.

"Mr. Crawford, some day you're gonna be prouda me."

Mr. Crawford looked up and suddenly he was frightening again. His eyes seemed to fill with a wild fervour. He flung out his long arms and lifted his face to the ceiling and for a terrible moment Sandor thought he was going to embrace him.

Instead he placed his hand on Sandor's head.

"In such a moment I am thanked," he said, and grew silent.

His hand grew heavier and heavier and Sandor, unable to move and growing tired, stared at his vest that gaped where a button was missing — the dark aperture opening and closing to the rise and fall of his laboured breath, a sad, black mouth with only one word to say, and that word unknown, to remain forever and always a mystery.

Sandor's head felt cold. Mr. Crawford had removed his hand and was smiling at him.

"Good night, Sandor," he said. "Bless you."

Sandor turned to the door.

Outside on the church lawn, he burst into a peal of clear, untroubled laughter.

"I got a job," he said hoarsely, "Cripes-aw-mighty, I gotta job." He plucked a blade of grass and dusted it off and looked at it. A restless urge came over him. He wanted to do something, to tell somebody, to shout the news aloud. He began to run.

Tomorrow a new life started. Tomorrow he would take the first step. He ran on until he could run no more.

Five

FRESHLY washed and scrubbed, dressed in a clean blouse and his Sunday pants, Sandor sat impatiently dangling his legs in the Academy Road streetcar.

Soon, he thought; and looked imploringly across at the conductor. He had been doing so ever since they had crossed the bridge, and at every glance the conductor had winked and motioned to him to remain seated.

But this time he nodded and pressed the buzzer. Sandor sprang to his feet. The car ground to a stop. He got off, walked a short distance up the street, and suddenly he stood still.

It was as though he had walked into a picture in one of his childhood books, past the painted margin to a land that lay smiling under a friendly spell, where the sun always shone, and the clean-washed tint of sky and child and garden would never fade; where one could walk, but on tip-toe, and look and look but never touch, and never speak to break the enchanted hush.

It grew real. There was the faint murmur of the city far in the background and overhead the whisper of the wind in the trees.

The green here was not as he had ever seen it on leaf or weed, but with the blue of the sky in it, and the air so clear that even the sky looked different here.

In a daze he moved down the street. The boulevards ran wide and spacious to the very doors of the houses. And these houses were like palaces, great and stately, surrounded by their own private parks and gardens.

On every side was something to wonder at. There were waggons and toys lying on the lawns as though no one here had even considered that they might be stolen.

He passed a lawn on which children were playing quietly with long wooden hammers and loops through which they drove wooden balls. He stopped there until a little girl drew the attention of her playmates to his presence.

As he approached the address which Mr. Crawford had given him, his heart swelled with pride, for it was one of the finest and largest houses on the street, built of solid stone.

He followed the path down the side of the house to the back and there suddenly found a woman sitting on a canvas chair under a tree, reading a letter.

Very leisurely she lowered the plump, jewelled hand which held the letter and looked out across the lawn, her gaze sweeping past him to return slowly and settle upon him, in an unexpected, careless way, Sandor thought, an insulting way, subjecting him to a long scrutiny from head to toe and back again several times, but without the flicker of an eyelid or the faintest expression of interest — much as he himself, he felt, might look if he should happen to glance absent-mindedly at a fence post. And yet in spite of this he could not help feeling that there was something in her manner which was appropriate and fitting, something which caused his resentment to fade and filled him again with pride; he was going to work for her, and so in a sense he belonged to her house and some of this splendid high arrogance of hers would be his too. This was the way it should be, he thought. This was how the rich English should act, this was the way they should look, dignified and cool-eyed and distant.

She beckoned, and as he approached her he saw that she was no longer young. Her hair, high and tight-coiled, with a comb like a crown in it, was turning grey, but her face was still smooth and her mouth was as red as a cherry.

"You're the little boy Mr. Crawford sent," she said. "I'm . . . afraid I've forgotten your name."

He had expected this, or rather had expected that she would ask him how to pronounce it; people he met for the first time always did. But to tell her now was suddenly impossible. She would smile and there would begin again the familiar, terrible ritual of mouthing it, and there would come over him again the feeling that he was exposing something naked and ugly to the world's gaze.

But to lie outright and give her some other name would be stupid. Mr. Crawford would . . .

Mr. Crawford like most other people made such a mess of Hunyadi that she would not suspect anything if he gave her the name he was trying to get his father to adopt. And it was just as unlikely that Mr. Crawford would notice the difference if she repeated it to him.

"Alex. Alex Humphrey," he said hoarsely.

"Alexander Humphrey," she repeated, and explained briefly what she wanted him to do.

Sandor began to breathe again. It was all right, then.

A few minutes later he was running the mower back and forth across the front lawn. It was easy work, clean and deeply satisfying to watch the grass billowing up behind the blades like green waves in the sunlight, to breathe in the smell of it and feel it fresh and cool on his arms and his face. For the first quarter of an hour or so he worked furiously, anxious to impress her with his industry. Then it occurred to him that the sooner he finished, the sooner he would have to leave. And besides, she was not paying him by the hour; she would be far more pleased if he did a good job.

He leaned on the handle of the mower and looked out across the lawn. Two houses away, some older boys and girls were playing the same game he had observed earlier that morning. He looked at them more closely, at the fresh colours of their clothes against the green of the hedges and the lawns. It was as though they were living in a fairy tale, he thought. They played, not as he and his friends played, hot and eager and hungry to win, but easily, quietly, without any strain.

A tall girl dressed in white appeared among them carrying a tray which she placed on a table beneath a large coloured umbrella. The children walked over; only the young ones ran. He heard the tinkle of glasses and their laughter.

Something stronger than envy seized him. He hated them. What had they done to deserve all this? Nothing. Nothing at all. They probably didn't even appreciate it. While he, if he were ever to live on a street like this, would have to fight and push and work all his life — the way Mr. Nagy was doing.

He returned to work. But he would do it, he thought. The day would come. The things he had seen this morning would some day be his.

He gave himself to the sun on his body, to the warm fragrance in the air, to a peace such as he had never known.

When he had finished, he pushed the mower to the back of the house. The canvas chair was empty. He moved it out of his way and set to work again. In a little while, it would all be over, he thought, and he would be back on Henry Avenue. In a few days the things he had seen here would grow unreal and he would begin to wonder if he had only imagined them.

He looked up as a small boy appeared on the walk, a boy a few years younger than he, with blond curly hair and dirty hands, in a white sailor-suit with white stockings and sandals. Sandor glared at him. "You want sumpin'?" he asked.

"Yes, mother wanted me to ask you if you'd mind cutting our lawn."

Sandor's eyes widened. What a fool he was not to have thought of it. There were probably dozens of women around here looking for someone to take care of their lawns. "How much does your mother figure on paying?" he asked.

The boy shrugged his shoulders.

'At's all they're good for, Sandor thought scornfully. Playin' with girls and drinkin' pink tea under umbrellas. Too delicate even to cut their own grass.

"Soon as I'm through here," he said. "I'll be over. . . . Where do you live?"

"Right across the street. There."

"Okay." Sandor set the lawn-mower in motion. I better tell Mrs. Creighton first, he thought.

When the pathway was swept and the tools put away, he walked up to the back porch, stood there for a while considering, and then turned and presented himself at the side door.

A stout, matronly woman appeared in a white lace apron with black ribbons and a cap to match. She reached out her hand to pat him on the head.

Sandor drew back indignantly. People were always patting him on the head, and besides she was only a servant. "I'm Alex Humphrey," he said. "And I wanna see Mrs. Creighton."

She nodded with mock severity. "I'll tell Mrs. Creighton right away," she said.

He watched her as she walked up the hall to the stairs. At the end of the hall was an archway. Beyond it he caught a glimpse of the living-room. Wonder crept into his eyes. He tip-toed through the hall to stand there and look, to hold his breath and keep looking, so that he might seal this room within him forever.

It was unbelievable, from the great dragon vase in the corner — big enough to crawl into — to the rich luxury of the dark plush sofa with golden nails on the arms and legs. There were satin cushions everywhere, and lamps; one, twice as tall as he, with a gold-tasselled shade; another, smaller but carved in the shape of a lamp-post with two boys climbing up, and pictures in gold frames, so many he could scarcely see the walls. To match the sofa there were dark red curtains that stretched from the ceiling to the floor. In the far corner stood a piano, beside it a gramophone, and next to that a long table under the window, covered with glass dogs and horses and flowers. This was it, he thought — the real thing. Comfort, wealth and beauty.

It was big enough and high enough to take the whole Kostanuik shack, with room to spare. . . .

He heard footsteps on the stairs. He tip-toed back, dreaming of what the future held for him, a future now so immeasurably widened and filled with things to possess.

When Mrs. Creighton appeared she seemed more splendid than ever. He looked at her, his eyes shining with admiration. He was proud of her. But on the back lawn she saddened him by getting down on her haunches and scrutinizing it from all four corners.

That was at the back. On the front lawn she merely walked about, letting her feet glide over the grass to see if he had raked it properly.

"I am really pleased," she said at last. "You may tell Mr. Crawford so when you see him." She looked at him intently. "That will be on Sunday, will it not?"

"Yes, Mrs. Creighton . . . at Sunday School."

She seemed to have become friendlier. Sandor took heart. "There's sumpin' I wanna ask you, Mrs. Creighton," he said. "The lady across the street over there wants me to cut her lawn too. Is 'at awright?"

For the first time she smiled at him. "You're quite a little business man," she said, "aren't you?"

Sandor grinned proudly. "It's awright then?" he asked.

She nodded. "Now here is fifty cents for your work," she said, "and twenty-five cents for your car fare for the next month."

He thanked her. When she had gone he deposited the money in his blouse pocket, from which he had extracted a large safety-pin. Then he unbuttoned his blouse and from inside finally succeeded in pinning the mouth of the pocket securely shut.

The money jingled pleasantly as he crossed the street. The boy was waiting for him. He should have been a girl, Sandor thought.

"Wot's your name?" he asked.

"Eric. Eric Hamilton. What's yours?"

"Alex . . . just call me Alex."

"I'll tell Mother you're here," the boy said, and led him into the front hall and asked him to wait.

The hall was almost empty; only an unframed mirror and a bowl of flowers on a table that looked like two smooth boxes nailed together. He stuck his head into the doorway of the living-room and drew back profoundly shocked by what he had seen. He looked again. A picture of a blue horse hung above the fireplace. It annoyed him. He liked pictures to be real; the kind of pictures Mrs. Creighton had, of coloured trees and ships and horses — real horses. But this . . .

He shrugged his shoulders. The room looked bare. The furniture was like the table in the hall and not even painted. And yet this house was spacious, all sunlight and air. And that cost money, he reflected. This immense room with all its windows would cost plenty to keep warm in the winter. There was money here, all right. But what kind of people were they to spend it on such things? He thought of Mrs. Creighton's living-room and sniffed disdainfully as he returned to the hall.

At the far end the boy appeared with a woman beside him. Not his mother, Sandor thought. She was far too young — so young she might be his sister. He watched her as they drew near. Eric was talking and she listened as a sister might, not at all the way most adults listened. She laughed, easily, freely, as though her first response to life and all that had happened to her since had been laughter. She was fair and slender and so beautiful that his breath caught in his throat. Suddenly with all his heart he wanted her and Eric to like him. He wanted her to smile at him the way she was now smiling at her son, to accept him because she was English and beautiful and rich and could give him the feeling of belonging not only because he worked here but because he had friends here too.

Eric moved a pace forward. "Mother, this is Alex. I . . . don't know his other name."

Alex flushed.

"Why, Alex, you're practically anonymous." Her lips parted slowly and beautifully. Eric was smiling. They stood there, she with her hand on her son's shoulder, both of them looking at him.

And for a long terrible moment he was afraid. How many times had people held infinitely greater promise of friendship, only to fail him in the end; how many times had closer acquaintance with things that were beautiful exposed only worm-eaten ugliness in their hearts?

But he had the feeling that they not only expected but wanted him to join them in this mild appreciation of her little joke.

He found to his surprise that he was laughing with them. "My name is Alex Humphrey," he said finally, and then grew embarrassed, wondering how he could bring himself to talk to such a woman about money.

But she raised the question herself and in a few minutes everything was simply and easily arranged.

"Since you have just finished working, I think you had better rest for a while," she said. "Suppose you and Eric go out to the back. I'll have Anna prepare something."

Sandor scarcely dared to look at her. Ah, my God, what a day this had turned out to be. Who would have dreamed that there could be English as friendly as these? If he had understood her properly she was going to give him something to eat.

In a daze he followed Eric to the back lawn. There was a table there with an umbrella over it such as he had seen earlier that morning.

He sat down. But what was there to talk about? This boy was rich and English and happy. He probably had all the friends he wanted. And to make things worse, he was almost a head shorter than Sandor. What could they possibly have in common?

"You play much with the kids aroun' here?" he asked.

"Not so much," Eric said. "Oh, sometimes. They call me a plumber," he blurted out.

"A plumber!" Sandor cried. "But — wot — wot for?"

"Just because I like fixing things." His eyes were like a little old man's, grave and deep-set and sad. And yet sad in an odd way. It made one smile to see those eyes above his pink, round cheeks.

"Wot kind of things do you fix?" Sandor asked.

"I fixed my bicycle," Eric said. His face, clouded the moment before, now brightened. "A tooth in one of the gears was broken," he explained. "I took it out and now it runs just like new."

"'At sure is swell," Sandor said. "But wot about those kids? Do they fight you or anythin' like that?"

"No. They only call me that to make fun of me. I call them farmers."

"Farmers! Why?"

"Oh, just because they're dumb, I guess." He smiled scornfully. "They can't even fix a bicycle bell."

Sandor considered this. "Wot else do you fix?" he asked.

"I fixed a lock," Eric began.

It appeared that he had fixed the metronome — whatever that was — and the toaster and the electric-iron cord.

In the middle of his recital, a maid appeared with a tray. Eric waited until she had gone and then continued. but Sandor no longer heard him.

He stretched out his legs. If only Louis could see him now, or his parents, or better still, the English gang, see him sitting here with his rich, English friend, with all the ease and assurance of a person born to this kind of life, eating little sandwiches that melted in his mouth and sipping pink lemonade — there actually was such a thing. There were real raspberries in it.

He gazed up at the sunlight in bars of gold and green and orange shining through the fabric above him, and looked beyond the horizon of the umbrella rim, and knew that as long as he lived he would only have to close his eyes and this would all come back to him again.

Eric was still talking. Sandor watched the play of expression on his face. Every passing mood was reflected there. If he ever tried to tell a lie he'd be sunk, Sandor thought. He was looking unhappy again. But that sailor suit he had on must have cost plenty. He had a bicycle; he looked well fed. He lived here in this rich house with a maid to look after him. What did he have to be unhappy about?

The poor young punk's just talked himself into sumpin', he thought. It was not going to be too difficult to become friendly with him. The trouble was that he would have to get himself involved in this crazy excitement about fixing things. . . .

" . . . do you?" Eric asked fiercely.

"Yes," Sandor replied, and saw that this was wrong and shook his head emphatically.

"I'm sorry it's finished," Eric continued, "because now there's nothing left to fix. Last week I started to fix my waggon but Mother sent it to the repair shop. She thinks it's dirty work and she likes things to be clean. And Father doesn't like me to fix things either. He says it's not proper."

He looked up angrily. "And that's why he won't let me look after the lawn any more. That's why you're going to do it. And I like looking after the lawn."

"But —"

Eric glared at him.

"But 'at's not my fault," Sandor said. "Is it 'cause o' the money? They paid you, eh?" He had decided on the desperate expedient of offering him half of what he would get, but Eric shook his head.

"It's not fair," he said tearfully. "They make me put my money in a bank, and at Christmastime and people's birthdays I have to buy presents with it. And all the presents I get are things I don't want."

"'At's tough," Sandor said. "'At's tough, awright. but wot are you mad at me for?"

Eric raised his eyelids languidly and looked at him as though he were not there.

"Okay," Sandor said. "If 'at's the way you want it. Then just tell me where the lawn-mower is."

Eric smiled slyly, and remained silent.

Finding the lawn-mower under the porch, Sandor set to work. Eric watched him glumly. Finally he disappeared, to return a few minutes later with the maid, who announced that his mother had given him permission to help, but only on the back lawn. It remained impossible, however, to get a word out of him. When they were done he vanished again.

On the front lawn Sandor saw him wandering aimlessly down the street. He looked at him long and thoughtfully.

"The poor young punk," he murmured, and suddenly he ran to the road and called to him.

Eric hesitated and sauntered back.

"I think maybe I kin get you sumpin' to fix," Sandor said. "We got a coupla old clocks around the house I think maybe I kin . . ."

"Clocks!" Eric cried. A small boy's greed leaped into the little-old-man's eyes. He smiled, but suddenly his face clouded with fear. He clutched Sandor's arm.

"For sure," Sandor said. "Next Saturday."

"Clocks!" Eric cried again, and did a wild caper on the lawn. "There's nothing I like to fix better than clocks. I'll be able to . . ."

"You better ask your mother first, eh?"

"I can't get dirty fixing a clock."

"I know, but maybe you better ask her anyway."

But Eric was already on the front steps. He was gone so long, Sandor began to wonder whether he had done the right thing.

The sight of him a few minutes later drove all further apprehension out of Sandor's mind. Eric came toward him, smiling, his hands behind his back.

"Mother said to thank you," he began, holding himself very erectly.

Out of the corner of his eyes, Sandor saw Eric's mother standing at an upper window, watching them.

"Mother said to say she was very pleased," Eric chanted. "And she said it was thoughtful. And . . . here."

He held out an incredibly misshapen package wrapped in brown paper.

"But . . . I'm on'y gonna give you a coupla old clocks," Sandor said.

It was difficult to keep his eyes from the upper window. Why had she done this? The clocks were not a present. They were just junk. Maybe she didn't know this and didn't want him to feel that they owed him anything. Was that it? If he were a friend — a close friend — would she have felt that she must immediately give one gift for another? He didn't know. Maybe that was the way people did things here. Maybe they were just being polite and it was up to him to refuse. Much as he wanted to accept, he wanted still more to impress her, to do what she would consider was the right thing, to make her feel that he wanted to be a friend.

It occurred to him that she might ask what he had said.

"I didn't promise to give you them clocks 'cause I wanted anythin' back," he said. "I just wanted to give them to you 'cause you had nuthin' to fix."

He gulped and considered what he had said.

Eric thrust the parcel into his hands. Sandor noticed that his hair had been brushed and his hands washed.

He thanked him with what formality he could muster. Eric was still holding himself stiffly erect. "An' say thanks to your mother too, eh?"

He turned and clearly within his line of vision he saw her, one hand upheld on the curtain, the other holding her bosom which was rising and falling with laughter.

He had done the right thing then in accepting, or she wouldn't be laughing. He tore open the package. A book and a wallet. The book didn't matter. But the wallet had a maple leaf cut in the centre and two compartments for bills — a man's wallet of gleaming brown leather that felt alive in his hands.

Eric looked on, a small boy bursting with pride, struggling to hold back his excitement.

Sandor raised his hand to clap him on the shoulder. But she was still watching, still laughing. She might consider this too great a familiarity.

"Thanks," he said. "Geez, thanks a million."

They shook hands. "I'm sorry I was such a farmer," Eric smiled, and suddenly he let out a whoop and began to caper about the lawn again.

He sat down finally on the front steps.

Afterwards it seemed to Sandor that the last few hours of this day had been the best. He had spent them quietly in the cool shade of the front lawn, playing croquet and talking to Eric, indulgently allowing him to win, smiling when he sulked, not at all through fear that he might lose his friendship, but prompted by a strange and hitherto unknown feeling, a half-shameful, embarrassed affection, the desire to protect him somehow and look after him as an older brother might.

The street lay in the shadows of the great houses when he left.

He was at the car-stop looking back when unexpectedly there flashed before him the mean and dirty clutter of the street he lived on, as though he were seeing it for the first time, crawling with pale, spindly kids, green-nostrilled, their mouths agape in the hot fury of play; and the battered houses with the scabrous walls and the shingles dropping and the walls dirt-stained and rain-streaked; like a silent herd of monstrous beasts stricken with some unnameable disease, slowly dying as they stood there, their members rotting and falling from them.

That was where he belonged — not here.

Sandor raised his head. It was true, a vast gulf separated this world from his, but he had spanned it; in one stride had crossed over to taste, to see, and forever to invest his dreams with the vision of it. He laughed at the magnitude of his achievement. He had a friend here — a rich, English friend. Next week he would see him again, and the week after that, and all through the summer until one distant day he would return here to stay.

Six

FOR HOURS on end he sat on the roof of the woodshed silently contained within himself, re-living Saturdays that had come and gone, lost in unfolding fantasies that formed themselves sometimes about Eric, sometimes about his mother. He moved from the far circumference of her life to its centre. He related himself to her, subjected her to a thousand perils and saved her from them all—and sighed at their unlikelihood. Her presence hovered about him. Enough that she liked cleanliness; he washed himself half a dozen times a day: that she had once frowned at his manner of speech, and she accomplished by the mere lowering of a brow what school teachers and his father and Mr. Crawford had tried in vain to do.

The outer aspects of his life receded. He held himself proudly aloof from the affairs of his family. He moved through his neighbourhood with unseeing eyes.

The summer holidays arrived. He remained alone, snug and secure in the cocoon he had woven about himself.

One night, sitting in his accustomed place, he overheard his parents talking in the yard below. With an air of supreme condescension he raised his head and listened. It appeared that his father had made the last payment on Onkel Janos' ticket. Sandor curbed his excitement. It was undignified and out of keeping with his highborn rôle.

But a week or so later he became aware that his mother was

planning a party, and from the evidence that had begun to accumulate, a party such as Henry Avenue had never known.

The attitude he had imposed upon himself began to show signs of strain. A telegram from his uncle shattered it.

Early that Sunday morning on which his uncle was to arrive, the kitchen began to fill with women — friends and acquaintances who had been invited to the party and had come to help. It was sweltering outside; in the kitchen the heat was almost unbearable. The women moved around in their petticoats, long shapeless affairs with flounces and lace, black and purple and yellow — an amusing sight to Sandor who stood in a corner laughing until his mother sent him upstairs to make sure that his uncle's room was in order. Mr. Schwalbe had consented to sleep in the outer attic so that Frau Hunyadi's brother would have a room to himself, for the first few days at least.

In the doorway of the attic, Sandor paused. All the beds had been covered with thick flannel sheets and on them, sucking their thumbs in sleep, squalling, pink and gurgling or blue with moist anger, lay the babies. Watching over them were the grown-up daughters of the women downstairs.

Once he might have stopped to listen to them. Now he simply looked into Mr. Schwalbe's cubicle and passed them by. They reminded him too much of the maids he had seen in Eric's neighbourhood. They laughed too loud and too long. Their clothes were too bright and too fancy.

He went into the toilet, took a small fragment of mirror out of his hiding-place under the floorboards and, holding it at arm's length, examined his new blue serge sailor-suit which his mother had bought — by instalments — with the money he had earned. He straightened the collar and continued to look at himself until he heard his mother calling to him from the foot of the stairs. It was time to go. He was to meet his father at the station.

A few minutes later he was on his way. He came to the hotel and reverting to his former rôle, passed proudly and sedately below the windows of the lobby.

Then he saw the crowd moving toward the station and

became Sandor Hunyadi again, pressing excitedly and eagerly to the great doors. He saw his father standing there in his best black suit which he wore at Christmas and New Year. It was like new. Whenever he removed it from the closet, he smiled and stroked it and clicked his tongue at Old-Country craftsmanship.

Sandor waved to him. His father waved back. They had been on good terms ever since the summer holidays had started. His father took him by the hand.

They followed the crowd into the vast echoing cavern to a rope barrier. Sandor had been here before and it had always been crowded, but now for the first time he sensed the expectancy of the people around him. Now and then the station reverberated to the jargon of the train-caller. On the platform above, he heard the familiar, ponderous clatter of the engines. The suppressed excitement of the crowd began to affect him. He heard his father call out a greeting to a friend and realized that his father was as excited as he was. His father did not quite approve of Onkel Janos. Was it only because he was an adventurer, or were there other hidden reasons?

From the upper level came the interminable slow creak and groan of a train coming to a stop. Behind him the crowd strained forward, pressing him against the rope barrier. All was still. There reached them the shrill cry of a child; a voice in English giving directions. Then the long-awaited tramp of feet, growing louder and louder, reaching the head of the stairs, and finally the first of the new arrivals emerged from the gates and looked about them timidly and fearfully, bent under the weight of their belongings. Reluctantly they moved forward, pushed ahead by those who came behind.

Sandor turned pale at the sight of them. They stood there, awkward and begrimed, the men in tight-fitting wrinkled clothes, with their wrists and ankles sticking out, unshaven and foreign-looking, the women in kerchiefs and voluminous skirts and men's shoes . . . exactly the way his grandmother looked in that picture in the front room. And it was this that was frightening. They were so close to him. Only a few months or years — a few words and recently acquired habits

— separated his parents from them. The kinship was odious. He knew how hard it was for his parents to change their ways. But they were changing. They used tinned goods sometimes at home now, and store-bought bread when they had enough money. English food was appearing on their table, the English language in their home. Slowly, very slowly, they were changing. They were becoming Canadians. And now here it stood. Here was the nightmare survival of themselves, mocking and dragging them back to their shameful past.

Sandor looked up at his father. His lips trembled at the expression on his father's face. It was as though the embers of something long forgotten had been stirred into flame by the sight of these people and now cast an ardent glow upon his features. His eyes half-closed, he murmured something to himself in his native tongue. Sandor tugged at his arm. His father never noticed. Sandor turned back and glanced at the newcomers. The foremost among them had faltered and finally come to a stop at the sight of the crowd in front of them.

The two groups stared at one another. Then a man's voice cried "Ilonka!" The new arrivals wavered. A woman shifted the child in her arms and waved. The man called to her again, and before they were in each other's arms the barrier was down and the two groups were one. The station echoed their gladness in many tongues. They touched one another and cried. They embraced and smiled and stood apart and stared into eyes familiar and yet grown strange.

Sandor scowled. There were probably dozens of people here who could call his father "landsmann." As he followed his father with reluctant steps to the foot of the stairs, he wondered with a sudden shudder of disgust whether his uncle was as foreign-looking and as dirty as these others. Off to one side of him, he heard someone calling his father by his first name. He caught sight of a tall, dark man moving toward them, with an enormous wickerwork trunk on his shoulders and a miscellaneous array of packages and boxes in his hand. His teeth against dark lips and a swarthy complexion flashed in a dazzling smile. Onkel Janos, Sandor thought with a sinking heart. He was unshaven; he wore a collarless shirt, and a faded green jacket that looked as though it had once been part of a uniform. Ten feet away he shouted a greeting at them, dropped his belongings, and sprang forward to meet them with outstretched hands.

"By gollies, hullo," he shouted, and laughed uproariously. The two men began shaking hands and talking excitedly in Hungarian. Sandor caught the sound of his mother's name, and once, while his uncle's glance swept appraisingly over him, his own. He stood still while his uncle patted him on the head and shouted "Kolossal!" For his uncle everything was evidently "kolossal." Sandor crept around behind his father and waited. The only thing to look forward to now was the food and possibly, though not very probably, his uncle's present.

The two men began collecting the parcels and boxes. On the street, Sandor dropped a few paces behind them. Gollies hullo, he moaned. So this was the Pirate Uncle. This was how an adventurer looked and smelled. This was the man who had fought the Turks — who had been captured by the Arabs and who had been a millionaire several times over.

He had arrived just in time. With his ticket paid for they were just beginning to lay aside a little money every week. Now they would probably have to buy him clothes and feed him until he found a job.

Half a dozen steps or so behind them, Sandor stood still while his uncle looked about him. He drew a little nearer when he discovered that they were speaking German. His uncle wanted to know if there was a place where he could wash and shave before going on. Joseph Hunyadi explained that he had already thought of that. He hoped Janos wouldn't mind; he had taken the liberty of buying him a few things: underwear, a shirt, a pair of socks.

Yeah. That's how it was with his father, Sandor thought. He could make a gesture worthy of a millionaire and borrow the money to do it.

There was a place only a few blocks away, his father continued, where Janos could have a bath and a shave.

Sandor walked on behind until they reached the barber

shop. His father and his uncle went downstairs. He sat down despondently in the empty pool room until a barber who had once lived with them as a non-paying boarder called to him and asked him if he wanted a haircut. The boss was out, he explained. Sandor nodded, and thanked him as he walked back into the barber shop. He sat down and closed his eyes. It was warm and quiet here, the air filled with the odours of the lotions and the soap. A fly droned on the ceiling. From the basement came the faint hiss of escaping steam; above him, the rhythmic snick of the scissors.

He had been up since early morning. He nodded and fell into a light slumber, from which he was awakened by the sound of laughter. He opened his eyes to discover his father, two barbers, and a stranger, all smiling at him. Sandor blinked, smiled back weakly, and felt his hair. It was cool and moist. He blinked again, and then turned back to the stranger, who was still laughing. He was tall and elegantly dressed. There was an air of distinction about him.

Sandor rubbed his eyes. The stranger laughed uproariously and cried, "Kolossal!" It was a complete transformation. His uncle was a foreigner no longer. He reminded Sandor strongly of the men in the hotel lobby.

He jumped to his feet. "Onkel Janos!" he cried.

His uncle bent down and with a swoop raised him aloft. "Hullo," he roared.

"Hullo," Sandor cried joyfully.

"By gollies, hullo, hullo, hullo," his uncle echoed. "I spik English? You will learn me, ya?"

Sandor nodded, too happy to speak.

He felt as though he were walking on air as they left the barber shop. The wickerwork trunk had been left behind to be picked up later. But the shoe-box, Onkel Janos said as he thrust it into Sandor's hands with a promising wink, this box was to be handled carefully. Sandor winked back and tucked it under his arm; it felt reassuringly heavy and solidly packed. He took his uncle's hand as they turned down Logan Avenue.

He snorted impatiently as his father and uncle began talking Hungarian again. Finally, he caught his uncle's eye. "Onkel Janos," he said, "please talk German. I can't understand."

"You don't speak Hungarian?"

Sandor shook his head. "I've forgotten."

"I've tried to teach him Hungarian," Joseph Hunyadi said. "Maybe when he's a little older . . ."

"But you speak English?" Onkel Janos asked, turning to Sandor.

"I talk English very well," Sandor said, and repeated it in German.

"Of course, you speak English. And why not? This is an English-speaking country isn't it? You want to get on. I can see just by looking at you that you're the kind of boy who's going to get ahead."

He turned away from Sandor and looked across at Joseph Hunyadi. "What does the boy want with Hungarian?" he asked. "Take my advice, Joseph, don't addle his brains."

Sandor tightened his grip on his uncle's hand. They turned down Henry Avenue, and walked on. A few hundred feet from the house, Onkel Janos suddenly raised his head. "I smell goulash," he roared, and lengthened his stride.

"The back way," Sandor cried, tugging at his hand. "Ma said to use the back door."

The back yard was full of children. On the roof of the woodshed sat the sons of the invited guests, taunting those who now gathered below, having nosed their way to the origin of the odours that had been drifting through the neighbourhood all morning. In their midst stood Frau Hunyadi handing out cookies. The invited urchins screamed. They were not being given any on the fantastic ground that it would spoil their appetites. From their perch on the roof they yelled down their defiance and threats.

As Frau Hunyadi turned back to the screen door, she caught sight of her brother. In an instant she was in his arms. "Ach, Janos, Janos." She held him close to her. They embraced and beheld each other at arm's length as well as their tears would allow. The children grew silent. Sandor shifted uncomfortably. His mother and Onkel Janos began to talk to one another in Hungarian.

Now a woman's face appeared at the window, and then another. Frau Hunyadi, catching sight of them, whispered something to her brother. To Sandor's relief they spoke German. It was very hot in the kitchen, his mother explained. And the front room was filled with tables and chairs. They had arranged a little party. Would Janos mind . . .

Onkel Janos kissed her. The women streamed into the back yard from the kitchen, red and smiling. And behind them came their husbands, their hands and faces burned dark with the sun, painters and carpenters and sewer-diggers; and a pale shoemaker, a Hegelian philosopher and close friend of Joseph Hunyadi.

The women began gathering around Onkel Janos, to be introduced. Sandor grinned from ear to ear at his uncle's performance. He had drawn himself erect. Now he twirled the ends of his moustache, and with a faint click of his heels and a slight bow, bent over and kissed Frau Szabo's hand. Frau Szabo flushed and giggled. Then Frau Gombos.

Their husbands smiled indulgently. The kids on the roof looked on in silent delight. Sandor laughed to himself. He felt he was beginning to understand. His uncle had a way with him that made people smile.

When the introductions were over, the women returned to the house; there were still a few things to be done in the kitchen. The men had been told to stay where they were. They pulled some logs off the woodpile and settled down to a comfortable smoke.

Sandor followed his mother and uncle upstairs into Mr. Schwalbe's cubicle. He remained in the doorway while they seated themselves on the cot. To his annoyance they began to talk in Hungarian again, and they talked for a long time. He caught the names of other uncles and distant relations. His mother began to cry. Sandor shifted impatiently. Finally his uncle noticed him, reached out, and took the shoe-box from him.

"Guess what?" he asked as he broke the string.

Sandor smiled and shook his head. This was going to be something, a real present. He knew it. Everything his uncle did exceeded one's expectations.

Onkel Janos opened the box and handed him a long shining cardboard tube, gaily decorated with laughing fishes and mermaids, with sailing ships and benign, droll monsters cavorting in a sky-blue sea.

Sandor eyed it with dismay. It looked like a kid's toy. From the expression on his uncle's face, he suspected that a joke was being played on him. "What is it?" he asked.

"Kolossal!" his uncle shouted, and burst into laughter.

"It's a joke," Sandor cried. "It's not my present at all."

Onkel Janos slapped his knees and roared with laughter. "Here, I'll show you," he said at last. "It's called a kaleidoscope. Look." He took the tube, held it up to the light, and peered through it. "So," he said, and handed it back.

Sandor placed his eye to the peep-hole and gasped.

"Turn it," his uncle said.

He turned it. There was a click, and behold, a new world. Another turn and another in a riot of colour, like a splintered rainbow; cool, deep-green gems, and frivolous pink ones, water-blue and orange jewels in triangles and squares and crescents glittering and flashing before his eye, ever changing, ever new.

He set it aside, finally, and gazed across at his uncle with a look of deep affection.

"Thank your uncle, Sandor," his mother said.

"Ho, something for you too," Onkel Janos cried, handing her a small leather case.

She opened it. A slow flush came over her cheeks. Sandor craned his neck and saw a pair of gold ear-rings with small red stones, and a brooch. She kissed her brother tenderly. "You shouldn't have done this, Janos," she said. "You know you shouldn't. But they are beautiful."

Onkel Janos was already engrossed in pulling out more shredded paper from his shoe-box. "For Joseph," he said, extracting an amber-stemmed pipe. "I'll give it to him later."

"You really shouldn't have done this, Janos. You've spent all your money, haven't you? . . . And a new suit," she exclaimed. "I never even noticed. It's very becoming."

Onkel Janos grasped her hand. "Here. Feel," he said. "English tweed."

"It reminds me of so many things, to see you sitting here like this," she said quietly. "You haven't changed a bit."

"And neither have you. You're as beautiful as ever, Helena."

Sandor's eyebrows rose. He watched the colour ebb and flow on his mother's cheeks.

She laughed softly and shook her head. Her laughter had a girlish trill. Sandor's incredulity grew. He had never heard his mother laugh like this.

"The whole village went into mourning the day Joseph took you away," Onkel Janos continued. "At least, the young men did. . . . The girls? Hmm!" He rolled his eyes, raised his right hand, and gave his moustache a twirl.

Frau Hunyadi laughed.

Sandor looked on in astonishment. His mother's lips, always so tightly pressed together, were now parted softly in a smile. He scarcely knew her. She looked strange and beautiful. He shifted uneasily.

As she raised her arm to fit her ear-rings in place, he bent over impulsively, threw his arms about her, and kissed her.

"Why, Sandor!" she said in surprise. He drew away, embarrassed, and looked at his uncle, who merely laughed and caught him between his knees and rumpled his hair some more.

His mother rose to her feet. "There's so much to talk about, I don't know where to start," she said. "But I'll have to go downstairs now. . . . Come, Sandor. Onkel Janos is going to have a little nap."

Sandor wandered about the kitchen until his mother asked him to leave. The men in the yard were talking about the Old Country. With the exception of Willi Schumacher, the kids on the roof were all too young to play with. He went into the lane and looked into his kaleidoscope until his arm grew numb holding it to his eye. He smiled to himself as he lowered it. Next Saturday he would take it along and show it to Eric, and maybe even lend it to him for a week.

As he walked back into the yard, Willi Schumacher called down to him, asking him what he was carrying. Sandor paused. The thought that flashed across his mind was fully developed by the time he was up on the roof.

Five minutes later he was doing a roaring business. None of his customers had any ready money, but their fathers were down there in the yard below and feeling in an expansive mood. A few of the boys came back with nickels. These were permitted to hold the tube in their own hands. Some, who had been able to raise only a few coppers, found their exclamations dying in their throats, the tube was snatched away so fast.

When it was over, Sandor thrust his hand into his pocket and let the coins trickle through his fingers. In fifteen minutes, he had made forty-three cents — almost as much as he earned for a morning's work. As he climbed down, he caught sight of his father and Onkel Janos looking down at him from the attic window. Onkel Janos was smiling. But in that brief glance at his father, he knew that there was going to be trouble. His father motioned to him to come upstairs.

Sandor walked slowly through the yard, wondering what was wrong. He shrugged his shoulders and went upstairs. They were waiting for him behind Mr. Schwalbe's cubicle. If he was going to be shamed, he thought, at least it was not going to be in the presence of all those girls. . . .

His father turned on him the moment he appeared. His face was livid. He raised his hand, dropped it — and Sandor, looking straight ahead, saw the clenched fingers in a convulsive fist, darkly veined, opening and closing and opening again.

"You demanded money of your friends before you would let them see your gift?" his father asked in German.

Sandor looked up at him in astonishment.

"Sure," he said. "Why not?"

"You're not ashamed," his father asked, "to make your friends pay?"

"They're not my friends," Sandor replied. "And anyway, what did I do that's wrong? They'da done the same to me if they were in my place . . ."

"They are our guests," his father shouted. "You sent them down to their parents for money to pay you. Have you no shame at all? Your gift has not been an hour in your possession and already you have turned it into something dirty by contaminating it with money."

Sandor lowered his head. To be humiliated like this in front of his uncle, on the day of his arrival, and for no reason that he could understand!

"I didn't do anything wrong," he cried tearfully. "Anybody woulda done the same as I did." He saw his uncle shaking his head at him, but with a faint sympathetic smile on his lips. "It's my present, isn't it?" he shouted. "I can do what I like with it."

He fled into Mr. Schwalbe's cubicle. At the door, he saw Onkel Janos remonstrating with his father, and as he closed it, caught a glimpse of his brother on one of the beds outside, lying peacefully there on his back, playing with his toes.

Poor little punk, he thought. He doesn't know yet what kind of a family he's in. . . .

He lay down on the cot, his eyes tight against the threatening tears, his mind filled with the familiar pain and pleasure of crushing his father and humiliating him as he himself had been humiliated. Then he thought of how things might have been if he had been older. And he remembered that Eric too had trouble with his father. It was something you had to bear until you were grown up. He thought of how his uncle had taken his part. He wiped his eyes.

The door opened suddenly and his uncle entered the room. He sat down, sighed, and removed his shoes. Then he yawned, flinging out his arms as far as they would go, which was not very far, for the cubicle was only five feet wide and as a result the knuckles of his left hand struck the beaverboard partition a blow that seemed to Sandor to rock the entire attic. The plaster between the sheets of beaverboard shot out against the far wall. Sandor began to smile. His uncle merely raised his eyebrows and asked Sandor to move over. The springs groaned under his weight.

"Your father has great plans for you," he began. "A fine life is in store for you. A good education, an established position. Some day people will call you Herr Doktor. You will be a wealthy man. Does this please you?"

Sandor shook his head. "Pa doesn't want me to be rich," he cried. "He wants me to be like him, instead of like other people. He thinks everything that's got anything to do with money is wrong. Honest-to God, Onkol Janos," he continued passionately, "Pa won't ever make enough money for me to go to University. He just talks like that. . . . And even if I could go, I wouldn't. You don't have to go to University to get rich."

His uncle stared up at the ceiling for a long time. "But your father works very hard," he said at last.

Sandor raised himself on his elbow. "Pa works hard," he admitted. His voice broke. "But he doesn't make enough," he continued. "And what makes Ma so mad is that he takes in boarders even when they don't pay."

His uncle turned and looked at him in silence. "I see," he said.

"Some day, I'm going to make a lot of money," Sandor said. "And Ma won't have to worry any more. I won't let her take in any boarders, and Pa won't have to work. I'll look after the whole family."

His uncle smiled and nodded. "So? That's fine," he said. "It's good to hear such things. But how will you earn this money?"

Sandor flushed. "I'm going to quit school as soon as I can, and get a job. In an office. That's how people get rich in this country. Working in offices. And I'm already earning money," he added. "A dollar every week, cutting grass for rich people. Next week maybe I'll be making a dollar and a half when I get another customer."

"But that's a great deal of money," his uncle said.

"That's how things are in this country," Sandor explained.

Onkel Janos sighed and pulled a package of cigarettes and a box of matches from his pocket. He flicked the package open and popped a cigarette into his mouth, then lit it and letting the cigarette dangle from his lower lip, he gave a snort and blew at the flame of the match in a great sweeping gust that quite extinguished it and sent a shower of sparks and ashes into the air intermingled with the smoke from the bright-glowing end of the cigarette.

Sandor looked at him, hungrily intent upon the mighty inhalation which caused the cigarette so visibly to shorten, almost tasting the long-drawn, thin blue smoke streaming slowly and deliciously out of his uncle's hairy nostrils. His uncle had a way about him, a special way. Everything he did was just right. You felt that the way he did a thing was the only way it could ever be done.

He lay on his back watching the smoke trickle out of his uncle's nostrils. He watched until he could stand it no longer. "Onkel Janos," he pleaded, "give me a puff, will you?"

His uncle raised his eyebrows. "You smoke already?"

"I've been smoking for years."

His uncle looked at him thoughtfully as he handed him a cigarette. "And girls, too," he said. "I suppose you know all about girls."

"What is there to know?" Sandor asked. "They're all the same, aren't they?"

"You think so?" his uncle inquired, and nodded. "Maybe you're right," he said.

Sandor felt himself flushing. Out of the corner of his eyes he glanced at his uncle to see if he was laughing at him. But Onkel Janos was very soberly crushing the remains of his cigarette in the lid of a jam tin.

"So you're already earning a dollar and a half a week," he said. "You've been smoking for years and you know all about girls. It is as I said to your father. He doesn't have to worry about you. You're the kind of boy who's going to get along in this country."

"And so will you," Sandor cried. "You look like an English millionaire in your new suit. Nobody could tell you just came to Canada a few hours ago."

Onkel Janos laughed. Grabbing him by the middle he lifted him in the air for a moment, then dropped him on the cot and pretended to wrestle with him. Sandor screamed with pleasure.

He was weak with laughter when his uncle finally let him go. He was about to retrieve his cigarette which had fallen to the floor when he heard the sound of footsteps on the lower front stairs. He listened intently and crushed his cigarette in the jam-tin lid. "It's Ma," he said.

His uncle grinned. "Go and tell her you'll wake me," he whispered, and winked. Sandor winked back. He opened the door and ran down the steps to the first landing. His mother stopped and looked up at him.

"You want me to call Onkel Janos, Ma?"

"Yes, call him, Sandor. Everything's ready now."

Sandor ran back upstairs. Onkel Janos was lying on his side, breathing heavily. Sandor smiled softly.

"Onkel Janos. It's all right now," he said.

His uncle rose, combed his hair, and put on his shoes. They went downstairs.

Sandor's mouth fell open as he entered the living-room. All the tables they had borrowed from their neighbours that morning had been placed end to end. With wedges under their legs they were now all the same height, and since they were covered with several white tablecloths whose edges overlapped, the whole thing looked like one table, long and immense in the little room. The linen gleamed, the dishes sparkled. But Sandor's attention was fastened upon the head of the table where, in all its splendour, stood the Hunyadi geranium. For the occasion, the jam tin in which it stood was covered with a piece of green crepe.

Sandor looked at it in astonishment. Against the cool crisp background, where everything glistened so invitingly, it seemed to have taken on fresh colour and life. Its blood-red blossoms gave an air of festivity to the room. How it had ever managed to survive at all was a mystery. Year in and year out, it stood on the front-room window-ledge. In winter, the panes froze over; in summer they were black with rain-smeared grime. The Hunyadis had not only to water the plant, but also, since the window faced the freight-yards, to dust its thick limp leaves and blow away the specks of soot that lay like so many black sins upon its petals. Sometimes, they forgot to water it; sometimes in the winter when they were short of coal for the front-room stove it was kept above the kitchen range. His mother had tried to grow other things, delicate fragile things with subtle odours and gracious forms, but one season on Henry Avenue and they were dead. Only the geraniums survived. And in window after window on Henry Avenue they stood, earthy and sturdy, throwing up leaves so that they might blossom and give their colour in lonely splendour to a neighbourhood whose only workaday tone was an abiding grey.

Now it stood at the head of the table to welcome Onkel Janos who, as he passed by, plucked a blossom and stuck it in his lapel.

Sandor followed suit and trotted after his uncle into the kitchen.

A moment later he heard the strains of an accordion in the back yard. The screen door banged as Long Thomas, a neighbour, entered with his accordion, flanked on either side by one of the Nemeth twins. Long Thomas was well over six feet tall, sad and gaunt. The great bald nodding heads of the twins came scarcely to his elbows. With their fiddles under their arms, they walked sedately beside him, their dark eyes infinitely guileless. Upon a few rare occasions Sandor had visited them in their shack by the river. In the winter they made raffia baskets; in the summer, willow flower-stands. But no matter what the season, there was always time for music. No party was complete without them. By long-established custom their fee had come to consist of all the beer they could drink and as much food as they could eat.

Behind them swarmed the children, screaming with laughter. Long Thomas stopped, flung an incredibly long leg

into the air, did a short little jig, and walked into the front
room.

As though guided by some infallible sense, the twins made
straight for the corner where the beer barrel stood. They drank
in a way that made Sandor's mouth water even though he
hated the smell of beer.

When they had finished, they sat down with their mugs of
beer beside them, adjusted their instruments, and began to
play. They played with verve, gusto, sweat, and love. Their
eyes closed, their bodies swayed, their pink domes nodded,
their fingers flew. Long Thomas finished his beer and joined
them.

But now without warning the song changed to a Hungarian
dance. Played by the Nemeth twins to a houseful of Hungarians, it was irresistible. From the kitchen came the sound
of shouting and laughing and the impatient clacking of heels.
Then to the loud delight of Sandor and the children, who had
gathered around the musicians, Onkel Janos came waltzing
into the front room with Frau Szabo in his arms. Sandor could
not make up his mind whether to look at his uncle or receive
the admiring glances of those around him for possessing such
a relative. For Onkel Janos did not merely dance. There were
times when Sandor could have sworn that neither Onkel Janos
nor his partner had their feet on the ground. He spun her
around, did a series of weird little sidesteps and then, while
she whirled alone, leaped up, snapped his fingers, clicked his
heels in mid-air, and shouted incomprehensible rhymes in
Hungarian. Frau Szabo's face grew flushed. She smiled happily. Her bosom strained alarmingly against the fabric of her
bodice.

The twins, watching them, nodded and grinned. Then their
eyes and their mouths closed simultaneously and sublime
smiles settled on their faces. The tempo of their playing
became frenzied. More and more of the guests came from the
kitchen and back yard; a man would laugh, look shyly at his
wife, and step out. The room grew so crowded one could
scarcely move. The narrow aisle between the wall of children
and the row of tables was filled with people dancing.

But no one danced as his uncle did, Sandor thought. Everything he did became appropriate, but only because he himself had done it.

When the music stopped, Sandor followed him to the corner where the twins were. With a few words, he had them laughing uproariously. They looked droll with their pink little tongues flickering in the dark caverns of their mouths.

But now the guests were beginning to respond to Frau Hunyadi's pleas. They were gradually seating themselves at the table. Frau Hunyadi's friends helped her to serve.

Sandor pushed his way forward to the table set up for the older children. He sat down where he could watch his uncle.

The food arrived, the hot steaming fragrance of it filling the room, savoury and varied and as spicy as an adventure, rich with the treasured cooking-lore of the whole of Europe. Crumb by crumb the women had garnered the skills and details, the piquant flavours and the subtle aromas from a thousand sources — small ingenuities that came from poverty, recipes taken from the vanquished and imposed by conquerors, graciously given by neighbours or stolen from friends, handed down from mother to daughter so that at last in Frau Hunyadi's kitchen there came to fruition an age-long process, proudly, lovingly, and painstakingly fulfilled.

Soup came first. But this was merely to prepare the guests for the more serious business of eating. Immediately after, there appeared an enormous bowl of chicken goulash, steaming hot in its red sauce of paprika, with great fat globules floating on the surface. As a side dish for soaking up the gravy there was a mound of home-made noodles, accompanied by small green gherkins with flesh clear as glass from their long immersion in brine, with the pungent aroma of dill and garlic and the young tender leaves of horse-radish. And there were pickled red peppers — for the adults who knew how to get them into their mouths without touching their lips — and horse-radish grated into crushed beetroot that went with the sausages, which were made by a landsmann who had been a butcher in the Old Country and who could be depended upon to season them liberally with paprika and garlic among other things.

Sandor rose after every course, with twitching nostrils breathing in the food that was carried past him, following it with his eyes to the adults' table, listening to his uncle's exclamations and the remarks of guests with a deep feeling of pride. This was a party. No one — not one guest — had been asked to bring anything. The pickles and preserves and things were offered out of friendship. Their equivalent would some day be returned. A fleeting image of the Kostanuiks, Mary and her mother and father, came to him. He saw them, their long-drawn hungry faces pressed to the front-room window, their eyes imploring him for food, "Yaah," he muttered, "that would be good for them."

He sat down, satisfied, only to spring up again as the aroma of another dish came to him. Sarma, it was called, made of ground meat and rice flavoured with paprika and chopped onions, wrapped in sauerkraut leaves. The thought of the paprika seeping through the finely shredded kraut almost made him swoon. He sat down. When he had finished the last course, he closed his eyes.

The clatter around him slowly diminished. Above the murmuring voices he heard his uncle's laughter. The twins began once more to play. He smelled coffee — real coffee with no chicory in it. His eyes opened.

The dishes had been cleared away; the cakes and pastry were brought in, heaping platters of kupfel, the bright outer pastry caressingly flaked around apricot, cherry, or plum centres. Mohn strudel — ground poppy-seeds with sugar and raisins, enfolded in a pastry like a jelly-roll. The apfel strudel and other tidbits, crisp bubbles of fruit-sugar and egg-white beaten to a froth and browned, with a walnut or an almond in the centre.

And last of all, the crowning achievement, the Torte, made of ground hazelnuts and a few spoonfuls of flour with five whipped-cream layers and a glazed dark chocolate covering. Sandor bit into it ecstatically. He felt as though he were eating his way into heaven. A few gulps later it was gone. He sipped his coffee and discovered that there was real cream in it.

At the adults' table, the men were getting up and beginning to smoke. Sandor got to his feet, just as the change of shift occurred at his table. The children were told to go outside and play. The girls who had been watching the babies upstairs, and the women who had helped to serve, seated themselves while their neighbours waited on them. Sandor sauntered slowly to the corner where the men were talking.

He sat down on the floor beside his uncle and listened, and watched the coming and going of people, and leaned back against his uncle's chair, contented.

Unfortunately, his uncle was speaking Hungarian. He got up after a time, passed a woman, a neighbour from across the way, who alone among the guests did not appear to be enjoying herself, and glared at her ferociously as he passed by.

The kitchen was full of women washing dishes and cleaning up. He helped himself to a handful of assorted pastries. Beside the dish stood a decanter and a brandy bottle with a few thimblefuls left at the bottom. He uncorked it and a sweet pungent odour reached his nostrils. He had never tasted brandy. His mouth began to water. He unbuttoned his blouse, thrust the bottle into it, and ran happily upstairs into his uncle's cubicle. He sat down, smoked the remainder of his cigarette, and then, raising the bottle to his lips, swallowed its contents in a gulp that suddenly sent him leaping to his feet to go reeling and gasping around the cubicle, clutching at his throat. In trying to get cold air into his lungs, he tore open the door and staggered across the attic and down the stairs.

At the bottom, just as suddenly, he stopped. From the pit of his stomach there began to spread the most agreeable feeling he had ever known, a warm, satisfying glow that rose languidly to his head and darted like little tongues of flame in his veins, slowly to his loins. He sat down and grinned vacantly. A great peace came over him. Above him he heard the sound of footsteps. He turned and saw two girls come mincing down the stairs, one of them Emma Schumacher.

Emma's name had been a byword in the gang. Fragments of sex lore flashed through his mind, but most of them had become established as neighbourhood fact only so that they might fit into the sorry scheme of some dirty joke or other, and they only made things more confusing. He looked up. He caught a glimpse of the margin of Emma's black cotton stockings and above them the pink flesh of her thighs. Emma was small and slender, but the size of her thighs was appalling. He grew frightened lest in some future time he should prove unequal to what would be demanded of him. But then he remembered. The last time he had gone swimming with the gang, it had not escaped his notice that he was almost as big as Hank and certainly as big as Louis.

Emma's skirt swished past his ears and for the first time in his life he felt an unmistakable tremor in his loins, as though of a power long dormant now stirring at last to brief wakefulness, to fill him with a delight that was indescribable, that seemed to transport him to a region deep within him, where his passionate affection for himself, far from laughter and derision, could unfold and flower.

As though entranced he returned to the front room to his place beside his uncle's chair. Distantly he heard the party coming to life. He felt his uncle's hand on his head and fell asleep.

When he awoke, it was to the sound of his uncle's voice singing a Hungarian song. Onkel Janos stood in the centre of the room, keeping time with a glass of beer to the music. The refrain consisted of a few bars of laughter. His uncle's voice, Sandor thought, no less than his laughter, was deep and rich and splendid. It was fine to see him standing there.

The assembled guests clapped loudly when he had finished. He lowered his glass and in bowing caught sight of Sandor who had risen to his feet to applaud. With a shout Onkel Janos swooped down on him, caught him under the armpits, and raised him to his shoulders.

"A toast," he cried; the rest was a Hungarian rhyme.

And Sandor looked down at the smiling, friendly faces upturned to him, all happy, all willing to raise their glasses to him, and thought that it was only fitting that they should do so, that they should look up to him. Somehow he felt he had deserved it. He saw his parents smiling up at him and in that moment he forgave them everything.

Seven

THE DAYS grew short, the nights cold. The puddles in the back lane froze. Sandor noticed that the sun no longer wakened him in the mornings. Up and down Henry Avenue the houses creaked and groaned. Window-panes were stuffed with newspapers and rags, storm doors fastened, ashes banked against the outside walls, and, in the houses themselves, ancient cracks in foundation and wall, open all summer, began to close and draw together as though preparing for a siege.

Men came home with lunch pails, and some, the daily labourers and plasterers, the bricklayers and sewer-diggers, laid them away and in the established order of things set out to offer arm and sinew to city clerks against days of snow — heavy snow, pray God — that by social alchemy would still the empty ache of hunger.

At night Sandor lay listening to the drip of water from the tap, left on against the frost. Under his pillow was his first postcard from Eric. And yet it was not of Eric he was thinking, but of Onkel Janos who was now unemployed. They had expected this; sewer-digging is seasonal work. But who could have expected that on the self-same day that his uncle's work had come to an end, his father should lose his job? The boiler in the shop had burst. In putting the fire out, Joseph Hunyadi had scalded himself and had had to remain in bed for a few days. When he returned to work he had found another man in his place.

Sandor raised his head. His parents were talking in the front room, his mother reproaching herself for the money she had spent on the party. They had saved very little. But at least, with Onkel Janos' contributions, they had paid off what they owed to Mr. Schwalbe's partner. Even if they went hungry, Sandor thought, he would still be glad that his father was not working for Mr. Friedel any more. They wouldn't starve. There were still a lot of watch-repair shops in town which his father had not yet visited, and if nothing came of that, then perhaps with all the money they had paid on the house they might be able to raise a second mortgage and so enable his father to open his own shop. Yes. . . . The important thing was that his father had at last got out of that hell-hole. In the end, it would probably be the best thing that had ever happened to them.

With this last consoling reflection on his family's affairs, his eyes closed. He let his mind drift to his uncle Janos, Janos Daffner. John Daffner. He repeated his name and smiled. Even in adversity his uncle was unique. He magnified his misfortunes, his sorrows, his unsuccessful attempts to find a job, until they reached almost epic proportions. It was difficult, even in his most solemn moments, to take him seriously.

Lately he had taken to going out at night. Sandor frowned as he recalled his own and his mother's attempts to draw his uncle out. . . . They were no match for him. He fell asleep wondering where his uncle went on those mysterious visits.

A few days later, sitting in the kitchen, their English lesson done, his uncle had unexpectedly inquired whether he thought he could get his mother's permission to go for a walk with him.

Frau Hunyadi consented readily enough. With two sweaters under one of his father's old jackets — he had outgrown his overcoat — Sandor set out with his uncle. At the end of the first block he was informed that they were going to visit a lady.

Ah! A *young* lady?

This was a question one never asked where a lady was

concerned. She was as a matter of fact neither young nor old. She was a widow.

What was her name?

Fraulein Kleinholtz.

But how "Fraulein," when she was a widow?

Onkel Janos turned to Sandor with great earnestness. The lady preferred to be called Fraulein. Would Sandor call her that — as a favour to his uncle?

Sandor agreed to do so.

Another thing, Onkel Janos continued. He was not prepared yet to inform Sandor's mother about Fraulein Kleinholtz. As man to man, would Sandor promise not to mention where they were going tonight or what had passed between them? Only for a little while. It was difficult, but it was better not to speak at all than to say what was not true.

Sandor began to enjoy himself. He promised. But why had his uncle taken him along?

A delicate matter. Fraulein Kleinholtz lived alone. Did Sandor understand?

Not quite. Hadn't Onkel Janos been visiting her by himself all this time?

Well, yes. But the situation had changed somewhat. . . .

They walked on, to a house not more than half a block from where Onkel Janos had worked that summer. It was while working there, Sandor discovered, that his uncle had met Fraulein Kleinholtz. One noon-hour he had gone to ask her for a pail of drinking-water; she had given him a pitcher of lemonade.

Sandor met her a few minutes later and for the next two months, although he saw her two and sometimes three times a week, could not erase that first, fearful impression from his mind. When she opened her mouth, he had half expected a moth to fly out. Her face was long and angular with sunken cheeks. From the corners of her mouth two deep furrows ran vertically down her chin. And this part of her face, between the furrows, always reminded him of a trap door, hinged at the bottom and likely to spring open at any moment to expose a gullet that would swallow him wholly.

She was obviously not rich; he had seen better clothes than the ones she wore hanging on racks at rummage-sales. She was old and ugly.

Then what did his uncle see in her?

On a night late in December he found out. It was a cold night. He was glad when they finally arrived.

They walked up the stairs to the porch. His uncle knocked. The door opened and Sandor caught the familiar, sour odour that pervaded Fraulein Kleinholtz's home.

She emerged from the darkness and to Sandor's horror bent down, clasped him in her arms, and kissed him. He squirmed helplessly. She had probably just finished kissing her dog, he thought, and it was not as though she were kissing him out of affection; it was only her way of showing that she was displeased with his uncle for arriving so late. He wiped his mouth as she turned back into the hallway. Not a word yet, to his uncle. It was going to be one of those nights.

The dog, a nervous little beast, barked furiously at them as they entered. Sandor lowered himself cautiously into his chair. But it was useless; the mothball fumes rose up and enveloped him. The only light in the room came from a lamp above him. It was a room that always reminded him of a story he had heard in his history class; of an ancient king who upon his deathbed had been placed in his tomb with all his possessions. Every time Sandor sat in this chair it came back to him. He imagined that Fraulein Kleinholtz had died and been buried, but had somehow revived and set up housekeeping in her tomb.

The springs in the settee below the window squeaked, and he knew without looking up that his uncle had seated himself beside Fraulein Kleinholtz with the dog between them.

The dog began to bark again, with a shrill high-pitched yap that set Sandor's teeth on edge. Now the performance would begin.

"He's sad," Fraulein Kleinholtz cried in a tender screech. "My little one's sad. Putsi doesn't like strangers. . . . No he doesn't. . . . Ah, my little heart." She raised him by his forepaws. "Come," she pleaded. "Stand up for Mother. . . .

Come, up, up, my little man. Up now, or Mother will be angry.

"Now he's standing," she cried, "all by himself. . . . Isn't Mother proud of him? All alone on his little feety." She fondled him affectionately. Suddenly she caught his snout between her hands and kissed him passionately. Then she laid him upon her lap and raised his paws again. "Just like a little man, my little Putsi," she screamed. "Standing up for Mother. Yes. Yes. Mother loves you best."

It went on and on, in a peculiar kind of German, so full of neighs and brays, her words so slurred, Sandor could scarcely understand what she was saying. He waited for the sequel, and lowered his head and grinned as his uncle finally leaped to his feet, grabbed the dog by the scruff, and ran out into the hall with him. Fraulein Kleinholtz followed.

The house grew silent.

Sandor gazed absently at a figure of a shepherd and shepherdess entwined about the lampstand. Since his last visit, the shepherdess had acquired a dress of sorts. She had always been naked, but in a strange sexless sort of way. . . . Or had he been mistaken? He considered this, then lifted her skirt and examined her. There was nothing there. He dropped it with disgust and lowered his eyes as the springs in the settee squeaked again.

"All right then," he heard his uncle saying. "I'll apologize. I'm sorry I came so late."

"It doesn't matter," Fraulein Kleinholtz answered. "I'm sure I never noticed. What time is it?"

Sandor looked up at the clock on the mantel. "It's nine o'clock, Fraulein."

His uncle sighed and let his watch slip back into his pocket. "I was out looking for work today, Kathie," he continued, and placed her hand in his. "I didn't get back until late."

"Not until after seven," Sandor explained. Onkel Janos and Fraulein Kleinholtz looked at him thoughtfully.

"Would you like your milk and cookies in the kitchen now?" she asked. "I'm sure you must be hungry after such a long walk."

Sandor shook his head.

"Not even a little bitsy hungry?"

Whenever she ogled him and talked like this, it made him squirm.

"No," he began, but saw his uncle beseeching him with his eyes to say yes.

There was nothing to do but agree.

His uncle accompanied her to the kitchen. In their absence, he walked casually over to the two sliding doors that led to the dining-room and drew them about half an inch or so apart. A few minutes later, having drunk his milk and thrown the two mouldy cookies into the stove, he tip-toed through the kitchen doorway to the dining-room, and seating himself there in the dark, began shaking his head at the extravagance of his uncle's words.

He grew sad as he peered at him through the crack between the doors. His uncle could have had any woman he wanted. The girls and the young women on Henry Avenue had not yet stopped talking about him. Why, then, had he chosen this one? Was he blind? Couldn't he see that she was as thin as a floor mop, and ugly and old, with patchy skin?

" . . . like a flower," his uncle continued in an impassioned voice. "Still blossoming in the midsummer of your bloom. . . . And you wonder that I should love you?

"How can you doubt it?" he cried, and placing a finger-tip under her chin, drew her head up and gazed at her in silence.

"Greet your image in my eyes," he cried. "See yourself as I see you and tell me again you question my love.

"Tell me," he challenged, with his hand pressed to his heart. "Why does it surprise you that a man should say he loves you? You are beautiful — oh, I know you deny it. In every other way you are a sensible woman. You are a good housekeeper, but do you think I want to marry you only for your housekeeping and cooking? My wife must be beautiful. I insist on it."

Fraulein Kleinholtz laughed and shook her head. She looked horrible when she laughed, Sandor thought. He leaned forward as his uncle took her suddenly by the shoulders and began to shake her. "You have been alone too long," he shouted. "You no longer see yourself as you are. In a roomful of beautiful women you would shine. Shine, I tell you!

Sandor stared at him incredulously. The whole thing was sickening. She was in his uncle's arms now, leering coyly, her head resting on his shoulder. In the uncertain light she looked almost presentable, he conceded. But that was probably because she was beginning to cry. She always looked her best somehow when she was crying. It seemed to take the hardness out of her face and made her look younger. She cried easily, almost as easily as Eric's mother laughed, he thought, with scarcely any effort, and without any attempt to check herself.

His uncle was still talking, trying to convince her that she was still young and beautiful and that he loved her.

Sandor wondered angrily why he bothered to sit here. He might have known, he told himself angrily, that nothing new would happen. He had seen this same performance more times than he cared to remember.

He nodded sagely as he watched his uncle's arm glide slowly around her waist. She withdrew. He tried again. Her lips tightened. She pulled away from him.

That's because she's been a widow too long, Sandor thought. A woman needed a man. Once, up in the attic, he had overheard the boarders talking about women. The talk had turned to widows. Before a man married a widow, one of the boarders had warned, he should make sure that she had not been a widow too long, because it was only a man's juices that kept a woman looking and acting like a woman. Too long without and she turned into a man, with a man's desire to be master. That was why widows and old maids were always so hard to handle. If such a female were caught in time, however, she could be saved. But only if she were caught in time and by the right kind of man.

Sandor continued to nod his head. This made sense. It was exactly what had happened to Fraulein Kleinholtz. This was why she looked so old and so horribly withered and why she refused to let his uncle put his arm around her waist. She had been deprived of a man's juices for so long she was turning into a man. And this was the kind of person his uncle wanted to marry! He bit his knuckles thoughtfully. If only he had remembered this earlier. But maybe it was still not too late. On the way home tonight, he would tell his uncle what he had heard about widows.

He rocked himself back and forth for a while, considering this, then leaned forward once more and peered into the living-room. His uncle and Fraulein Kleinholtz were seated at opposite ends of the settee, talking.

"I don't suspect you of anything," she was saying. "I just think you're ashamed to be seen there with me."

So they were quarrelling about that again. Sandor grinned as his uncle jumped to his feet. "I've told you a thousand times, Kathie," he shouted. "I'm not ashamed of you. I love you. But how would it look, to take the woman I want to marry to my sister's home and expect her to entertain us, when I'm not even paying my board? How can I ask that of her? It's humiliating. . . ."

"You needn't shout," Fraulein Kleinholtz interrupted. "We're not married yet." She lowered her head. "It's all right to humiliate me . . ."

"Humiliate *you*!" he cried.

"Yes, me. To propose marriage to me and then refuse even to let me meet your family, isn't that humiliating? Why don't you admit you're ashamed of me? You're ashamed because I'm too old." She burst into tears.

He threw his hands in the air at this, and muttered something under his breath.

"What possible difference can it make to you, whether you meet my sister or not?" he asked finally. "We don't need her consent, do we? We're both of age . . ."

Fraulein Kleinholtz uttered a hoarse cry. "That's right," she sobbed. "Throw it in my face — even before we're married."

To Sandor's utter disgust, Onkel Janos sank down on his knees beside her. "I never meant it that way, Kathie," he said.

"And if it means so much to you, I'll arrange a visit — next Sunday."

As Fraulein Kleinholtz raised her head, he caught her in his arms and pressed his lips to hers.

Sandor heard her moan. He watched his uncle stroking her; with bulging eyes he saw her body slowly begin to shiver and then to twitch as though in torment in his uncle's embrace. It corroborated fully what he suspected. No normal woman would act like this. The sound of her voice was heavy as though with a strange pain. In a sort of trance she rose to her feet, swayed, and then still moaning, she fled into the hall. His uncle followed her.

A moment later he came into the kitchen. Sandor was waiting for him.

"What's wrong with her?" he cried.

His uncle helped him on with his sweaters and his jacket. They walked silently down the steps.

"I heard Fraulein Kleinholtz crying," Sandor said.

Onkel Janos stopped in the shelter of a doorway to light a cigarette and, as the match flamed, Sandor noticed that his eyes were wet. This was certainly not the time to warn him about Fraulein Kleinholtz's long widowhood. He slipped his hand into his uncle's as they continued down the street.

They came to a wood-yard, on the corner of which stood a shoemaker's shack, its shingles glistening in the moonlight. Sandor tugged at his uncle's arm as they approached it. One night when he had had two glasses of milk to drink, he had stopped here. His uncle had joined him. Since then, it had become a sort of ritual that Sandor looked forward to. It was pleasant to stand there manfully beside his uncle and watch the silver stream arc out against the logs; to try to reach as high as his uncle did. Once, by exerting himself and by standing on his toes, he had actually done so. His uncle had laughed and patted him on the back and said something in Hungarian which Sandor knew was complimentary.

He continued to nudge his uncle until he nodded and followed him. It was dark and secluded here. Three sides of the yard were stacked high with cordwood. The smell of the birch and the tamarack was clean and pungent. He looked back as he walked into the shadows. His uncle was sitting on a log, his hands pressed to his forehead.

Sandor sighed. The dull cordwood grew wet and then luminous. He arched his body and tried to reach the next log — a small one. "Yaa, Kleinholtz," he muttered, and sprayed it furiously.

He turned back. His uncle was groaning and striking himself on the chest.

"My God," he cried. "My God, what shall I do? My soul is in agony."

Sandor threw himself into his arms. "Don't marry her, Onkel Janos," he cried. I wanted to tell you about widows. She's not right for you. I heard the boarders talking . . ."

His uncle drew him down on his knee.

"Don't marry her," Sandor whispered. "Stay with us at home, Onkel Janos. We want you to stay with us."

His uncle's laughter made him shiver.

"What kind of a life is this for a man?" he asked. "Have I grown so unfeeling that I can steal the bread from your mouth? For months I have been begging your mother for car fare and cigarette money. Did you know that? Your uncle begs pennies from your mother. Ach, my God, better if I had never seen her again than she should see me in my shame like this."

Sandor looked at him through his tears. "Don't marry her, Onkel Janos," he pleaded. "She's too old for you. You could have any girl you wanted."

"Don't marry her!" his uncle repeated bitterly. "She is rich. Do you understand?" he shouted. "So rich she could buy the whole street you live on and not even miss the money it cost."

"But her . . . but she dresses like a scarecrow. Her house . . ."

"She has so much money that I would sell my soul to possess her. Did you think your uncle was capable of such a thing? Did you?"

He fell silent. When he began talking again, it was as though he had almost forgotten Sandor.

"In this country I felt a new life would begin for me," he

murmured. "Here, I said, everything will be different. An end will come to this empty wandering. . . . Here, I said, in this new land, a homeless buffoon will find his home and his manhood. Was it so much I wanted? A wife; and a roof over my head." He stopped.

"And she suspects me," he cried in a voice so loud and so filled with loathing that for a moment it drew Sandor out of the dream into which he had fallen — a dream of splendid affluence. Now he opened his eyes and in the pale clear light he saw the anguish on his uncle's face.

"She suspects that I have no affection for her," he said. "God help her — she is in love with me, worm that I am. This is what I have come to."

Sandor patted him on the arm. Try as he might, he could not resist the bright vision that swam before his eyes, a vision of the golden life that would be his, and his family's too, if his uncle married Fraulein Kleinholtz.

It lured him on, in spite of himself. They could move away from Henry Avenue. They would have a whole house to themselves, new clothes, and all the food they could eat. In one extravagant moment he saw himself living next door to Eric. Then with a guilty start he drew his uncle into the orbit of his fantasy, but only to see himself in his uncle's office. His uncle was in business for himself. In the background, sitting at a desk, Sandor caught a glimpse of the man he himself would some day be. The future beckoned. . . .

His uncle broke the spell. "Come," he said wearily. "It is late. This is no place for a prospective bridegroom to be spending the night."

Eight

SANDOR groaned as he came into the kitchen. His mother had been washing. The air was heavy with the smell of steam and soap. The clothes-line strung across the kitchen sagged under the weight of napkins and underwear. In a corner by the stove she sat sewing, with the baby at her feet.

"It's four o'clock awready?" she cried, and began to clear the table.

Sandor dropped his schoolbag and shook the snow from his jacket. He opened the oven door. "Noodles and potatoes. Two times already this week we've had noodles and potatoes."

His mother sighed. "Put some wood on the fire," she said. "The noodles should be ready when your father comes home."

He raised the lid and stared gloomily into the fire and wondered what his uncle was doing. What was he thinking about, this very minute? Maybe sitting in a hotel somewhere in that town in Saskatchewan, where they had gone for their honeymoon — sitting there, probably smoking a cigar over a glass of beer, laughing and talking as only he could talk, and not thinking at all of his sister and his nephew. And after what had happened, one could hardly blame him.

He had a rich uncle, he thought, and what good did it do him? His parents had not even had the sense to hide their feelings. . . . At the ceremony his mother's sobs had been heard throughout the whole church. At the wedding party,

114

neither his mother nor his father had spoken more than a word to the bride. And to make things even worse, Sandor had discovered that the bride's best friend was a certain Frau Kostanuik.

He threw a log angrily into the fire and dropped the lid back into place.

"Don't take your coat off," his mother said. "Mr.Crawford came today . . ."

"I won't go," Sandor shouted. "I'm not going to any more rummage-sales."

"It's not a rummage-sale," his mother answered. "Mr. Crawford says everything is private there. The church ladies give things free,"

She reached into the cupboard. "Here's the address. You should give this to the lady and you'll get an overcoat, and maybe shoes. With the coat, don't forget — look at the but-tonholes, and feel the material. It should be thick, and never mind how big. Better to get a man's coat. I kin fix . . ."

"I'm not going."

His mother continued. "I kin fix . . ."

"I kin fix," he mimicked. "Noodles and rummage-sales, and Pa can't even get enough money to open his own place. And all you and Pa had to do was be nice to her. Just make a little joke with her and tell her something and laugh. Now she hates us. She hates even me because of you. And she liked me before. She even wanted to buy me a new coat so I'd be nice at the wedding. She told me. And you and Pa wouldn't let her. . . . You thought I didn't know."

"You said enough," his mother warned. "Don't think you're so big I can't give you a slap yet."

"Ma, listen to me," he pleaded. "Fraulein Kleinholtz wants you to like her. She wants to help us. All you have to do is write and ask her how everything is and say you'll be glad to see her when she comes back. She can fix everything. She's richer'n you think. Honest-to-God, Ma. All our troubles would be over. Pa could open his own place and wouldn't have to shovel snow no more and you could send your clothes to the laundry instead of washing them by yourself. . . . We could move away from here, Ma. We could live where it would be good for the baby. You always said the baby . . ."

His mother was really angry now.

"You're not ashamed to talk like this?" she cried. "To beg from her? She gives with her head, that one, not with her heart. Everything she does with her head. How else did she catch your uncle, tell me? You think she loves him? If she loved him she would let him marry somebody who is half so old."

She burst into tears. "Not enough she put one husband under the ground awready," she continued. "No, she wants another one to swallow."

Sandor shrugged his shoulders. It always ended like this. He would have to go, not so much for the overcoat as for the shoes. The ones he was wearing were almost falling off his feet. He reached for the envelope with the address on it.

"Come right away home," his mother admonished him as he walked to the door. "Mr. Nagy comes again tonight and I want you should be home when he talks to your father."

Sandor wrapped his scarf around his neck and pulled his cap down over his ears. The street lay in darkness. The snow had stopped falling. On the sidewalk piled high with hard-packed snow his heels crunched with a hollow echo.

He thrust his hands into his pockets and hunched his shoulders against the cold.

Maybe something would come of all these talks with Mr. Nagy. Maybe after all these years his father was finally going to get his own shop and be his own boss. A mortgage of four hundred dollars on the house was not so much to ask. But if his parents — aw, they were stupid, both of them. Hadn't they accepted the money from his uncle to pay back the cost of his steamship ticket? All right, then. But who had actually given them this money? Fraulein Kleinholtz, that's who. Fraulein Kleinholtz who would have done almost anything they asked of her, if only they had been willing to accept her.

He slipped on a broken icicle and kicked it angrily out of his way.

The next moment he was swearing and hobbling around on

one foot. The cap of his right shoe had come off and the cardboard in the sole had either worn through or had shifted; he remembered now that he had intended to replace it and to dry his stockings as soon as he got home from school. He sat down on a doorstep and removed his shoe. The cardboard had turned into a soggy mess.

He searched through his pockets for something to put in its place, found nothing, and began to swear in earnest.

On Logan Avenue, he crept into a fruit store to get warm but had no sooner opened the door than the bell attached to it summoned the proprietor who, remembering him as a member of a certain gang, drove him out. A few blocks from Main Street he stepped into the hallway of a small apartment block and sat for five minutes or more in a stupor on the radiator, examining the envelope which Mr. Crawford had given his mother. It was sealed.

He ran the rest of the way and arrived finally at a grey-brick structure above whose sagging door hung a faded sign.

Sandor walked in. In the hall was a framed New Testament text, and a finger pointing the way upstairs.

He obeyed its injunction, and a moment later entered an enormous room occupying the entire floor. About him lay heaps of magazines and books, and row upon row of apple boxes filled with kitchen utensils, corsets, and ladies' hats. Beyond these were several tarnished bird-cages, a few floor-lamps, a barrel filled with toys, and several enormous mounds of miscellaneous clothing. At the far end was a long rack of coats and dresses and suits.

He walked circumspectly to the small partition in the corner of the room, took off his cap, and knocked.

The woman who opened the door reminded him very much of Mrs. Creighton. She was no longer young, her face was unlined, her manner cool and distant but familiar and therefore reassuring.

She opened the envelope which he had handed to her, and looked at him.

"You want this overcoat for yourself?"

Sandor flushed. "Yes, Ma'm, and a pair of shoes . . ."

"I'm sure I haven't the slightest idea where Miss Farley keeps things," she said.

"Maybe I could just look around," Sandor suggested. "I'm sure I'll find something that'll fit me. It'll save you the trouble."

"Well, that's fine," she said. "You see what you can find and then bring it to me here, so I can record it."

Sandor thanked her and made straight for the rack on which the men's clothing hung. Hidden from view, he made a systematic search through the pockets of the suits and over-coats. Once at a rummage-sale he had found a ten-cent piece in a suit pocket. He was not so fortunate this time. When he was through, he had only a handful of toothpicks and an old comb to show for his trouble.

He returned to the coats and tried on the one he had chosen. It came down to his ankles. The shoulders dropped half-way to his elbows. He thrust his hands into the pockets and doubled over to reach the bottom of them. But the material was unbelievably thick and soft. He examined the buttonholes and the edges of the cuffs, the way he had seen his mother do at rummage-sales. He scrutinized the lining and the armpits and the collar. There was no sign of wear. Gloating over it, he put in on again and began to look for a pair of shoes. In the course of his search, he discovered a small tin basin filled with gloves. He selected a pair made of soft black leather, and with rising spirits came upon a foulard scarf with silk tassels. He thrust these added possessions into the pockets of his coat and suddenly he stood still. Lying under a table he saw a pair of tan shoes, narrow and long and pointed, with brown buttons — the kind that Willi Schumacher's brother used to wear. But that was the trouble. They belonged to Henry Avenue. Reluctantly he put them aside and picked up an ordinary black pair. He stuffed paper into the toe-caps and buttoned them. They had leather heels and made a satisfactory clatter when he walked. He bent over, spat on the caps, and polished them with an old sock. The leather began to shine. But there was not the joy in the wearing of them that he would have felt had he chosen the tan ones. He looked back sadly at those and returned to the office.

The door was open. The woman was sitting at a desk reading a magazine. She looked up. Her eyes widened. "Isn't it a trifle large?" she asked.

"My mother can cut it down for me," he explained. "She's got a sewing machine."

The woman shook her head doubtfully.

"But it's a man's coat," she objected. "And it's still in perfectly good condition. It would be a shame to . . ."

"I won't be able to go to school if I don't get a coat," he broke in.

She looked at him and sighed. "Well, all right then," she said. "But I'm quite sure Miss Farley wouldn't have approved."

She reached for a pen, opened a ledger, and examined Mr. Crawford's letter.

"Hun — Hony — Honaydiay," she murmured.

Sandor watched her silently as she wrote his name in the ledger. It ran from the red-lined margin to the centre of the sheet. Then his address.

"And what does your father do when he's working?" she asked, and turned expectantly to the door at the sound of approaching footsteps.

"Hello, Elizabeth. Are you there?" A voice from the landing — an incredibly soft and beautiful voice.

Sandor turned suddenly numb at the sound of it. But it couldn't be, he thought. What could she possibly be doing in here? His teeth began to chatter.

She came in. Their eyes met. Her lips formed his name . . . Alex. He saw the astonishment in her clear, untroubled gaze give way to a brief concern. She reached out her hand, drew it back, and a look of revulsion leaped into her eyes and spread to her features, which strained to an unfamiliar ugliness, to a reproach that screamed and screamed within him.

Through the doorway he saw Eric coming toward him with a bundle of old clothes in his arms, smiling amiably to himself, until he suddenly recognized him. Eric's mouth opened in astonishment. The bundle dropped from his arms.

His eyes blurred with tears, Sandor lumbered past him, his overcoat dragging at his heels, his sleeves flopping wildly.

Half-way down the stairs, he heard Eric calling him. He stopped. But there was only the sound of his laboured breathing and the creaking of the stair underfoot; then Eric called again, but only once, for suddenly there reached him the shrill cry of Eric's mother, calling her son back.

Sandor ran on until he reached the street. He noticed after a time that people were staring and laughing at him. It occurred to him vaguely that they were laughing because he was crying. The tears were cold on his cheeks. He wiped them away, lowered his head, and cried to himself as he walked on.

This was the way it was ending, then; the way everything in his life had always ended, in pain and ugliness with nothing left but empty longing and the prospect of crawling back to Henry Avenue.

Right now they would be learning the truth about him. They would discover that his name was Hunyadi, that his father was not a watchmaker with his own shop, but only a poor janitor. And if they wanted to they could find out that he was Hungarian and that his father shovelled snow for the City.

Eric would wonder at the lies his friend had told him, and his mother would take his clocks and watches away from him because the Hunyadi boy had probably stolen them. And in a few days they would stop talking about him, and by the time summer came again they would have forgotten him. And years from now, something or other would remind them of "that boy" and they would say "do you remember?" Eric and his mother would smile at each other and perhaps laugh at the way he had talked or dressed or acted at the table.

Sandor nodded. As he raised his head he saw his reflection in a store window — a small scarecrow.

"I wish I was dead," he said, and trudged on wearily until he reached the Hotel, where he stopped to look into the windows of the lobby, to gaze at the men who sat there.

Tonight they seemed infinitely remote. He made a half-hearted attempt to stir his dormant hopes to life again, but succeeded only in bringing back the sound of her laughter in the early dusk, floating out over the lawns that surrounded the great homes in which lights were beginning to glimmer. That was all, but the memory of it was filled with intolerable bitterness and yearning. He stood for a minute looking at the people around him. Holding his tears back, he remembered — how long ago it seemed now — returning from Mary Kostanuik's party, crying inside himself like this until he reached the red fence, there to be welcomed by the gang, who asked no questions, gave him what they had to eat, and accepted him for what he was. The peace, as he had lain there smoking in the cool weeds and listening to their talk, came back to him. And the carefree, happy times he had had with the gang! He had broken with the only real friends he had ever had. The gang was where he belonged. But they would never take him back now and he had only himself to blame. The old times were gone.

"I been a fool," he muttered to himself.

He walked on slowly until he reached home. He noticed that there were two sets of bicycle tracks leading from the road to the front steps. Mr. Nagy had come and gone.

The light was burning in the front room. On a sudden impulse he climbed to the pile of ashes that lay banked against the front of the house and looked into the window. It was clear of frost in the centre. He saw his parents. He had only to look at them to know that Mr. Nagy had refused them the mortgage. A sudden rage came over him. If his father had been a different kind of person he would not have had to lie about his name and the kind of life they led at home — he would not have had to go down there today for that overcoat. He might still have been friends with Eric. His lips quivered.

"Aw, the hell with it!" he cried. "It don't matter no more. Nuthin' matters no more."

Dropping to the sidewalk, he ran around to the back of the house, up the stairs, and to the toilet. He sat down on the floor beside the stovepipe, warming himself, listening to the roar of the draught in the chimney and the creaking of the frost-bound boards in the roof. Everybody, it seemed to him, had someone they could talk to; his father had his Saturday-night friends, his mother had her neighbours. The kids in the neighbourhood had the gang . . . only he had no one. He began to cry.

After a time he got up and raised the floorboards that covered his hiding-place. Eric's postcards were under the junk box. He lifted them out and saw what appeared to be a blue and gold picture in the shadow under the floor. He remembered then the books Eric had given him. There were two. He had never read either of them. He opened one and in the fly-leaf read "To Alex. From his Pal Eric." Above this line, the words "Eric from Aunt Margaret" had been firmly crossed out.

He sat down, flicked a few pages absently, and began to read. His eyes widened. How could anyone have written such a book?

He noticed that both books were by the same author.

It was the story of a poor, honest farm-boy; an orphan in an infinitely worse plight than Sandor had ever found himself. His name was Jack. He had come on foot to the great city with his few belongings wrapped in an old handkerchief, and on the very first night had been robbed of the few dollars his mother had given him on her death-bed. That night he had cried himself to sleep under a bridge. The next day he had set out to look for work.

Every night he slept under the bridge. But he kept himself clean and presentable, for his mother's last words to him had been that if he remained honest and neat and tidy there was no height to which he could not rise. He did everything that honest pride permitted him to do. And yet at the end of the week he was still without work, and so weak with hunger he was on the verge of collapse.

Little did he know, said the author, that the following Monday would prove to be a turning-point in Jack's career. Sandor, gnawing at his finger-nails, was glad to hear it. Jack was now a mere shadow of his former self. He crawled out of his shelter on this particular morning and, after washing and brushing himself, walked forlornly to the centre of the city, still doggedly determined to find an honest job.

At a busy intersection he stopped for breath and surveyed the carriages that went rolling by. He wondered if he too might not some day ride to work in this fashion. Suddenly as he stood there, lost in thought, he saw something drop from one of the carriages. He ran forward, dodging carriage wheels and horses, and discovered that it was a leather wallet.

He raised it aloft and shouted to the occupant of the carriage from which it had fallen.

The carriage rolled on.

Jack opened the wallet. It was filled with documents, business cards, and a large amount of money — two hundred and ten dollars, in fact.

Sandor's eyes bulged. How many times had he not envisaged this very scene. But what would Jack do? Give it back?

Jack was already walking in the direction which the carriage had taken. The decision to return it had not really been a decision at all, the author said. Jack had acted instinctively.

Sandor groaned as he followed Jack to his destination. "Awright," he muttered. "See where it gets you."

Jack entered an enormous office building. Above the doorway in bronze letters was the name of the man he sought. He made inquiries and asked to see him. People laughed and rebuffed him.

Sandor took a deep breath. Surely, now, Jack was entitled to keep the money. He had tried to return it, hadn't he? Wasn't that enough?

"No!" said the author, "not for an honest man."

Jack persevered until he finally reached the office of the great man, who took the wallet from him and fervently grasped Jack's hand.

He was asked to sit down. The great man smiled, reached into the wallet, and offered him a ten-dollar bill.

Sandor glared at him indignantly. He nodded when Jack refused it. The great man smiled paternally. He took in the boy's threadbare clothes, the hungry look in his eyes, but observed also with evident signs of pleasure his manly bearing and clean and tidy appearance. He held out two, then three of the notes. Still the boy refused. The wallet was not his, he said. He was not entitled to anything for returning it. It was simply a matter of honesty.

But the paper in his wallet, the great man explained, was a contract worth many thousands of dollars. Surely the finder was entitled to something?

"Honesty is its own reward," Jack answered promptly.

Sandor grinned, as he caught the drift of this. This Jack was not so simple after all. How long would ten, twenty, or even thirty dollars have lasted? A few months at the most. And then what? He would be out on the street again looking for a job.

"Sir," Jack now said respectfully but boldly. "I have spent the past week seeking a position. I am not afraid of hard work. I appeal to you not because I seek a reward but because I should like to work for you."

The great man's brow furrowed, but only for an instant. He got up and held out his hand. "This country could do with more young men like you," he said. "I am sure I can find a place for you in our organization."

It was Sandor who felt the great man's handclasp. A lump came to his throat as he tried to thank him. But the great man was already asking Jack his name and something about himself. He began to shake his head sadly. Poverty was certainly nothing to be ashamed of, he said, but Jack's lack of education was most unfortunate. A man without schooling might be able to do the work of a junior in his organization, but he would never be able to get ahead, and it would be unfair to the man himself to employ him under such circumstances.

Sandor turned pale as he sat staring with dull misery at the great man who wanted to help him but was unable to.

But Jack was made of sterner stuff. He began pleading with the great man for a chance to show what he could do. His words were Sandor's own. He found that he was speaking manfully, forcefully, and yet respectfully.

He had confidence in his ability to achieve what so many others had done, he cried. By the time he was ready for advancement he would be prepared to meet the demands of his new position. He would go to night school. He would persevere and study hard. All he wanted was an opportunity. The great man had said that poverty was nothing to be ashamed of. And yet he was punishing him for his poverty, depriving him of the opportunity to make something of himself. It was only because his parents had been poor that he had been unable to get a proper education.

Sandor wiped the sweat from his brow. The last few lines had choked him into silence.

The great man had risen to his feet. But what was this?

The great man was smiling and holding out his hand. He would permit no one to say that he had punished a boy because his parents were poor, he said. The position was his.

Sandor almost collapsed. Jack, faint with hunger and excitement, swayed on his feet. The author closed his chapter with a lengthy dissertation on the fruits of virtue, which Sandor skipped.

Jack was now at work. But one of the clerks in the office, a lazy, dishonest, untidy fellow and a nephew of the great man, was plotting his downfall, and Jack, poor, honest, simple Jack trusted him.

Sandor shook his head and read on, filling his mind with the daily events in the life of the office. Jack's struggle was as eventful as it was arduous. Sandor toiled and strained at his side, rising with him in assurance and prestige until the day when the great man led him silently to the office beside his own and pointed to the name-plate on the door. Sandor turned the page.

He knew, although Jack did not, that behind that door, in the new Vice-President's office, there awaited him the great man's niece, whom Jack in his innocence had imagined he had forever lost when he had exposed her brother as a liar and a thief.

The great man's eyes were misty as he opened the door and pushed Jack gently over the threshold.

At that moment on a street corner some twenty-odd storeys below there crept through the shadows a figure with bloated, ravaged features — the great man's nephew, whining as he begged the price of a cup of coffee from the passers-by. The story had come to an end.

Sandor rose stiffly to his feet. The light hurt his eyes. He turned it off and walked to the window.

In a dark sky, the stars glittered, distant and yet smiling down as though to encourage him.

His father was wrong. That was the most important thing. But that he should have been proved wrong by a book, that was subtly and deeply satisfying.

The great men his father talked about, what were they after all but talkers like himself? The great ones in this book were the doers, the men of wealth and power, the men who counted, whose words people listened to. And one had only to work hard and devote oneself whole-heartedly to the things they believed, to become one of them.

He stood there filled with wonder that there should be such a book, giving him back his own dream, his own secret longings that had stirred within him so long — dreams which his father had tried so hard to destroy. From the very beginning it was he who had been right, not his father. He would do as he had planned. When the time came he would get a job with Mr. Nagy. He knew now how to ask for one.

And when he was old enough he would change his name. And as for the English . . .

Sandor smiled. The day he changed his name he would have nothing more to worry about. The day was coming when all this would be behind him. It would remain there forever. When he looked back there would be only the memory of this book. Of all the things that had happened to him, this was the only thing he wanted to remember.

PART TWO

Nine

THIS WAS the hour of the night he liked best of all. It was quiet and peaceful in the office; only the occasional creaking of the springs in Nagy's cubbyhole, the old man's laboured breathing, the footsteps on the pavement below the window.

The office lay in darkness but for the cone of light from the green reflector above his desk. The cigarette on the ashtray beside the ledger burned itself out unnoticed. He worked on steadily for an hour or so, his head bent over his desk, immobile but for the restless movement of his eyes, which periodically swept across the office from the window at his right, to the counter a few yards in front of him, to the door of the old man's room, and back to his desk again.

In the course of this almost unseeing, habitual inspection, his glance fell upon his name-plate — his name in black enamel on brass. *Alex Hunter*, it read, *Assistant Manager*. "Alex Hunter." He repeated it softly, reached for his pen, and wrote his signature on a clean sheet of paper. But it was still not right.

He tried again. Something bold was wanted here, particularly in the A and H; something with the imprint of his character in it, the statement of a man who has nothing to conceal; something that inspired confidence, that mirrored the man of affairs, too pressed for time to write legibly because he must affix this signature on perhaps half a hundred pieces of correspondence in a day.

129

Yes . . . that was what was wanted. It was, he conceded, rather a heavy burden to place upon a signature.

By a happy chance, he managed to obtain what he sought. A steep incline for the first stroke of the A, then a short plateau at the top, a formidable downward thrust, another parallel to it, and one horizontal bar that served both A and H. The rest of the name looked something like the teeth of a buzz-saw. But this was it, he thought jubilantly, and copied it down on a fresh sheet of pape together with the month and the year — June, 1924 — to mark the occasion on which he had succeeded in shaping it to his final satisfaction. He held it up before him. He would have preferred the name Humphrey, the name he had set his heart upon as a boy; it had a quiet English elegance, it seemed to him, that Hunter lacked. But it was too soft. It sounded too harmless. He sighed.

Out of the corner of his eye he observed a small boy at the window, his nose flattened, his lips ballooned against the pane — a hollow-cheeked and grimy boy with large, hungry eyes. He vanished the moment he was seen. Alex turned thoughtfully back to the sheet on which he had written his signature. He lowered it. Old memories came to life.

He saw himself looking through the glass panel of the door, watching Mr. Nagy coming toward him in answer to that early morning knock. Now he was standing inside, afraid that he might speak foolishly, and yet through his fears came the knowledge he had gleaned from the books, sharp and bright in his mind, giving him the courage to go on.

For what seemed an eternity he had stood there, trying to persuade the old man to give him a job; twice Nagy had turned to go, twice the boy had clutched him, holding him back until finally in a burst of anger the old man had ordered him out of the office.

Alex shook his head incredulously at the impudence of this urchin who now calmly sat himself down, stared boldly across at the old man, and announced that he would not budge until he was given a job. He wanted to be a business man like Mr. Nagy.

This was the turning-point. "So you want to be like me?" the old man had asked.

"All right," he continued. "You will start as I did — every morning at seven. We work until eight. But if you lie, or repeat to anyone what happens here, or steal even a penny stamp, you will be fired. Is that clear?"

He had gone into his cubbyhole and returned with a broom, a pail, and a mop. But the presumption of this fourteen-year-old brat was almost beyond belief. He stood there with the pail in one hand, the mop and the broom in the other, and coolly remarked that he had no use for postage stamps; he was more interested in becoming a business man than in stealing pennies; and he blandly concluded by remarking that before he began washing the floor, he would like to discuss the question of his salary.

For a moment Nagy had looked at him with his mouth open. Then he leaned forward and patted him on the head. And yet, Alex recalled, the old man had suppressed his approval quickly enough, for in spite of the boy's objections his salary had been set at three dollars a week.

But the salary didn't matter. . . . It was the beginning, when everything was fresh and exciting and filled with wonder, when it was a momentous thing just to fill an inkwell or to rule a line in a ledger, when it was a joy to get up in the morning because another day at the office awaited him.

These were the golden years, filled with the feverish desire to know, with days and nights spent poring over the office records, listening to the talk of salesmen, insurance agents, aldermen, plumbers, carpenters, painters, business competitors; crawling into basements with Nagy to poke at foundations, intent upon the old man's every word; squirming under porches, climbing into attics and up scaffolds, learning the tricks of the trade.

Three nights a week for three years at night school — book-keeping, typing, business English, and a short course in commercial law. Alex nodded. He had loved it, just as he loved every corner and crevice of this dark, dismal little office. On the other side of the counter was the high wooden bench upon which he had seated himself so defiantly that first morning. And across that counter, nine years ago, he had brought to a successful conclusion his first small business deal.

Here in this office which had become more than a home to him, he had found himself.

He looked about him until his eyes fell upon the door to Nagy's cubbyhole.

"The old buzzard," he murmured affectionately.

He owed the old man more than he could ever repay. It was Nagy who patiently, day in, day out, had explained what no school could ever have taught — the simple yet intricate business of how to earn a dollar, and what was more important, how to put that dollar to work.

His eyes narrowed. If only one could trust him.

"Alex!" The old man coughed and groaned. "What are you doing?"

Alex nodded absently. "Right away."

"And don't forget to lock the door."

"I won't forget."

Holding his name out at arm's length again, he looked at it intently, his head cocked alternately to right and left. "Alex Hunter," he said under his breath. "Alex Hunter."

With this signature it became really his. No one started, snickered, or gaped when this name was spoken; it came easily to the tongue. Eyebrows remained in place at its mention. A new name . . . that seemed to absolve him of all he had done in his previous existence.

Looking at it, it was as though he could see the tattered husk of his former self. He felt he had left behind all that was worthless and had been born anew — an act not so long ago accomplished. It had taken longer than he had expected. But under threat of changing his own name, he had finally persuaded his father to do so.

"Alex Hunter," he murmured, and the identification was complete. This was he, his will and purpose, his highest aspirations — they had a name now, a name which represented that young man over there, reflected in the plate-glass window, who in his attempt to add age to his years had grown a small moustache, and changed the parting of his hair from centre to side. A smooth young man in a quiet blue-serge suit and polka-dot tie, perhaps a little unusual in manner and dress in most North End crowds but indistinguishable from his fellow diners in the hotel, where he managed by dint of considerable sacrifice to have his lunch on Mondays and Fridays. A young man who had an affable and disarming smile — he smiled, to prove it — but who could also upon occasion set aside his more congenial qualities and become almost as unaccommodating as his mentor.

He was still thoughtfully gazing at himself when the light in Nagy's cubicle was switched on. At the same moment he became aware that the old man had been repeatedly calling him.

He found him sitting on his cot in an old flannel dressing-gown, stuffing bread between his toothless gums, bread softened with water and flavoured with paprika and salt. The old man raised his hand, opened his mouth to speak, crammed more bread into it, and continued to gesticulate and chew. His teeth lay on a chair at the head of the cot. For two years after he had had his own extracted he had gone without any. They were too expensive. Now he had become accustomed to eating without them.

As he munched his bread, long, deep lines spread in all directions from his mouth so that it took on the appearance of a black sun, etching its malevolent rays upon his countenance. The heavy, baggy pouches reaching to the upper level of the cheek-bones were so swollen and distended they looked like some monstrous fruit, ripe and ready for plucking.

He had stopped chewing now. A dark hand, discoloured with splashes of brown pigment, reached out and clutched a battered coffee mug upon which the letters CPR were still visible.

The coffee ran in gleaming rills from the corners of his withered mouth down to his chin, vanished, and then reappeared in the hollow of his throat.

Alex turned away as the old man smacked his lips. They were no longer grey; the hot coffee had turned them a deep red. He smacked them appreciatively, reached out for his teeth, and deftly inserted them.

"About that grocer," he said. . . .

Alex scarcely heard him. His teeth had transformed the old man. The wrinkles around his mouth had vanished. His lips were full now. They gave him a revoltingly youthful look, he thought. And suddenly he shivered as Mr. Nagy clicked his teeth.

The old man was slow and sick and no longer sure of himself. He had never been very fast in closing a deal. But there was something about him, in the way he sat there, his body tensed as though ready to spring, his hands with their thick yellow nails, half-closed and twitching on his knees — something in the moist red lips and the white glistening teeth that reminded him of an old, lean, and hungry wolf. One could almost hear those teeth cutting through bone and tissue, and hear them crunch as they bit into their victim.

Alex stared at him in fascination. "How high will he go?" he asked finally.

"Eighteen thousand, and one-third down."

They looked at one another in silence and shared a slow, mirthless grin.

Then the old man nodded and sank back into his cot. His lips were beginning to turn grey again. His eyelids, heavily veined and almost transparent, trembled and settled to rest. His breathing grew heavy, and then rasping, and suddenly he broke into a long convulsive cough. He sat up holding his chest until he recovered his breath. Then he spat, removed his teeth, wiped his lips, and motioned impatiently to Alex to go.

His cough had grown much worse. Alex looked at him with concern. "Can I get you something?" he asked. "Some brandy?"

The old man snorted at the extravagance of this, and waved him away. "Turn out the light," he said.

Alex reached up to the light-bulb and unscrewed it half a turn.

"First thing tomorrow morning I want you to call Kostanuik," Nagy continued. "Tell him for God's sake to finish that job. The people are moving in on Monday. . . . Now what else was there? Yes — cancel the appointment with Halpern tomorrow."

The springs creaked. He coughed again.

"But he's got a clear title," Alex objected. "I spent nearly three days . . ."

"Leave me in peace," the old man cried petulantly. "And what are you standing there for? For God's sake go home. There's no work to do. Why do you come back here night after night and shine that light in my eyes? Go home and let me rest."

He sank back with a groan. Glancing at his assistant out of the corner of his eyes, he added by way of appeasement, "You can take over the Naturchik mortgage."

Alex stared at him incredulously. For the first time in nine years the old man was allowing him to use his own judgment. "This calls for a celebration," he said.

"Celebrate, celebrate," Nagy muttered. "First we'll see how much money you lose."

He sat up. "All right. Get the brandy. Maybe you'll even make a few dollars."

They drank in silence. The old man sucked at his withered lips and dropped back in his cot.

"Go now," he said. "And don't forget to lock the door."

"I won't forget."

He switched off the light above his desk, reached for his hat, and for a long time stood in the outer doorway looking into the office. Then he locked the door and walked out and was no sooner on the pavement than he turned back and looked through the window. Where should he go? He began to wander down the street. For a while he stood on the corner watching the cars go by. He walked on aimlessly. A block from the office, he retraced his steps, looked into the office window again, and sighed. It was still early, only a few minutes after ten. But there was no place to go. After a while he turned north and homeward.

Ten

A LEX TURNED uneasily from the bills he was checking to the old man's cubicle. He was still sleeping. His snores filled the office with a gurgling wail that rose and fell and at odd intervals took on the accents of an impassioned dispute in some foreign tongue. It was nearly nine o'clock. He had been sleeping for almost eleven hours.

Probably something in the medicine which that herbalist had given him, Alex thought, and returned to his work, only to lay his pen aside and turn again with anxious eyes to the door beyond which the old man slept.

There was no longer any doubt that he was seriously ill. For weeks now he had not done any work.

Sooner or later he would have to let go the reins, and then . . . Very slowly Alex began to smile.

The old man moaned in his sleep, grew silent, and began to snore again. It was raining outside. Alex's thoughts drifted. "If only one could trust the old buzzard," he murmured, and looked up as the front door opened.

A short, thick-set man in overalls, with massive shoulders and heavily corded forearms appeared behind the counter. He walked stolidly into the office, dropped his cap on a chair in front of Alex's desk, and began vigorously to scratch his head. His eyes, deep-set above high cheekbones, slowly closed. His nose crinkled. A beatific expression came over his face. Alex glared at him.

Kostanuik paid no attention. When he had finished, he

replaced his cap, reached into his pocket, and pulled out a three-inch finishing nail with which he began to scrape out the debris which had accumulated under his fingernails during the previous performance.

Alex's lips turned livid.

"Nagy's sleeping," he whispered. "What do you want?"

Kostanuik interrupted the operation upon his fingernails. "Herr Nagy telephoned this morning he wants to see me," he said. "Wot for I dunno."

He dropped the nail back into his pocket. "How is your auntie, and your uncle?" he asked.

"They're fine . . . thanks."

"I finished that liddle job on Magnus," Kostanuik continued.

"You charged too much," Alex said.

"So? Herr Nagy says I charged too much?"

Alex flushed. "No," he shouted, and instantly lowered his voice. "*I* say you charge too much. Nineteen dollars for a kitchen cupboard, five dollars for a few feet of baseboard — it'll take two months before we get that back in rent. Do you have to build everything as though it's got to last for a hundred years?"

He was about to go on when he noticed that Kostanuik was cleaning his nails again.

Alex handed him his cheque and jumped to his feet as Kostanuik crossed the office to Nagy's door.

"I told you Nagy's sleeping," he whispered. "He's sick."

"He telephoned he wants to see me," Kostanuik repeated impassively, and continued on his way.

"I'll wake him," Alex said.

A wave of warm air struck him as he opened the door of the old man's cubbyhole — the smell of old socks and brandy, of mice and paprika and the backflow of the water in the sink. Only the affection in which he held everything associated with the office mitigated the full horror of it. He found it necessary nevertheless to stand back for a while before entering.

Nagy was still asleep. As Alex bent over him, the old man

began to mutter and then to cough in a long-drawn liquid spasm. Alex drew back.

What did Nagy get out of all this, he wondered. A man worth sixty-five thousand dollars at the very least, living in this hole year after year, denying himself the comforts of life; yes, and even begrudging himself its necessities, living alone here almost like an animal. Why was he saving his money? There were things Alex understood about him, but his inner purpose, the vision that had kept him here all these years — that still eluded him.

He bent down and touched the old man gently on the shoulder.

Nagy's eyelids trembled. His eyes opened with a soft, guileless gleam in their dark depths; then they narrowed, blinked, and opened fully with their hard, metallic, everyday glint.

"Right away, right away," he mumbled, and reached for his teeth. "What is it?"

"Kostanuik's here."

Nagy raised himself, groaned, and fell back with his hands clutching his chest. He lay still. Then he sat up.

"Tell Kostanuik I'll see him in here," he said. "Get me the brandy and put on the light, and — no, don't go — I want you to hear what I've got to say. I think you might be interested."

There was a quality in his voice that caused Alex to tremble. The uneasiness he had felt ever since the old man had taken to his bed came over him again.

Kostanuik came in and sat down. Alex lowered himself to the edge of the cot. They waited while Nagy raised the bottle to his lips and then set it in a fold of the blanket between his legs. The old man gazed intently first at Kostanuik, then at Alex and back to Kostanuik again.

"I have news for you," he said, and began to cough. "I thought you two gentlemen might be interested to hear," he continued, "that I intend to retire."

Alex controlled himself with difficulty. This was it, the taste and the feel and the substance of achievement, nine years' labour come to fruition . . . here in this little room where fittingly enough, on his twenty-first birthday, the old man had first intimated that his assistant might some day succeed him.

But Nagy's eyes had at last come to rest. Alex felt them upon him and lowered his head in what he hoped was an attitude of regret.

"I'm sorry to hear that," he said, looking first gratefully at the old man and then dispassionately at Kostanuik, who was bent over, his elbows resting on his knees, his head clutched in his hands.

Nagy's quick, darting eyes were moving again with metronomic regularity between Kostanuik and himself.

"I can promise you one thing," Alex said. "I'll do my best. But you know that. And anyway, it's not as though I won't be able to consult you when I — "

He stopped at the cool amusement in the old man's eyes.

"I think there's a small misunderstanding here," Nagy said. "I must apologize for not making myself clear. Let me put it this way. The Agency is up for sale."

It was not only the silence that devoured. Was Kostanuik smiling? No, but Nagy was — in broad enjoyment.

"A misunderstanding?" Alex whispered. It was a trick, he thought. The old man was only testing him — his last lesson, to see how he conducted himself.

But there was a mordant, familiar gleam in the old man's eyes, an expression hitherto reserved for the oncoming client . . . or the departing simpleton.

"A misunderstanding!" Alex shouted. "There's no . . ." His voice fell. "You promised," he said, and flushed as the old man's smile widened contemptuously.

Alex lowered his head.

The last lesson, he thought bitterly. It was finished, and the day dreams too. But the old man had promised. They were not just dreams. He looked up. "But why sell?" he asked tremulously. "We're operating at a profit. Why don't you just let me look after things the way I've been doing? It's in your own interests. I could take care of the office. You could have an accountant come in every month. You could drop in yourself to see —"

The old man looked at him as though he were a fool.

"I'm not asking you to trust me," Alex cried. "You'd still have your lawyer to keep track of things and . . . and you'd have Kostanuik to look after the new construction and repairs."

Kostanuik raised his head at this and looked expectantly across at the old man, who merely reached for his bottle and raised it to his lips again.

Kostanuik got up and walked slowly out of the cubicle. The floorboards in the office creaked. There was the familiar and suddenly heart-rending sound of the hinges in the counter gate, then the deeper creak of the main door, and the office grew silent.

"Go and see if he closed the door," Nagy murmured absently.

"That's quite a trick you played on Kostanuik," Alex said, "letting him buy that equipment and dump-truck when you knew you were selling out. How is he going to pay for it now?"

Nagy chuckled. "You're worrying about Kostanuik?" he mocked. "In nine years I have learned something about you, my boy. You fool me not at all. You're thinking about yourself, not Kostanuik. If anything, you would have got rid of him long ago."

"That was no misunderstanding," Alex said bitterly.

"What?"

"You know damn well what," Alex continued. "You told me more times than I can count that when you left I'd take over. Just a trick to hold me here and make me work my bloody fool head off for you, that's all it was."

He lowered his voice. "Why couldn't you at least have told me first?" he asked.

"Your feelings are hurt?" Nagy asked in mock credulity. "You disappoint me. I feel that I have failed in my . . ."

"What's happened to you?" Alex cried. "You've changed so much, sometimes I don't know you any more. You weren't like this before — at least not with me —"

His voice broke. He turned away so that the old man could not see his face.

The springs creaked.

"Mere childishness," the old man said in a tired voice. "Are you the only one who ever lost a job? Maybe you expected me to make you a present of this business on a silver platter like in one of your story books?"

He began to cough. "Go and leave me in peace," he cried petulantly. "Why do you make all this uproar? Do I owe you anything? Turn out the light and go home . . . and make sure the door's locked when you go."

Alex returned to his desk.

"Go home," he said under his breath. But this was home, home and family and the breath of life to him. There was nowhere else to go. He had cut himself off from everything that even remotely threatened to disturb his life within these four walls. He looked across at the doorway to the old man's cubicle.

"I used to think of you as though you were my father," he said. "I used to say to myself, 'Someday I'll be like Mr. Nagy.' That's a hell of a joke, isn't it? For anyone to want to be like you."

He got up and adjusted the angle of his name-plate.

The old man called to him as he opened the front door. Alex slammed it shut, turned, and watched him hobbling around switching off the lights.

"Nine years," he said, "working my damn fool head off, and for what?"

He walked on to the car-stop. Tomorrow he would have to start looking for a job.

A few blocks before Salter he got off and crossed the street to a barber shop. Directly below the window was his father's "establishment," a few square feet of space, a work bench, a wall board covered with green baize — the shop of which he had dreamed when he was a boy.

He looked up at the three figures in the background: his brother Rudolph sitting under the hat rack, gazing intently at his father who stood mildly gesticulating with his back to the window; Mr. Schiller, the barber, sitting in his chair, his thick-lensed spectacles flashing as he nodded his head.

The mirrors, facing opposite walls, projected the barber shop and its array of lotions, its calendars and gleaming light-clusters into an endless series of images far beyond the confines of the little room.

It looked cheerful and friendly; the three figures so intent upon themselves seemed untroubled and at peace, not only with themselves but with the world around them. If only he could walk in and sit there as his brother was doing, and let the peace and quiet settle upon him!

His brother was talking now. How old was he? — Eleven; twelve, maybe. He'd better watch himself, Alex though absently. First thing he knows, he'll turn out like the old man. And that . . .

"By God!" he exclaimed. "Imperial Crown Investment. They're the biggest." He paused. "I'll call their real-estate man tomorrow. . . . And don't forget," he said. "Look him straight in the eye. You've got something on the ball. The people in the North End know you. They trust you, and God help them, some of them even love you." He surveyed his image for a moment in the plate glass, and straightened his tie. "Listen, Mr. Crown," he said. "I'm your man. I've got nine years' experience dealing with these people. I know them. They're suspicious of Anglo-Saxons. You understand, sir?"

"Now I'm convinced that the men you've got representing you in the North End aren't doing as well as you think they might."

He's going to stop breathing there, Alex thought. He'll object. He has to; he hired them. On the other hand he probably gave them hell only the night before for not being on their toes. Anyway I better tell him first what a fine bunch — what a fine group of men they are. . . .

"But they're working at a disadvantage, sir. They're handicapped, and for no other reason than that they're Anglo-Saxons."

He laughed, and drove his right fist into his left palm. By God, that's it, he thought. All I have to do is dress it up a bit. Getting out of that hole is probably the best thing that could have happened to me.

He opened the door, walked briskly into the barber shop, and sat down. They had stopped talking, he noticed, the moment he entered.

"Hello, Ruddy. How are you?"

"Oh, okay, I guess."

Alex glanced at his father. "Hello, Dad. Hello, Mr. Schiller."

"The table is either there or it is not there," Mr. Schiller shouted in German. "And why is my belief in its existence inadequate? I can see it, can't I, and touch it and even sit on it if I want to? Isn't that enough?"

Alex looked at him in astonishment and turned to his father, who, he noticed, had a book in his hand.

"Why do you get so excited?" Joseph Hunter asked. "It's merely a restatement . . ."

He opened the book. "But how well he has expressed it! Listen. All he says is that the table is not what it appears to be from a commonsense viewpoint. For example, if a number of observers sit around and examine it, each one depending upon his position will see it differently. Each one sees a different table."

Mr. Schiller jumped to his feet. "Therefore it is impossible to arrive at the truth about the table or anything else," he shouted. "I'm a couple of premises ahead of you. This is a dangerous doctrine, Joseph. Can't you see where such reasoning leads one?"

"Ach, listen to him!" Joseph Hunter threw back his head and laughed. "You've heard this before. Why so vehement?"

"This man is dangerous, I tell you," Mr. Schiller cried. "An enemy of humanity."

Joseph Hunter looked up. "Listen," he said softly and opened the book again. "For whom is this dangerous?" He read slowly, translating into German. " 'Love, beauty, knowledge and the joy of life: these things retain their lustre however wide our range of vision. And if philosophy can help us to feel the scheme of these things, it will have played its part in man's collective work of bringing light into a world of darkness.'''

He lowered the book. "Are these the words of an enemy of humanity?"

"He uses nice words," Mr. Schiller conceded, and pursed his lips.

"Nice words," Joseph Hunter cried. "Your stubborn conviction that that table embodies only its apparent characteristics illustrates perfectly one of the defects in common beliefs which he is trying to replace with a ... a ..." He opened the book once more, thumbed it rapidly, and read, " 'with an amended kind of knowledge, which shall be tentative ... ' "

"Tentative," Mr. Schiller cried triumphantly. "Why tentative?"

Alex glanced at his brother, who appeared to be following the discussion not only as though he understood what was being said, but as though he were deriving considerable amusement from it.

Does he really understand all this stuff, he wondered, or is he just pretending?

"Do you know what they're talking about?" he whispered.

"It's about a book by Bertrand Russell on philosophy," Rudolph answered, tearing his eyes away from his father. He flushed and added, proudly, "I brought it home from the library."

"Philosophy," Alex echoed. "About men sitting around tables? What's the use of talking about that?" he asked, somewhat louder than he had intended.

"The use!" Mr. Schiller repeated. "The question of the nature of reality is under discussion, and he asks, what's the use?"

Alex groaned. Mr. Schiller had few pleasures in life, but one of these was baiting the eldest son of Joseph Hunter.

"I'll tell you," Mr. Schiller continued. "Instead of examining this table, let's examine you. All around you are observers.

From every angle they sit and observe. But this doctrine says no two will see the same thing. You comprehend? All of them see something different. Ho, says one, I see a Hungarian. Ha, says another, an Englishman. No, no, says a third . . ."

Alex leaped to his feet. "The only thing wrong with your theory is that I'm not English," he shouted, and growing aware of it, lowered his voice. "And I'm not Hungarian," he said. "I'm Canadian."

"So you are a Canadian," Mr. Schiller said. "Tell me something, Mr. Canada. . . . What do you believe?"

Talk for the sake of talk, Alex thought wearily. Night after night, year after year. What a way to spend one's life — talking about whether tables existed or not.

"Mr. Crown," he murmured to himself. "I'm not just looking for a job. I've got one. What I want to do is to associate myself with a . . . an organization that's alive and growing and big enough to provide opportunities for advancement."

By God, that's good, he thought. All I have to remember is that it's just like any other sales talk, except that I'm selling myself.

He turned impatiently back to Mr. Schiller.

"What do you mean," he asked, "what do I believe?"

Mr. Schiller had returned to his chair. "Every man," he said, "believes in something. Tell me, what do you believe?"

"I just believe in things the way they are," he said, and moved toward the stairs. "The way things are is all right with me."

"At least consistent," Mr. Schiller intoned. "In fact a perfect answer. . . . And what of you?" he continued, waving his hand at Rudolph, who suddenly flushed beet red at the question. "What do you think of all this?"

"Well," Rudolph said finally, "I think I'll just suspend judgment."

The young punk, Alex thought. Where does he get those words?

His father and Mr. Schiller were laughing. Alex smiled as he mounted the stairs.

In the kitchen, seated at the table, he discovered his mother and Mrs. Schiller playing cards. Between them on the table stood a box of toothpicks and a pitcher of lemonade. The two women smiled warmly at him as he entered. His mother inclined her head as he approached; he kissed her on the cheek and laughed as Mrs. Schiller turned her head too. He brushed his lips against her forehead and sat down, with a sigh.

"They're making jokes downstairs for a change?" his mother asked in English.

Alex shrugged his shoulders.

"And who pays the groceries and the milk bills while the father makes the world better for the neighbours?" Mrs. Schiller asked.

"The neighbors, maybe," Alex smiled.

His mother and Mrs. Schiller nodded in agreement.

"You look tired," his mother said, and removed a thread from his shoulder. Her hand remained there. "You shouldn't work too hard," she admonished. "Like I told Mrs. Crossman. With brain work it's even harder than with the hands. You should watch you don't get brain fever."

In her eyes, he could do no wrong. He knew that she lauded him shamelessly to her neighbours. He was a successful business man and a dutiful son — the highest praise that any woman in the neighbourhood could bestow.

The sound of the telephone ringing in the living-room brought him abruptly to his feet with the wild thought that Nagy might be calling. As he ran into the hallway, he grew certain that the old man had changed his mind.

At the head of the stairs he almost collided with his brother who ran on ahead of him, only to stand there sheepishly with the receiver in his hand and announce that it was their aunt.

"Not tonight," Alex groaned as he took the receiver. "God damn it, I had enough for one night. . . . Why can't he get drunk at home?"

"He's drunk again?" his mother cried out. "Aiee, that woman! I told him, but who am I?"

Rudolph quietly closed the door.

Alex listened impatiently to his aunt's lament. "I just got

home from the office," he broke in. "I'm tired. I had a hard day."

She was crying. She was always crying. . . .

"Where is he?" Alex asked.

"He's at that place called Nick's," she answered, and began to plead with him.

"All right, all right, I'm going."

A few minutes later he was in a cab speeding down Main Street. He would have to weigh his words a little more carefully when he mentioned that those North End agents weren't doing so well. In fact, he had better not mention it at all, but merely outline the obstacles they faced. Yes. They're a fine group of men. Build them up, you're so good yourself you can afford to. . . . But don't, for God's sake, talk too much. Don't oversell it . . . And don't rush in. Just take it easy. Wait and find out what kind of a guy — of a man you're dealing with. Just throw the ball in his direction and give him a chance to send it back. Don't throw the damn thing at him. And smile, damn you, smile. . . .

When he finally looked up they were in the outskirts of the city.

The car lurched as they turned off the highway and coasted to a stop. Nick's place was only a few hundred yards away, hidden from the road by a small clump of trees.

The night air was cool and fresh. In the distance, in a bright haze, gleamed the city lights. From the shadows in the trees and from a nearby creek there came a lonely chirp, a myriad-tongued murmur, punctuated now and again by a resonant, lugubrious croak.

"What the hell are those things?" Alex asked. "Every time we come here they're making that racket."

They crossed over the creek on a narrow bridge.

"Grasshoppers," the cab-driver said helpfully.

Alex shook his head. "Frogs," the cab-driver suggested. "Crickets, maybe."

But frogs slept at night, didn't they? And crickets sounded English and unreasonable. Were there crickets in Canada?

The cab-driver shrugged his shoulders.

"Well, they sure make a hell of a racket," Alex said. "It makes you wonder how the farmers around here ever sleep at night."

They made their way in the darkness past a row of cars to a small frame house.

Alex knocked twice, waited, and knocked again.

The outer door opened. There was no light. The warm reek of alcohol and stale tobacco reached his nostrils.

"Is that you, Mr. Hunter?"

"Nick?"

"Yeah."

"How is he? He isn't sick, is he?"

"No. Just like always, Mr. Hunter."

"All right, Nick. Bring him out."

Onkel Janos came staggering out, flaying the air and roaring a Hungarian song.

"He pay you?" Alex asked.

"He paid me, Mr. Hunter."

Alex motioned to the cab-driver. Together they half carried, half dragged his uncle to the bridge. The year before, in the early spring, while fighting them off, he had fallen into the creek. The shock had sobered him instantly, if only temporarily, and ever since, no matter how belligerent he might be, he invariably grew passive as they approached it.

They hurried across it, shoved him into the cab, and drove off. On the way to the hotel, while the cab-driver stopped off to order the black coffee, Alex reached for his uncle's wallet. Ten dollars. Very thoughtful of Nick.

He forced the coffee down his uncle's throat and they drove on again. The whole procedure had long since taken on the form of a ritual. It was though every step had been rehearsed. When they reached the hotel, Alex signed a bill for the fare and handed the driver two dollars. The doorman saluted them; the cab-driver left.

The aged elevator man, sitting idly at the door of his cage at this hour of the night, rose with a greeting and escorted them to the steam bath where for a fifty-cent piece he blessed young Mr. Hunter and hobbled back to his cage. The steam-bath attendant led them with mincing steps into the locker room.

Naked in the steam bath, his elbow on his knee, his chin resting on the knuckles of his right hand, Alex let his mind drift and grow pleasantly vacant.

He looked up as his uncle staggered in. Only yesterday, it seemed, he had seen him lithe and buoyant, his most trivial actions invested with inimitable grace. Now he sat there, a fat, ungainly man in a drunken stupor, his eyes dull and empty, his features bloated. The flesh below his chest and under his armpits lay in thick, red corrugations that quivered with every breath he took.

He grew docile under Alex's gaze, took his nephew's hand like a child, and allowed himself to be placed under a shower. As the cold water struck him, he began to yell. He flung his arms about wildly, straining to tear himself away, and yet remained as though rooted to the spot while a look of sobering agony spread over his face.

Alex watched him with mingled disgust and pity.

In the steam bath again, the attendant adjusted the valve above the hot iron globe in the centre of the room. The first drop of water spluttered and shattered. A second drop followed.

The air in the room, warm and moist when they had entered, filled rapidly with steam.

Alex began to nod. It's going to be all right, he thought. Best thing that could have happened to me.

Through half-closed eyes he saw his uncle sitting on the bench facing him, clumsily soaping his paunch.

Alex turned away and watched the steam billowing slowly and softly above the iron globe, listened drowsily to the sound of the water dripping, and let his eyes wander from the immaculate tiled floor to the walls where a mosaic depicting an underwater scene with queer marine creatures seemed to take on life in the steam-laden atmosphere.

His thoughts drifted, moved down a bypath of memory.

"Those were the days," he murmured. "No troubles, no worries or anything."

His eyes closed. He dozed for a few minutes. His thoughts veered. "Nine years," he said. "And what did I end up with? Twenty lousy bucks a week. He must have laughed to himself every time he looked at me. . . ."

"Alex, your uncle wants to talk to you."

Alex groaned.

"Alex, don't be impatient with an unhappy man."

"All right, all right! What is it?"

"Are you sure nobody got hurt, Alex? I think I remember . . ."

"Onkel Janos, nobody got hurt," Alex shouted. "Honest-to-God. Believe me for once. Nobody got hurt."

"Don't be angry, Alex."

"I'm not angry. But why do you always keep asking the same question?"

"Then nothing happened to her?" his uncle asked.

Alex sat up. This was something new.

Onkel Janos looked up at the ceiling ecstatically. "Alex," he sighed. "That girl had a pair of milkers." He shook his head incredulously. . . . "My boy, I would sell my soul to feel them again."

His hands cupped, closed gently, opened, and traced a voluptuous line in the steam-laden air.

"Ah, the sweet, sinful joy of her," he exclaimed.

"Alex," he said. "Listen to your uncle who thinks only of your comfort and of what is good for you. If you ever get married, my boy, get a woman with flesh on her to cushion her parts. Such women are most agreeable, my boy, let people say what they will. . . . Are you listening, Alex?"

"Did I ever tell you?" he continued. "I knew a girl once in Fiume . . . no, in Trieste . . . or was it Fiume? A girl with eyes like a song at evening over still water. The stars shone in her . . ."

There was a rumble in his paunch. " . . . in her eyes," he burped, and fell silent.

Alex's eyes had closed. There came back to him an evening in his fifteenth year. He was in Mrs. Waldchuk's kitchen, sternly demanding that she pay her rent. The kitchen stank with cabbage and mouldering wood and old clothes, and from the corner beside the stove where her husband slept in a drunken stupor, the acrid odour of beer.

The house swarmed with children, and in their midst she sat, huge and dirty and genial, limp in her chair, her massive legs sprawled wide.

She smiled, Alex recalled, and he saw himself, a small boy banging his fist on the table, making the bread-crumbs dance. Unexpectedly she reached over and while her left hand stroked his hair, her right began to fondle him.

"You want?" she asked in a deep voice. "You want?"

And as he drew away, overturning his chair and fearful that her husband might waken, she suddenly roared at the children to get out. They vanished, all but the youngest, who sat on the floor, gravely rolling a beer bottle to and fro. Her husband slept on.

"Ah, little sonny," she cried. "Little sonny, I won't hurt you."

Alex Hunter stared into the swirling vapour about him. "Little sonny," he murmured.

She had almost dragged him into that summer kitchen, but it was not until he had seen with greedy and terrified eyes the enormous quivering volume of her that he had tried to run away.

She had simply reached out and enveloped him and, long after wonder and lust had fled, held him to her.

He had proved himself. Now he knew what there was to know. He raised himself and looked out of the window. The stars were in their accustomed places and there was the sound of children playing on the street.

Yes. Now he knew. Then why did he feel like crying?

Before Alex's eyes there appeared the women he had known, shrill and modern, and in the modern manner all skin and gristle, very often drunk, and generally embodying everything of which he disapproved. Tawdry, short-lived riverbank and hallway affairs.

His uncle swam into view. He stared at him enviously; then he thought of his aunt with her spindly shanks, her grey, grim visage, and the collarbone that bit into him every time she kissed him.

"You want to stay here for the night?" he asked.

His uncle nodded, and while the attendant finished dressing him, Alex telephoned his aunt.

Later, in an adjoining room while his uncle slept, Alex interlaced his fingers behind his head and gave himself to his thoughts. It was just as well he was leaving the Agency. Sooner or later he would have left anyhow, if only to get out of the North End. He would get himself a job on Portage Avenue, perhaps even at Imperial Crown, with a salary that would enable him some day to open his own agency. What was he complaining about, then?

He closed his eyes. He saw himself in a walnut-panelled office, seated behind an enormous desk. He was the Investment Manager of Imperial Crown Investment, held in fear and respect by all below him, and rated by all above as the up-and-coming young man in the organization. That Alex Hunter was a man worth watching.

Variations on this theme flashed through his mind.

"Alex Hunter," he said to himself, and repeated it endlessly over and over again.

He reached for his jacket which hung upon the chair at his side, and searched the pockets until he found one of the slips of paper upon which he had written his signature.

He sprang out of bed and opened the window. Far below him he saw the street corner where he had stood so long ago. He tore up the slip of paper with his name on it and shredding it into tiny flakes let the wind suck them out of his hand. They scattered far and wide. It was a foolish thing to do, he thought, but it gave him pleasure. He laughed as the wind carried his name east and south — tiny bits of himself falling through the night upon the city.

Eleven

TWO DAYS later he stood before Imperial Crown Investment, thoughtfully surveying its massive granite front. It was a mere three-storey structure, shadowed by its neighbours. But above its doorway was carved the simple declaration: "Est'd 1705." That was all. And it was enough, Alex thought. What better statement was there for an investment house than the fact that it had been in existence for more than two centuries; for more than a hundred and fifty years before the incorporation of Winnipeg as a city? It was as blunt and direct as a hammer blow. The mentality that had conceived this manner of proclaiming its identity appealed to him.

He looked at his watch.

Precisely at half past nine, he strode briskly into the office of the manager of the Real Estate Division. A tall, sad, lean man with a small greying moustache rose from behind his desk as he entered and with an affable "Mr. Hunter?" extended a sinewy hand, motioned to a chair, and offered him a cigarette.

The sound of his name, Alex thought as he seated himself, was like a song on this man's tongue, vowelled with a precise and beautiful clarity. His first impression of him was of an impeccable grooming; his second, during the brief but inevitable weather and state-of-business discussion, that there was something in the half smile which punctuated his thoughts that made one feel he was smiling not with the desire to be friendly, or in self-appreciation, but rather as if he hoped and expected momentarily to be told something which would amuse him.

It was only an impression, but in the course of his business dealings Alex had acquired a profound faith in this kind of almost unthinking assessment of people.

His eyes still intent upon the man's face, he took a deep breath and, rejecting the carefully thought-out introduction he had prepared, remarked that he had gone to considerable trouble to investigate the financial position of Imperial Crown Investment before deciding to inquire whether he might associate himself with it. Didn't Mr. Atkinson agree, he continued, that a young man had to be very careful of the Company he kept?

There was silence.

For a moment he felt the irregular beating of his heart. Had he been too presumptuous? His joke, if one could call it that, was old and hoary, but applied to Imperial Crown, it was so outrageously inappropriate that it was . . .

He discovered to his astonishment that Mr. Atkinson was laughing, silently and sadly and not with his mouth all, but with his body.

"Ah, my dear fellow," he said finally, and sank back into his chair. "So you investigated us?" He smiled and raised his cigarette to his lips.

"Hunter," he said reflectively. "Any relation of Colonel Hunter?"

Alex felt that he could not trust himself to speak. He shook his head.

"Well now," Mr. Atkinson continued. "Tell me something about yourself."

For the next few minutes Alex found himself facing a leisurely barrage of questions. He made several vain attempts to direct the conversation into business channels until it dawned on him that, for the time being at least, Mr. Atkinson was far more interested in his "people" than in his business career.

The questions grew more personal.

In addition to a number of other minor facts, he had now

disclosed that his parents were both living, that he had a younger brother, that his father was a watchmaker, and that they lived on Selkirk Avenue. At the mention of Selkirk Avenue, he thought he detected a flicker of expression in the man's eyes, too transient to be interpreted.

At the next question, framed in the same courteous, almost off-hand manner as the others, he felt the colour mounting to his cheeks. He cleared his throat.

"Hungarian," he said.

The silence in the room was edged with old fears that set him trembling, with suddenly remembered North End talk of discrimination beyond the invisible barrier at Portage and Main, talk which he had always disregarded as having no possible reference to himself, but only to half-qualified, dime-a-dozen clerks. For nine years Nagy had been beating it into his head that this kind of prejudice was a luxury no business man could afford, and he had come to believe it, even though he still found it distasteful to deal with North End people. Business came first. Your personal feelings were of no consequence. And it was true. He had corroborated it himself hundreds of times in his relations with the builders' supply houses, with the bank, with inspectors and lawyers and salesmen.

Was he mistaken about the man's motives? He might possibly be; he knew that he was unusually sensitive on this point. He fought back his apprehensions and waited while the man across the desk very slowly lit another cigarette.

Another question. Under the meticulously clipped moustache he saw the sad lips begin to form it. It hung in the air, and with its utterance there was no longer any room for doubt. And yet he should have expected it; it was a logical extension of what had gone before. . . . Hunter was scarcely a Hungarian name.

"Hunyadi," he said, as much to himself as in answer to the man sitting across from him, who surveyed him with no affability now and no sadness, but quite dispassionately, with all expression drained from his face.

Alex wiped his palms on his knees. He felt it again and was

surprised that it should be the same, the same uncoiling disgust, the revulsion he could not bring himself to direct outward, but must turn in upon himself. And there was nothing to do or say — only to sit and watch the long, slender fingers crushing a fresh cigarette into an ashtray, absently and yet thoroughly until it was pulverized.

In his ears there still rang the vowelled vulgarity of that last question, a vulgarity that seemed suddenly ineradicable and universal and that would plague him forever, that filled him with a loathing for himself so deep that he could only think of running out, and crawling back into Nagy's office, to draw the blind and sit there, dark and secure behind his desk.

Mr. Atkinson had risen. Alex reached for his hat. "So it's your policy . . ." he began, as the door opened and a girl with a stenographer's notebook appeared.

Mr. Atkinson motioned to her to be seated. He looked up. "I have no recollection of having discussed policy, Mr. . . . Hunter," he remarked.

Alex stopped for a moment in the doorway. What was he going to say? It didn't matter.

It was cool outside. But at the first breath of air he felt his stomach heave. He swallowed and crossed over to a café where, after ordering coffee, he sat down and stared vacantly before him. Another version of Humpy Ya Ya; more refined, that was all. . . . He saw them again over his shoulders, in the sunlight with their mouths open red and their white teeth gleaming. Hunky, Humpy Ya Ya. . . .

It can't be, he thought. Not all of them. Business men weren't like this. They couldn't afford to be. A ferocious image flashed through his mind. He saw himself in Atkinson's office again and gave himself without restraint to an annihilating re-encounter from which he emerged feeling somewhat better.

His coffee arrived. He raised the cup and found that his hands were still trembling. A wave of self-pity came over him. He yielded to it, to its warm cradling comfort, and closed his eyes until it subsided.

They're not all like this, he said to himself. They can't be.

He spent the remainder of that day and the next two going from one establishment to another. In two, the mere mention of Selkirk Avenue and Nagy's office brought all discussion decisively to an end, and with somewhat less formality than in Atkinson's office. In another there was a misunderstanding; he was taken for a German and the interview closed before he had time to explain. (But here, in extenuation, he told himself, the man who had interviewed him was wearing a war-service medal in his buttonhole.) In five, he managed to finish his sales talk, but with his now heightened sensitivity and his nervousness, he found himself no longer able to judge how he had been received.

Late in the afternoon of the third day, he stood on the corner of Portage and Main and looked around him. Whether he had proved anything or not, he didn't know. He had had enough. Some day he was coming back here, he thought, not with his hat in his hand to beg for a job, but in his own right, to set up his own office and no questions asked. And God help anybody who got in his way.

In the meantime he would find a job; it would have to be in the North End. There would be no difficulty in finding one, but the opportunities for advancement would be limited; the firms were small; almost every second one was ridden with owners' cousins and uncles and bookkeeping nieces. The prospect was a dismal one. He would probably mark time for the next five years of his life, working for one small hole-in-the-wall outfit after another, crawling around through slums, spending himself in dreary quarrels over leaking roofs and plugged drains and rent. But that didn't matter. In one way or another, no matter how long it took he was coming back.

He turned down Main. An overwhelming sense of oppression came over him. It was easy to talk, but what had happened was so sickening he could no longer think about it.

He returned to the office and looked in at the window, and it was as though a wing tip brushed against awareness. Something that filled him with elation and sent the blood racing through his veins flashed through his mind, seemed about to burst into meaning, and eluded him.

He shook his head, walked into the office and, as Nagy called to him, continued on to the old man's cubicle.

"You still work here?" Nagy screamed. "What am I paying you for?" He sucked in air laboriously, sat up, and pointed to the doorway. "Go back to your desk," he ordered, "and from now on, ask permission before you leave."

Alex shrugged his shoulders. "I'll be out all day tomorrow," he said.

"I'll fire you!" the old man shouted at the top of his voice.

"You can go to hell," Alex said and walked back into the office.

"Stay by the phone at least for a little while," the old man wailed. "It rings and rings. How can I sleep?"

Alex sat down at his desk and continued with the task of posting the Agency's properties to Nagy's account. The first lot had already been sent on to his lawyer for the transfer of title.

"Alex."

"For Christ's sake go to sleep."

There was silence.

The old man began to chuckle. "Have you found a job yet, Alex?"

Five years, if all went well. He would be nearly thirty years old. . . .

"Alex, I said have you found . . ."

"I heard you. And I'll tell you something. I'll find a dozen jobs before you sell this hole-in-the-wall for fifteen thousand dollars. You couldn't get that much for it even if you went with it."

Nagy laughed. "You know who phoned again today? Mrs. Kostanuik." His high-pitched cackle ended in a cough.

Kostanuik had probably mortgaged his house to buy that equipment. Alex nodded grimly. Too bad he couldn't raise anything on his wife and daughter.

"What did she want this time?" he asked.

Nagy began to laugh again. "You." The old man was really enjoying himself. "Kostanuik must have told her you're the heir to the throne," he continued. His hilarity ended disastrously; when he had finished coughing there was silence.

And in the silence it came again. Something whose meaning was about to unfold . . .

"Alex."

If only that doddering old idiot would shut his mouth for a while . . . that unfolded, and at the moment of unfolding revealed itself as something so obvious that for several minutes he remained in a state of stupefaction.

That was why Mrs. Kostanuik had been calling him. She had not forgotten that he had a rich aunt.

"Of course," he said, and raising the receiver dialled his aunt's number to ask if he might come over and visit her that evening.

Twelve

H E SAT in his customary chair beside the marble shepherd
lamp, a doily under each elbow, a skein of wool between
his outstretched hands, breathing in the sour odour that pervaded her home, listening wearily to the story of her life, with
every feature of which he had long since acquired a detailed
and unhappy familiarity.

For the past two weeks now, night after night, he had done
little else than sit and listen. It was all right for her to talk
about herself, he thought furiously, but he had only to open
his mouth to mention the business that had brought him here
and she would waggle her finger and remind him of his
promise not to open the subject again until she had had time
to think about it.

As he flexed his thumbs to the unwinding wool he noticed
that she was looking up at the clock again. She had lately taken
to the use of cosmetics. From the corners of her mouth, which
she had smeared with scarlet, ran the two vertical furrows.
These she had evidently attempted to disguise with powder,
only to succeed in emphasizing their black depths.

Alex felt a wave of revulsion pass through his body at the
sight of her, and unmindful of the fact that it was upon his
suggestion, some months before, that she had begun using
cosmetics, and drawn for the moment from his own problems,
wondered that his uncle, following in the footsteps of his
predecessor, had not long since left her.

"Now what was I saying?" she asked.

Alex shifted into a more comfortable position as he let the end of the skein slip through his fingers.

"You were in . . . in . . ."

"Budapest," she said. "He left me, and I was young and alone and a stranger there."

She laid the ball of wool in her lap. Her features softened into a shadowed mask of grief. Her eyes grew lustrous with unshed tears.

"I was alone," she continued, "and I was hungry, and no one who has not been hungry can ever understand what that means. It is not the same for a man as for a woman. God forgive me, the pain and the shame of it grew until I hated the whole world. Soon it was too much trouble even to wash or to comb my hair or even to go and fill myself with water.

"Once I saw myself in the water in one of the great fountains," she continued. "There are so many beautiful fountains in Budapest. I remember it was turned off that day; the water was still, and I looked and saw a little cloud floating by. Then it passed and I saw myself. I saw what I had become and I began to cry. People looked at me. 'What is the matter?' a woman said. 'Have you lost something?'

" 'Yes,' I told her, 'I have lost something. I have lost my youth.' And I was seventeen, and what I saw in the water was not a girl in her first bloom any more but an old woman."

The room grew silent and Alex, who had been considering the possibility of taking his uncle into his confidence and had at that very moment decided against it, raised his head and saw that she had covered her eyes and was crying.

He looked at her thoughtfully and then got up and seated himself beside her, made an effort to touch her, withdrew his hand with a shiver of disgust, and finally let it fall lightly on her shoulder.

"You think I don't know I'm ugly," she suddenly screamed. "I know! I know! He laughs at me when I ask him if . . . if . . .

"The first time I saw him he was laughing," she said,

lowering her hands and glancing at the clock. "He laughed and I said to myself, dear God, how can a human being laugh like that? He stood out there with his shovel in his hand and looked at me, and when he came in for a pail of water he laughed and his laughter filled the darkest corner of my heart."

She clutched Alex's hand and clung to it until her crying subsided. Her palm felt cold and wet. Her body began to sway to and fro.

"What happiness have I ever known?" she murmured. "In Budapest I lived like an animal until the day I dropped in the street and they took me to a hospital. There for the first time someone was kind to me. I lay in bed for two months, first one sickness and then another. But I was happy. . . .

"When the letter came from my husband saying that he was in Canada and that soon he would send for me, I remembered the things he had done to me and I knew that I would never return to him. But I forgave him. I learned to pray again in the hospital. I prayed for him."

Alex gazed down mournfully at the worn and faded pattern of the rug. So this was what it had come to; to sit here and hold hands with a self-centred old witch whose face, what with her wrinkles and her rouge and her tears, was so revolting he could scarcely bring himself to look at her. A hell of a fine way this was of doing business. . . . But he had already done everything that was humanly possible, he told himself, and felt her eyes upon him and looked up and smiled.

" . . . this doctor who was a German," she was saying "took me into his home to be a housemaid. I was still weak, but every morning at five I had to get up for the children. I worked all day, not a minute even to sit down — sometimes not even to eat. His wife starved me, and not only me but the others too.

"What could I do? I went upstairs to the top of the house where my room was, and I cried. I cried every night in that room. What else was there to do?" She disengaged her hand and returned to her knitting.

"So there I worked for three years, then for four years in another house until one day what should happen but that I should receive a letter from a lawyer who asked me to come and visit him. My husband was dead in Canada, he said, and he had died a rich man."

She glanced up from her knitting. Her lips moved silently. "Alex!"

Alex raised his eyelids.

"I though you were asleep," she sighed, and looked up at the clock. 'Your uncle is going to be late again," she said. "Come, let's have our coffee."

It had become one of his minor chores, in the absence of his uncle, to grind the coffee.

In the kitchen he set to work, cursing her under his breath. He had flattered her, wheedled, coaxed and begged her. He had proved to her, irrefutably, he thought, the relationship between his uncle's idleness and his drunkenness; had shown her that she had nothing to be afraid of. It would be her privilege as owner to make all the important decisions, to examine the books, and to decide when to buy or sell. She had been looking after her own properties all these years, hadn't she? And astutely, too. Among real-estate men in town it was recognized and freely admitted how shrewdly she had managed her affairs. What was there to worry about, then? As an investment the only difference between the Agency and her properties was that, dollar for dollar, the Agency operated at a greater rate of profit. He had shown her copies of the office records to prove it and had in fact met every objection she had raised, and all to no effect.

The telephone rang. Probably Nick calling about Onkel Janos. He tip-toed to the door and drew it open a few inches.

She was talking to some woman . . . to Mrs. Kostanuik. He heard her mention his name and a few moments later saw her place the receiver on the table and come walking toward the kitchen.

"You've been flirting with some young man," he began as she entered the kitchen.

She leered coyly at him and shook her head. "I've been very naughty," she said. "I've been talking to Mrs. Kostanuik. She wants you."

Alex's eyes narrowed. "You told her about the Agency, didn't you?" he asked.

"I begged you not to," he shouted. "For God's sake, Auntie, can't you understand? My whole life depends on this. I told you not to tell anybody. Nagy hasn't advertised yet, and if word gets around, the Agency will be sold to somebody else."

This was nonsense and he recognized it as such, even as he shouted at her. But why couldn't that damn woman keep her nose out of his business? She had been calling him regularly at the office.

"God damn it," he continued, "what . . ."

"Alex!"

"What did you tell her?" he asked, in a quieter tone.

"She came yesterday for money and told me her husband would lose everything. She cried and I felt sorry for her, but I said no. And then it just slipped out. I told her that everybody was after me for money and that you wanted me to buy . . ."

Alex nodded. "So I'm just everybody. You meant me too when you said everybody, didn't you? That's very nice to hear. I never expected . . . "

"Alex, please. I did not mean it that way. You know I didn't."

"Why did she call me just now?"

"She wants you to come over." His aunt hesitated. "For a visit. She's waiting on the phone. She wants . . ."

"I know what she wants. She thinks I'm going to manage the Agency. She wants me to promise I'll keep her husband on as my contractor."

"But I never promised that I would buy it," his aunt cried, clutching his arm.

"I know you didn't. You'd rather see me out on the street and your best friend bankrupt. You'd rather turn your husband into a drunkard and lose him altogether than give up a few cents of your money."

He freed himself from her grasp.

"I'm just in the right mood to talk to her tonight," he shouted, and ran into the hallway and picked up the receiver.

"This is Alex Hunter. Yes," he smiled grimly, "I'll be glad to come over." He hung up.

His aunt stood in the kitchen doorway, her hands pressed to her lips. Alex drew on his coat. As he reached for the door she came running to him and threw herself into his arms. "Don't go like this," she sobbed. "I'm all alone in the house."

He caught her by the shoulder and held her at arm's length.

"Auntie, listen to me," he pleaded. "Doesn't it mean anything to you that Onkel Janos is lying out there drunk somewhere, not even knowing what he's saying or doing? If anything happened to him, would you ever forgive yourself? I tell you if he had a business of his own he'd stop drinking. Things would change between you and him. He's unhappy because he hasn't got anything to do. Every time I bring him home from that place he tells me how ashamed he is that he has to live off his wife. He feels that the whole . . ."

"How can you know what lies between us?" she cried. "For nearly a year now it has not been as it should be between man and wife. God forgive me, I shouldn't talk of such things. I don't know any more what I'm saying."

He felt the shudder that passed through her body.

"I don't know any more what I'm saying," she repeated, and moved her hands distractedly from her throat, to her mouth, to the lapels of his coat.

"I'm right, Auntie," Alex whispered. "You know I'm right. You told me yourself . . ."

"No!" She pushed him from her. "No," she screamed. "Even if you are right. Do you know how he would be in an office? He's like a child. He trusts everybody. Everybody is his friend. Everything he laughs at. How long would it be before he went bankrupt and lost everything?"

"But Auntie, don't you remember? I've explained all that. We'll make him president or something. I'd manage the Agency for you. How could he go bankrupt when the money would be in your hands? And in the office I could talk to him and keep an eye on what he's doing. I tell you, Auntie, he'd be happy there. He'd have work to do. He'd be an office man with a regular job and regular hours. In a few weeks you wouldn't know him."

"Please, Alex, no more . . . not tonight. We'll talk again some other time."

"Auntie, listen to me."

"Not tonight," she said, and sank down on the hall bench and with her eyes fully upon him began to cry. The tears streamed brightly down her discoloured cheeks. Her lips moved wordlessly.

Alex ground his teeth and turned to the door.

"What will you say to Mrs. Kostanuik?" she asked.

"I'll tell her," he said slowly, "that so far as you're concerned Kostanuik and I can go to hell — or go begging on the streets. It's all the same to you."

She sat there wringing her hands. "You won't tell her that, will you, Alex? You're saying that only to hurt me because you're angry with me."

"All right. Suppose you tell me what to say."

He caught the hardening of the lines around her mouth, the slow anger in her eyes.

"I'll tell her you haven't made up your mind yet, shall I?"

"Yes."

He opened the door and ran down the steps and out into the street. "This is gonna be good," he muttered. "Yeah, a real pleasure. By God, I'll make them jump!"

He walked quickly past the wood-yard to Salter, a block and a half — and then he stopped.

Nothing had changed. There was the mail-box, and below it the round bare spots where he had peeled the paint blisters away. It came back to him, as he stood before the door, as though it had happened only yesterday. He turned to the back of the house. There was the porch across which they had dragged him, and the steps down which he had fled. Nothing had changed — except their rôles, he thought, as he walked back to the front door. He was going to savour every moment of this.

"I should have brought flowers," he thought, and knocked on the door.

It opened almost instantly to disclose a dumpy, homely

little woman with a small button of a nose and grey-streaked hair, who began to make a prolonged and agitated effort to control herself. He had remembered her as terrifyingly vast and tall, and the discovery that he could look down upon her now filled him with an indescribable sense of well-being.

She helped him with his coat and welcomed him into the house in a strained whisper. He followed her and looked about him and shook his head unbelievingly. It was just an ordinary North End working man's house.

Mrs. Kostanuik waited for him at the living-room door, and, as he advanced, she opened it and stood aside until he had walked in. Then she scurried around and waved him to her husband.

Kostanuik rose from his chair, red-faced and bulging in a tight-fitting blue serge suit whose cuffs barely reached his wrists. He held out his hand gaping at his wife the while, raising and lowering his brows as though seeking further instructions.

Mrs. Kostanuik motioned stiffly to the chesterfield. Alex sat down and found himself looking directly at a young woman upon whose cheeks the colour ebbed and flowed.

"You remember Mary?" Mrs. Kostanuik asked hopefully.

He would not have known her, he thought. Not once in all the years that had passed had he met her. Now and again on lonely nights while sitting at the hotel window he would suddenly start from his chair and follow into the shadowy distance the girl he had imagined her to be. And sometimes in the hasty tumult of a paid embrace she would flash across his vision. As he looked at her now there crept into his mind the memory of their childhood. She was beginning to smile at him when he resolutely thrust all further thought of her from his mind. He had not come down here to be ogled at. She'd probably stop smiling when she heard what he had to say. It was all right for her and her parents to come snivelling around now that they were in trouble. Maybe they thought he had forgotten.

He turned away from her as her mother came into the centre of the room and placed a bottle of wine on the table.

"Why don't you set on the chesterfield?" she asked her

daughter. "Is more comfortable there. Mr. Hunter won't bite you. . . . Go set on the chesterfield."

"I'm comfortable here, Momma." The colour mounted to her brows.

Out of the corner of his eyes, Alex caught the look that passed between them. The old bitch was as subtle as a sledge-hammer, he thought. And that "Mr. Hunter won't bite you"!

They were seated in a circle, suddenly silent.

Alex sat back and waited. He reached for his cigarette case, extracted a cigarette, tamped it leisurely, and lighted it. They were all watching him.

The silence grew. He felt their embarrassment and let his eyes wander casually about the room. Ten by twelve he estimated; sinking in the N.E. corner; the baseboard tearing away from the walls. The floor . . . There was a sound ringing in his ears, the sound of laughter as they raised him from the floor — not more than a few feet from where he was now sitting. They were dragging him to the door. His cries rang in his ears.

Mrs. Kostanuik was clearing her throat. It was nice of him to come on such short notice.

He nodded, and studied the glowing end of his cigarette. It was a pleasure.

She was smiling now, settling back in her chair and looking at him expectantly.

Now, he thought, and raised his cigarette to his lips.

"I understand you're bankrupt," he said amiably, and it was as though he had suddenly cracked a whip over her head, but as suddenly he wondered what she felt, and this twinge of a thought — it was no more than that — passing so idly through his mind, disturbed him, because it was not just curiosity, but something . . . something soft, that had no place in his life, that threatened and must therefore be thrust from him.

He looked up. His eyes moved hungrily, intently, lingering upon each of them in turn, coming to rest finally on Mrs. Kostanuik, finding peace in the empty horror on her face. He saw her standing above him with tears oozing out of her bloated features as she bemoaned the loss of her table.

"Is about this we wanna talk," she began. "Please to lissen, Mr. Hunter. Excuse me . . . you will be the manager of Mr. Nagy's business?"

Alex shrugged his shoulders.

"Then is true?" she asked.

"Who knows?"

Kostanuik raised his head. "Mr. Hunter," he said earnestly, I been — I have work for —"

"For God's sake stop making a fool of yourself and talk German," his wife cried, and looked imploringly at Alex for some assurance that this would be acceptable.

"You know that I have been working for Nagy for a long time," Kostanuik continued. "Long before you came into the office, while you were still a little boy." He lowered his hand until it was within a few feet of the floor. "And never any complaints. Always good work . . ."

"And always too expensive," Alex broke in. "And everything built to last for a hundred years. What do you think people are in business for?"

"Mr. Hunter. Please to listen to me," his wife pleaded. "My husband will work cheap for you, cheaper than anybody else. Nobody makes better work, not in the whole city. Please to listen to me. He is not so good in speaking, only in working."

She glanced angrily at her husband and daughter, and then continued in an impassioned voice.

If he refused to help them, they would lose the roof over their heads. And they were old already, too old to start again. Mr. Hunter had to get somebody to work for him. Then why not her husband, who knew what was wanted and who was a good workman? She had never begged for anything, not from anybody. And Mr. Hunter was not the kind of young man who would let an old woman beg him for a favour. Why couldn't he just say yes? It meant so much to them and made so little difference to him. . . . She faltered, and clasped her hands, and grew silent.

The one thing he had hoped to hear she had left unspoken.

And yet she was anything but a fool. Alex inhaled leisurely. Perhaps she had forgotten. Well, he had not, and right now he would tell her something she would remember as long as she lived.

"I'm sorry," he said. "I've got a contractor already."

He scarcely heard her scream, for suddenly his blood ran cold. How could he have been so incredibly stupid? If his aunt bought the Agency she would unquestionably insist that Kostanuik be kept on. Mrs. Kostanuik was as close a friend as she possessed.

He felt numb. This was what came of mixing business with pleasure. He had made a glaring and unpardonable blunder. Then another aspect of the situation occurred to him. How was it that Mrs. Kostanuik herself was not aware of the strength of her position? Evidently she credited him with having far more influence over his aunt than he thought he had.

He looked up. Mary was standing in front of him. Her parents had gone.

"Tell your father it's all right," he said hoarsely.

"You mean —"

"Yes."

She hesitated for an inordinate length of time, he thought, and then she was gone. He felt ill and depressed as he walked into the hall.

As he slipped into his coat, he heard their tread on the stairs. Then Kostanuik was pumping his hand, his wife and daughter on either side thanking him and inviting him to stay for coffee — or at least a glass of wine. Mrs. Kostanuik pleaded with him to say yes.

"Business," he said, and reached for the doorknob.

They were still thanking him when he walked out. Mrs. Kostanuik accompanied him outside. She closed the door behind them.

"There is something I must say to you," she began in a quivering voice. "I hope you don't mind if I speak German. . . . You have made us very happy tonight and I want to thank you."

"Don't thank me too soon," he muttered. "The Agency's not mine yet."

"It will be," she answered. "I think in the end you will always get what you are after. But if I can help . . ."

"I don't want any interference," he whispered angrily. "You hear, I don't need any help, especially from you. Don't interfere, I'm warning you. Don't talk to my aunt. Keep out of it."

He saw that she was afraid of him, and the fostered hatred and the desire to humiliate her now suddenly gave way to contempt for the withered creature she had become.

"I did not come out only to thank you," she said. "I want to say something which is very difficult to say . . . about the last time you came to visit us. I know you have not forgotten and that is why I must speak."

There was a faint throbbing in his temples. It grew until the world seemed filled with the pounding roar of his pulse beat. Then it faded and there was something at once familiar and heart-warming in the words that reached him. In the rôle which he had assigned to her she had spoken them upon countless occasions while grovelling at his feet. A cherished pain began to tear itself reluctantly from him and in its place there came a feeling of profound relief.

Her voice had grown so low and uncertain that he had to strain to hear what she was saying. He observed the abject look on her face and heard her self-reproachful words.

"People do things sometimes for which they are sorry the rest of their lives," she continued. "I would have spoken to you long ago. I told your auntie many times I wanted to see you. . . . I want you to . . . say that everything will be well between us."

The air of unreality which had pervaded their relationship now suddenly lifted. He was himself again.

She was shrewd, he thought. That whole business inside proved it; everything had fallen on her shoulders and she had handled it well. Was it possible that this, too, was just part of her plan?

He conceded that this was unlikely. She might have used it

to better effect before he had refused to take her husband on at the Agency.

"And I would like you to think of my home as a place where you will always be welcome," she said. "To come to whenever you like."

"I'll think about it," he said. "I haven't any more time tonight. It's late."

He opened the door for her. She walked in. It closed softly.

"You sure made a mess of that," he said, but it was as though having once expressed this he could admit to himself that he was not dissatisfied with what had happened. He was going to be saddled with Kostanuik, but the picture of him in his house with a wife who practically led him around by the nose mitigated somehow the unpleasantness of the prospect of working with him.

He turned off the pathway to the street. Her bland assumption that he was going to succeed in getting the Agency raised his spirits. But the thought of his aunt and the struggle that still lay before him was sobering.

He walked on. "The next time he gets drunk she's going to see for herself what she's doing to him," he said. "And if that doesn't work, then . . ." He nodded thoughtfully. "Only one thing I know. Nothing's going to stand in my way. Nothing."

Suddenly he stopped. "You know, it's funny," he said reflectively. "You'd never think from looking at her that her parents were foreigners."

Thirteen

IT WAS as though the office had been transformed, as though the counter along which he now ran his hand, the ledger which he thumbed, the very walls, had suddenly become invested with a warmer, richer meaning, as though they had become extensions of himself through which he could see and feel and through which he could assess and face the world outside.

Pride of possession seized him. It was his! He flung out his arms as though to embrace it. It was his at last. He moved around excitedly, laughing to himself, and as though in answer to a long-awaited summons there flashed through his mind plans long since formed, near and distant prospects, the substance of dreams that floated clearly and triumphantly before his eyes. Their realization was now assured. The first and most difficult step had been taken.

He continued moving around the office until, worn out with the exertions of the day, he sat down at his desk and turned to the window. Now there would no longer be any need for him to sit in the hotel lobby, he thought. At night, when work was done, he could turn off the lights and sit here quietly and smoke a cigarette and watch people passing by.

It had stopped raining. The streets gleamed. There was something almost festive in the hundreds of light bulbs that swayed overhead, in the running play of headlights and the reflections of shop windows on the glittering roadway. There was something reassuring in the steady tread of the people who passed before the Agency.

And yet as he looked at them his elation fled.

It had not been pleasant. His aunt's cries rang in his ears. He saw her looking down at her husband, sprawled in a drunken stupor on the settee — staring at him with folded hands until through the mouldy odour of Nick's brew she had caught the sickly reek of cheap perfume.

No, it had not been pleasant, what had happened then.

"But I'll make it up to him," Alex said, and thought sadly that even if his uncle should some day find out how his clothes had come to carry that tell-tale scent, and discover who was responsible for it, he would forgive him.

I'll get him the biggest desk I can buy, he thought. I'll fix Nagy's room up into a private office for him. He'll like that. We'll work together and he'll be away from her all day and he'll be happy here.

He got up and wandered into what had been Nagy's cubbbyhole.

It was wrong, he thought plaintively, that he should have to be alone tonight. There should be someone to talk to — a friend or someone. He brushed the thought angrily from his mind. The Agency was his, wasn't it? He had what he wanted. Then why all this sentimental drivel? He switched off the light, lit a cigarette, and returned to his desk.

A random image of Nagy passed through his mind. The old man had barely had the strength to say goodbye that morning. But he had stubbornly refused to take a cab. A pedlar with an ancient horse and a waggonload of junk had carried him off, his cot and his ragged bundle of possessions, to the rooming-house to which he was moving. The last Alex had seen of him was his bowed and shabby figure, almost indistinguishable from the mound of paper and old clothes upon which he sat.

It suddenly occurred to him that Nagy, too, was without friends. Perhaps long before Alex had come into the office, he had sat here in this chair watching people pass by. Perhaps the person who sat here was fated to be lonely, to grow old and sick and ugly. He remembered that he had once wanted to be like the old man, and at the recollection sprang to his feet and switched on the lights.

"What's the matter with me?" he murmured. What was there so frightening about a man growing old? It had nothing to do with the office.

"I could go home," he said. But the mere thought of what his father and Mr. Schiller would say was enough.

He opened the ledger. Work, just plain ordinary work, that was the answer. Tomorrow morning he would call Kostanuik to come down to the warehouse with him. But why tomorrow? He would call him tonight.

He tilted his chair back, dialled, and had barely settled on the desk when Mrs. Kostanuik was on the line.

"Work!" she cried. "Ach, my God. Work!"

He heard her calling to her husband; far off there was a rumble of laughter. Then Kostanuik on the telephone asking incredulously if it was true . . .

Now his wife again. "Please to tell him, Mr. Hunter. He won't believe even his own wife. Such wonderful news!"

Alex assured him that it was true.

A faint rustle in the receiver, a thin but distinct whisper in German. Mrs. Kostanuik's voice: "Say something to him. Your parents can't talk like you. Go on . . . only a word you have to say. Tell him . . ."

A long silence, then Mrs. Kostanuik's voice again. "Mr. Hunter, we wanna say thank you . . . but is not easy on the phone. Maybe . . . Excuse me, if you're not too busy, it's not so late yet we couldn't make a liddle celebration tonight. Please to say yes."

"I'm very busy," he said.

"Only for a liddle while," she pleaded.

"I'm sorry. I've got more work here than I can handle."

"Mr. Hunter . . . to come if only to drink a glass of wine and make a toast. Please. We will wait for you. Awright?"

Five minutes later he was sitting on a Dufferin streetcar itemizing his possessions. He owned a tenement on Alexander Avenue with four families living in it; two sixty-foot lots in Kildonan; a warehouse — a renovated barn actually, but containing enough lumber to start building almost immediately. He owned all the office furniture. He had . .

Suddenly he sprang to his feet. "My God. I forgot to lock the door."

No. No, he remembered now. He had noticed that the door needed varnishing as he set the latch. He sat back and took a deep breath and grew aware of the wave of amusement that was sweeping the car. A typical North End crowd, he thought contemptuously, grinning at him, gesticulating, pointing him out to their neighbours. The hell with them. He dismissed them from his mind. A few blocks later he got off the car.

His thoughts drifted pleasantly to the reception that awaited him at the Kostanuiks'. There was something gratifying in the knowledge that they were almost obliged to welcome him.

He knocked, and from the moment the door opened he was glad he had come. Their congratulations brought his achievement back into focus again. He let the picture of the Agency glide into his mind, let it unfold until every detail glowed in clear bright relief. Their words gave it back to him. It was his. Tomorrow and tomorrow and tomorrow, he could go back and call it his own.

Mary had taken his coat. "We're glad you could come," she said, and before he could answer, Kostanuik caught his arm. "A special wine," he whispered in German. "Nearly four years old."

"Such a young man to be a boss awready," Mrs. Kostanuik exclaimed as they seated themselves in the living-room. "So young to be a manager."

They laughed easily, he thought, and reflected that it was owing to him that they could laugh at all.

Mrs. Kostanuik handed him a glass of wine and glanced sharply at her husband. He rose to his feet.

"To Mr. Hunter," he began. "To a happy . . ." He smiled sheepishly.

"So talk German awready," his wife broke in. "Nobody's gonna bite you."

"To Mr. Hunter's success and to a long and happy association," Kostanuik continued. "And to the houses we will build — good houses, but cheap."

Alex smiled. Kostanuik had not forgotten.

The wine was really good. His glass was no sooner empty than Mrs. Kostanuik filled it again.

He sank back into the chesterfield and raised his glass to Mary.

And suddenly and achingly against the dark stream of the years his memory flowed to an attic room where a small wide-eyed girl sat listening to his story of a fabulous captain uncle who sailed on an unpronounceable sea. She clapped her hands when he was through. "Say it again to me," she pleaded. And then, no less than now, it had been fascinating to watch her lips part so hesitantly, to press softly against her teeth and come together again so ripe and full.

He wondered if she ever recalled their childhood together.

"We're almost strangers," he said. "It's . . ." And in the silence of the room it was the voice of a stranger that he heard. Her eyes were darker than he remembered; the apple-round cheeks had vanished in the soft oval of her face. He recalled the little pigtails and the pink ribbons; her hair was bobbed now and blondly gleaming — like — like waves of gold, he thought, and knew that this was inadequate, and groped for something more appropriate.

But she was waiting for him to continue.

"It's funny we've never met," he said lamely.

"Every summer my daughter goes to Kipling," Mrs. Kostanuik chanted proudly. "You know where Kipling is, Mr. Hunter?"

Alex shook his head.

"It's in Saskatchewan," Mary said. "Only a small place, full of Hungarians. You're not there more than five minutes before somebody's trying to find out whether you're related or not."

Her voice delighted him. The words that fell from her lips were bright sounds, round and sparkling. She seemed to caress them as they parted from her. In the dark with her, he thought, one would be able to see what she was saying. But this was so extravagant that he set his wine glass firmly on the table.

"Instead of talking about the weather," she continued, "they talk about their cousins and their uncles in the Old Country."

He observed that her dress reached barely to her knees. The disturbing word "modern" insinuated itself into his mind. But one really could not tell that her mother was Hungarian and her father — what was Kostanuik? . . . It didn't matter. He glanced at her from beneath lowered lids and for the first time it seemed to him he really saw her, not as a playmate who had grown up, but as a young and beautiful woman who was a stranger.

The next moment he reflected gloomily that she was far too beautiful to have remained unattached. She might even be engaged. She was probably smiling at him now only because her mother had ordered her to be pleasant to him.

"What do you do when you're not visiting friends in Kipling?" he asked, and at the sound of his voice reached for his glass and drained it in a gulp.

"So tell Mr. Hunter," her mother urged. "Tell him. You stay home and practise on the piano."

She addressed herself to Alex. "Music lessons she takes from Professor Eltor, two dollars a lesson."

"Wonderful chicken goulash they make in Kipling," Kostanuik remarked.

"You would like to hear her play for us?" Mrs. Kostanuik continued.

Alex nodded. The old battle-axe had understood immediately and only too well. He turned to Mary and, at the flow of colour on her cheeks, wondered that his heart could ache and laugh all in a moment.

"Not tonight, Momma," she said.

"She's shy." A sickly sweet smile crept over her mother's face.

Mary lowered her head. "Please, Momma. Not tonight."

"You will play for Mr. Hunter tonight," her mother said

with a restraint so ominous that Alex shivered in spite of himself.

"Maybe some other time," he suggested.

"Tonight," Mrs. Kostanuik repeated, and smiling and glaring at her guest and her daughter in turn, pointed to the piano. "So why are you waiting? Go. Play something."

At this point, Kostanuik turned to Alex. "You like chicken goulash?" he asked.

"Chicken goulash!" his wife broke in. "We talk about piano-playing and he talks about chicken goulash. . . . You don't know chicken from horsemeat," she cried.

"Horsemeat!" Kostanuik looked at her indignantly. "At home we had meat twice a week, every week in the year. My family . . ."

"Your family! Cabbages and potatoes they stuffed themselves with."

"And yours." Kostanuik winked broadly at Alex. "On weekdays bread and onions, on holidays, onions and bread."

Alex sat back and laughed. In one form or another he had heard this argument all his life, and yet tonight it seemed hilariously funny. "I've been drinking too much," he thought, and suddenly he noticed that Mary had risen to her feet.

"I'm sorry," she began.

Her lips trembled. "I've got a headache," she said, and before he had fully understood, she turned and walked quickly from the room. He saw her in the hallway, reaching for a coat. The next moment she was gone.

"What's wrong?" Mrs. Kostanuik cried. "What happened?"

"She has a headache," Alex said.

"A headache!" she scoffed, and ran into the hallway. Alex and her husband followed her.

"Mary?" she called up the stairs. "Mary!"

"Poor girl," she said. "No wonder she has got a headache. So excited she was when she heard you were coming."

"I have to leave anyway," Alex said, and took down his hat and coat. "I've still got work to do."

"Not yet," she wailed, clutching his arm. "I will make coffee. Her headache will get better yet. . . . It's still early."

Alex opened the door. "Some other time. I enjoyed myself. Thanks."

"Tomorrow at half past seven," Kostanuik said.

Alex nodded impatiently.

"You will come again?" Mrs. Kostanuik pleaded.

Alex smiled. "Soon. Good night."

He closed the door behind him, took one breath, and went reeling down the pathway until he reached the gate. He clung to it until his head cleared. She could not have gone very far, not in such a short time.

He peered down the street. It was empty but for the lone figure of a woman some two blocks away. He ran to the first corner, observed that the side street was deserted, and continued to run until he was within a few hundred feet of her. She turned then, looking apprehensively over her shoulder, and quickened her steps. His anxiety flared into anger as he recognized her. She looked so small and defenceless. What if someone else had been chasing her? What would she do? He had almost reached her when she looked back again; it was so quiet that he heard the intake of her breath. She faltered and stopped under a street lamp. He saw that she had been crying.

"I'm sorry I laughed," he said. "I had too much to drink. . . . I'm sorry."

"It's not your fault." She began to cry again. "All night, Momma was waiting for a chance to brag about me. She would have made me play, too, if it hadn't been for Poppa . . . and she knows I don't like to. I just play for myself." She paused. "I want you to know what kind of people we are," she said. "This afternoon she made some strudel just in case you would come, and I was supposed to tell you I made it."

"But why?" Alex broke in. "She knew that your father would be working for me . . ."

His eyes widened. He stared at her incredulously. "But she doesn't have to do that," he blurted, and in shamefaced joy watched the flush of colour that came to her face. So that was where it started — high up on her cheeks, mounting to her brow where it was lost in a few blond tendrils, and down to the shadowed hollow of her throat.

"Now you know," she said, and turned her head in embarrassment. "We're not very nice people."

"There's nothing wrong with your family," Alex said lightly. "Believe me." She had stopped crying.

"But you shouldn't be out here alone at night like this," he continued. "When I was chasing you — I mean, running after you — no, I — " He floundered and turned angrily from her, but at the sound of her laughter glanced down and unexpectedly found himself looking into her eyes. There was laughter there too, but also an unguarded warmth in their depths that entranced and further embarrassed him.

"I mean you shouldn't be out alone like this," he muttered.

"I never go very far," she said softly, and her words were invested with that glowing colour which only she could impart.

They had been slowly walking back. Now they stopped at the gate. He could scarcely tell her that he had enjoyed himself, he thought. Not after what her mother had . . .

"You bad girl, you! Worrying your poor mother like this."

Alex looked about him in consternation. Where was she?

"You had a nice walk?" Mrs. Kostanuik continued.

He discovered her at one of the upper windows, leering down at them and waggling her finger like an animated old gargoyle.

"Mr. Hunter," she whispered. "Excuse me. Maybe Wednesday night? Something special for supper. Maybe . . ."

"Momma! Momma, you close that window this minute, do you hear?"

To Alex's surprise the window was slowly drawn down.

It was no sooner closed than Mary ran to the door. Alex caught her arm.

"I was going to ask you if I could come and see you again tomorrow," he said.

She lowered her head, "I'm just too ashamed to talk."

"Tomorrow night, then?"

"If you still want to." She ran in.

"Mary," he said. The door closed, and suddenly it struck him that for the past half-hour or more he had not even thought of the Agency. But there was no need to. He felt it as though it had really grown to be a part of him.

He opened the gate and as he looked back the second upper window flooded with light. "Momma, you close that window this minute, do you hear?" he said, and laughed. So she could be like that, too. But what was she doing right now? Probably sitting on the edge of her bed, perhaps looking into her mirror. Did it tell her how beautiful she was — that her lips were like . . . like petals?

Alex's brows rose. Now this was really too much. A feeling of uneasiness came over him. This whole thing was happening too fast. Where would it lead? To allow himself to become involved here was a poor piece of business. Kostanuik would undoubtedly try to take advantage of him. Well, if that happened he'd tell him off, and if that wasn't enough he would simply sever all further relations with them.

He looked back again and signed. He had the feeling that it was not going to be nearly as simple as this.

Fourteen

HIS EYES intent upon the ledger, he raised the cord of the venetian blind, drawing it up until he remembered that this was Sunday; the consequences of any of his North End clients seeing him at work today were not to be taken lightly. The blind clattered down. He raised one of the slats and peered out. A typical Sunday crowd. Where were they going, he wondered? What satisfaction did they get in just wandering around the streets?

He looked at his watch. Mary should be arriving at any minute now. It was pleasant at odd moments to think of her like this — to stop, if only for a moment, and let her come to him.

He cleared his desk, lit a cigarette, and moved happily and aimlessly about his recently-constructed private office, his mind pleasantly dwelling one moment upon seeing her again, the next upon the solid achievement reflected in the ledger. She would arrive with a picnic basket under her arm and stand there and wait until he admired her. Four houses constructed in the past six months, and more money earned in commissions during that time than Nagy had made in the last year. Her picture was on his desk where his name-plate had once stood. She looked across at him gravely; only in the corners of her mouth, very faintly, lurked the laughter of her childhood. He gazed at her from a distance, his head inclined, his lips unmindfully seeking the expression on hers. . . . He

was now earning thirty-five dollars a week, almost as much
as his father earned in a month.

He smiled and opened the door of what had once been
Nagy's cubicle. On the glass panel had been painted the words
J. Daffner, Manager. The room had been enlarged and, like
the main office, freshly painted. A window had been cut
through the back wall, a rug laid on the floor. In the centre
stood a massive mahogany desk with an elaborate combina-
tion lamp, inkstand, and calendar.

Everything looked new and impressive, but somehow
so infinitely pathetic that he could never stay in this
office very long. And yet there was nothing here to
reproach him. He could truthfully say that his uncle had never
been happier.

Every morning at ten he would come striding in, boom out
a good morning to his assistant manager, then, calling to the
office boy for his coffee, would light his cigar, loll back in his
chair, and read the newspapers until noon.

In Nagy's time, the nondescript North-Enders who had
streamed into the office for advice or money or someone to
talk to had been disposed of quickly enough. Now they were
welcomed and dispatched no less summarily, but to the
manager's private office or to the bench just outside his door.
On a good afternoon, two or three of them might wander in,
and nothing pleased his uncle so much as to come out and
find them there.

Alex shook his head. He had tried painstakingly to interest
him in the affairs of the Agency, only to discover that his sole
interest in the office lay in this riff-raff. The help he gave them,
the advice and the money, were given almost as an after-
thought. His main pleasure was to sit and talk to them.

"I've done everything I could, everything I promised to do,
even more," he murmured, and crossed over to his desk. "It's
just that . . ."

He smiled. How could one help but smile? That magnificent early-morning entrance in black homburg, cane and
stick-pin; that air of assurance! His uncle had a flair for this

rôle, there was no doubt about it. So a bank president or the chairman of a board might appear.

Alex sat down. Out of the corner of his eyes he caught a flash of white ribbon beyond the edge of the counter. She had arrived while he was in his uncle's office. He rose quietly, hesitated, then lowered himself into his chair again. She would be sitting there laughing to herself. If he were to discover her now her secret would be spoiled. He opened the ledger and thumbed through it, glancing affectionately beneath lowered lids at the spot where the crown of her hat bobbed up and down.

It was strange, he thought, how everything about her, her gloves, her shoes, her hat, should somehow, even when she was not wearing them, remain so unmistakably and appropriately hers alone.

The brim of her hat suddenly came to view, and between that moment and her appearance there came back to him the night when for the first time he had been alone with her. Sitting on the chesterfield watching her in her stockinged feet cross to the kitchen for refreshments, and about to follow her, he had found one of her shoes lying beside him; a high-heeled shoe, immaculately white. He placed it upright in the palm of his hand and laughed to himself that it should be so small and stand there so pertly. Then, sinking back and still holding it before him, he contemplated it and — what could have possessed him to do such a thing? To talk, not even to himself, but out loud and to a shoe! And worse; to address it with such fervour, with words he had not yet spoken to her. Stroking it tenderly, he laughed away her objections. He had still to hold her in his arms and kiss her.

He suddenly became aware that she had returned and was watching him. She must have seen and heard every word. The shoe dropped from his hand. He stared at it, calling himself a thousand different kinds of a fool, fearful that at any moment she would laugh at him.

"Alex," she said.

He closed his eyes and it was as though he could feel the

caress of his name on her lips, feel the affectionate reluctance with which she released it.

"Alex," she whispered. "What were you doing? Oh, Alex!"

There was laughter in her voice, but she could permit herself that, now that she had spoken his name in this tone, now that she so unexpectedly sank into his arms.

She appeared from behind the counter. He lowered his head until she called to him.

For all time, he thought, that room would be filled with the remembrance of her in her stockinged feet, of her laughter and her lips. A sad and lonely afternoon in his childhood had been bridged on that night, and his life before and after brought together and made whole again. . . .

"Surprise," she cried.

She was all in white, slender and cool. She came through the little counter gate with her picnic basket under her arm, and then, standing still, laughed as he continued to look at her.

Was it because she was in white that he remembered? So she had stood before him when they were children, in a starched little dress, like a cool little bell luring him to come out and play.

"Did I surprise you?"

He nodded and, rising from behind his desk, drew her to him, and on a sudden impulse, gathered her up in his arms and began dancing about the office with her.

"Everything I want in the world is here," he said. "Here in my arms, and around me."

"I love you when you're like this, Alex."

"And when I'm not?"

"Then, too," she said gravely.

He sank into his chair and kissed her, breathing in her freshness, feeling the smooth warmth of her body as she pulled away.

"Not now," she whispered. "Not till we get to our own little place."

He held her mirror for her as she arranged her hair. "It's so nice out," she said, "the nicest Indian summer we've ever had. The park will be all in colour with the leaves. It almost makes one sad. Let's go right away, shall we, Alex?"

He walked out first, glanced nervously up and down the street, and then beckoned to her to follow. He knew that it vexed her to leave this way, but it was unavoidable. It was also, unfortunately, impossible to explain this to her. She said nothing, but asserted herself nevertheless by sauntering very leisurely out to the pavement to stand there and wait for him while he made sure that the door was locked. Alex shook his head. For the moment, at least, there was no one passing by.

He took the basket from her as they crossed over to the safety aisle. On the streetcar, she nudged him and nodded at a middle-aged woman across the aisle with a sleeping child in her lap.

"Poor woman," Mary began. "Don't look now, Alex, but just see her face."

Alex smiled. Now it would begin. In cafés, on the street, or in the park, she would seize upon this or that passer-by and weave a story about his life.

"She wanted to be an actress," Mary continued. "Look now, Alex."

"An actress," he laughed softly. "I know her. She's just an ordinary . . ."

"Don't you dare tell me," she said. "She wanted to be an actress ever since she was little. Whenever she was alone she used to go to the mirror in her mother's bedroom and stand in front of it and practise expressions . . ."

What prompted her, he wondered, to make up these stories. They were interesting, most of them, but they were untrue, so what was the use of them? Holding her hand behind the basket, he smiled indulgently, listening to her voice, looking absently out of the window until in the outskirts of the city, sighting an insurance billboard, his thoughts focused upon Lawson and his friends — the kind of men he had known he would some day meet.

He had met Lawson a few weeks after the interview with Atkinson. Finding himself on Portage Avenue that day, he had yielded to the impulse to try once more, to prove to himself that there were men here whose only criterion in their business dealings was that which buying and selling demanded.

In Lawson he had found such a man. His friends were the same. Lunch with them on Wednesday was the high point of the week, a constant affirmation that he had been right. They were all young, alert and ambitious: the assistant manager of a grain company, an accountant, the manager of an office-supply house, an account-executive in the local branch of an advertising agency.

"But sometimes when she's alone," Mary said, "and her work is done, she sits in the kitchen and looks at herself in the mirror that hangs over the sink, and she cries to herself."

From the very first, Alex thought, he had sensed a kinship between this man and himself. If anything, Lawson went even further than he in condemning foreigners who refused to adapt themselves to Canadian ways; Lawson included Englishmen in his denunciation, and what was more, objected violently to being called anything but a Canadian. The best thing he had ever done, Alex reflected, was to accept the North-End insurance agency which Lawson had offered him.

" . . . and the leaves," he heard Mary say. "They look as though they were celebrating because they know spring will come again. Don't you think so, Alex?"

"Celebrating?"

"Yes."

They looked at each other.

"I could eat you up," she whispered, in far too loud a voice, he thought, and glanced about him, shocked not so much by this unabashed declaration as by the gleam of body hunger in her eyes.

It was unbecoming to a young girl to look like this and to make so open an avowal of her affections. He responded readily enough, however, to the pressure of her hand. It was not her fault; it was the fault of those crazy North-End gigolos and floozies who had been after her to join them ever since her return from Kipling. She had repeatedly pleaded with him to take her to one of their parties — and one was enough. The girls were loud and vulgar, rolled their stockings below their knees, necked and drank while they danced; and their boy friends . . .

Alex's lips curled derisively.

The sons of bricklayers and sewer-diggers hopping around from one jazz party to another with flasks on their hips, emulating the latest college-boy movie hero; with no ambition, with never a thought in their heads of what might happen to them tomorrow. The party had come to an end with all the lights out and the guests necking in whatever corners of the house were still unclaimed.

Suddenly he was grateful to her mother for watching over her so carefully. She didn't belong there, he told himself, and shuddered at the thought of what might have happened to her had he not appeared when he did. He glanced at her out of the corner of his eye. She was so unlike the person she tried to be, he thought — intent upon shocking people with her "modern" ways, trying so hard to rebel, and in the end merely overturning little unimportant things.

They arrived a few minutes later, walked arm-in-arm over the bridge and into the park to the zoo, where they stopped before the glassed-in cage of a lugubrious, lonely little gibbon, and when Mary's fierce sympathy for him had spent itself, they moved on past the bear pits and the pheasants and peacocks until they came to the buffalo run. Here they took to a narrow path where suddenly the world seemed to fall behind them and all was still but for the sound of their footsteps upon the fallen leaves; his slow, in even unhurried strides, hers quick and light until she left him, dancing on ahead, scooping up armfuls of scarlet and russet and golden leaves, tossing them above her, entwining her arms over her head as they fluttered down upon her and then darting back, showering him with their bright burden so that watching her he could not help but laugh and yet reflect upon his incapacity to key himself to these buoyant moods of hers.

She stopped before a slender white birch at a turn in the path and, leaning against it with heaving breasts, waited until he arrived. Then she took the lunch basket from him and he carried her a few yards through the underbrush into a small clearing beneath an overtowering elm. Here, after he had kissed her, she reached into the basket and brought out a small bottle of wine. She held it aloft triumphantly. "Momma gave it to me — for you," she said. "But you're not to say anything to Poppa."

She looked down ruefully at a bottle of coloured soda-water. "I'm going to drink some wine too," she announced.

Did she really want it, he wondered, or had she said this simply because she knew that he objected to women drinking? It was the same as when that crazy gang of yahoos had invited her to their party. If he had agreed, she might have forgotten about the whole thing. Since he had refused, she had insisted that they go.

He bit into a sandwich. The important thing was that she had not accepted a second invitation; as a matter of fact, she had not so much as mentioned what had happened that night.

"I sliced some wurst for you," she said, "because I know you like it, but you're not to eat any, or I'll have to eat some too . . . and I don't like it."

Alex burst into laughter. "Honest-to-God, Mary, I love you."

"And some gherkins, I brought, and the sandwiches, and a little cake. I baked it for you."

Alex crossed his legs. The sandwiches were so small he could scarcely get his teeth into them. "Wonderful," he said, and reached for another. "Did you make these too?"

She nodded.

"You're not eating," he said. "Is anything the matter?"

"I had a terrible time with Momma this morning," she said quietly. "She thinks I can't bake or cook or do anything by myself. I've been begging her for weeks for recipes and things."

She stopped abruptly, flushed, and looked away.

"Well, what happened?" he asked.

"We quarrelled. She just wouldn't leave me alone. And after I got her out of the kitchen, she sat in the hall nagging at me. You know what I think?"

Alex nodded absently.

"I think she's jealous of me," Mary continued. "She's jealous, that's what she is!"

"But how can you talk like that?" he cried. "About your own mother . . ."

"It's what I feel," she replied. "I just can't help it."

He saw that in a moment she might cry. "Well, there's one thing we won't have to worry about," he said. "All these stories about mothers-in-law — we won't have to worry."

"You're laughing at me."

He took her hand. "Mary, sometimes I don't know whether to laugh or to cry," he said in a low voice. "I only know I love you — just the way you are right now. So don't think about it any more. I'm going to take some of your cake now."

She handed him a piece and looked at him intently as he carried it to his mouth. "It tastes wonderful," he exclaimed, as much with relief as with astonishment. Some of her previous ventures had not turned out so well. "I'm going to have some more with my wine."

She flushed with pleasure as she gave him a second piece. "You thought I'd forget the corkscrew — didn't you?" she asked, and reached into the basket. "I brought a wine glass, too."

She took merely a sip when he offered her some. They finished their lunch. He watched her as she gathered the remains and placed them in the basket.

"You said you'd try not to think about it any more," he admonished, and taking her in his arms lay back against the trunk of the tree. "Promise not to," he said.

"I'll try," she replied.

In the silence he turned his gaze upward to the interlaced branches and twigs against the sky, and looked down and saw the shimmer of light that bathed them in a coppery haze cast down from the yellow and russet leaves in the sun.

"It's lovely here, isn't it, Alex?" She raised her lips to his. "But it'll never be the same again, so quiet and peaceful. . . . It makes one sad, to think that it will be over so soon."

"We'll come back next year," he said. "And it'll all be the same, you'll see."

"But it won't be," she whispered.

She stirred restlessly. "Say something nice to me, Alex — like you used to."

He pressed his mouth to hers. She yielded with an unexpected passivity that invited and inflamed, and suddenly heedless of resolve he pressed her to him and with his lips still upon hers, let his body follow hers to the floor of the clearing, and felt for the first time the sweet-flowing contours of her naked warmth beneath his hand. As her body arched itself to his, she tore her lips away and called his name, drawing him as though in a dream to herself.

He tried to rise against the clasp of her arms. Then her lips were pressed again to his, and a sob broke from his throat. — Not with her. Not until after. With those others it had been different.

Unexpectedly, there flashed before him an image of their flaunting thighs and breasts. A cold sweat came over him. In dark, tight compartments, remaining forever foreign to one another; the private locked-away picture of her forever insulated from them; that was how he wanted it to be. Now they were neighboured, and with faces lewd and simpering, lonely, drunk and debauched, they welcomed her to their sisterhood.

With his lips on hers, they faded from his mind. He recognized dimly what had driven him to them. Not only the animal quickening of loin. But out of the hunger of loneliness to find a lonely body to enter, that he might appease the denied longing for friendship and put an end, when work was done, to the endless quest for he knew not what. To leave the chair at the window and wander down dark, desolate streets, with triumph turned to ashes for lack of telling, and fretful, small defeats grown large and bitter. To exchange the tokens of achievement for an intimate word. But how could such things be spoken, that vanished like a mist even as they came to mind?

He drew away. Never had she seemed so beautiful. Her eyelids fluttered. Her eyes opened and in a glance dispelled his misgivings. This was for itself, clean and untroubled and

apart. He kissed her gratefully, straining her to him, and then
there was only the hunger for her body and the glimmer of
the light, the sinewed quick descent to the coral inner reaches,
and the cry that came from her lips, which passed unheeded,
for she received him fiercely and passionately to herself even
as she cried.

The shadows had lengthened when he sat up and in the
warm light looked down at her until she opened her eyes.

"Alex," she whispered.

It was as though she had spoken too soon, he thought. Still
intent upon herself, she had not yet seen him. The expression
on her face was not meant to be revealed. Perhaps alone on
an afternoon in the silent house, sitting at the window dreaming of what was to be, she might look like this, with tender
inward turning, forming her life to come, giving herself to it
with this unveiled longing. And as though growing aware of
her inner vision glowing in her eyes, rising to the light of day
and to his gaze, she let it sink back slowly into her depths.

Her lips parted and he wondered that a mouth so
miraculously formed should have felt his lips and spoken his
name. She kissed her finger-tips and placed them upon his
brow and traced his profile.

Her hand dropped.

He smiled sheepishly and looked away, and feeling her eyes
still upon him, flushed and busied himself with a few leaves
that had fallen in the basket. When he turned back to her, he
discovered that she was asleep.

For a moment he looked at her unbelievingly, with mounting indignation, watching the peaceful rise and fall of her
breast. He shook his head plaintively. He had expected some
further show of affection, some shy confession drawn from
reluctant lips, and here she was sleeping as though nothing
had happened. . . .

And yet, how like her to have given way. His features
softened into a smile. What could she have said? How better
reveal that he had satisfied her?

A song he had sung at school came to mind, the words

forgotten. He hummed the tune. From far away came the haunting bitter-sweet odour of burning leaves, around him the forest murmured, beyond the edge of the clearing there was the flash of dusky-orange and gold leaves. "As though they were celebrating," he whispered, and conceded that it might be so.

He looked up, startled by a sudden whir of wings.

A small bird with a short yellow beak lighted on a twig above him. It began to chirp, every note sharp and beautifully clear. He laughed to himself at the picture it brought to mind. It was as though he could see an iridescent rill of sound flowing from its beak. It winked, and he laughed again. "Winking Mary-buds," he said, and sang the words: "And winking Mary-buds begin . . ." The leaves behind him rustled. He turned and saw that Mary had awakened and was sitting up.

"I'm so ashamed — I've been asleep, haven't I? You shouldn't have let me."

Alex laughed.

"Alex — "

She paused thoughtfully for a long time.

"It's right that a man should be experienced in such things," she said.

"Mary! For God's sake . . ."

"But Alex . . ."

"Who told you that? Where did you hear such talk?"

She pressed his hand to her cheek, as though to comfort him, he thought, and he clenched his teeth to control himself.

"I read it in a book, Alex. It's all right."

"In a book," he echoed. He had heard of such books, passed from hand to hand in pool-rooms and . . .

"A wonderful book," she continued. "I didn't know anything until I read it; I used to be scared, because Momma . . . I'll show it to you when we get home."

She placed her lips to his. "It's different now, isn't it, Alex?" she whispered.

He nodded sadly. Yes, it was different. But he was afraid.

There were times, all too frequent, when she was alone, long hours during the day and sometimes unavoidably in the evenings when he was not there to protect her, times when those flibbertigibbet girl-friends called on her. God alone knew what they talked about. From the very first he had been concerned about their influence on her. And now this! Was this the kind of thing for a young girl to read? He watched her as she set her mirror in a fork of a tree and began to comb her hair.

He sat there unhappily brooding over her until he chanced to look up at the very moment in which she removed a leaf that had caught in her hair. She gazed at it for a long time, then she carried it to her lips, kissed it, and flung a quick glance in his direction. He had barely time to look away. Out of the corner of his eyes, with a sense of delight that dispelled all thought of his tribulations, he saw her place it between her breasts.

To think that she could do such a thing! Such a tender impulsive foolish thing. She would take it home and place it in the book he had once given her, along with the faded pressed flowers over which she had cried so bitterly.

Yes, she could be like that and on the other hand speak so dispassionately, with such cold-blooded knowing.

"A man should be experienced in such things," he repeated, and once more he began to spin a web of anxiety about her.

"Alex."

He looked up. She was ready to go.

"You haven't spoken to me for nearly five minutes, Alex."

He rose to his feet. "I was just thinking," he said, and picked her up, and pressed his face to her breast. She clung to his shoulder as he carried her to the birch beside the shadowed trail. Here he suddenly stopped.

"Mary," he said hoarsely. "When can we get married?"

The silence swallowed his words. In the dim light he could barely see her face. But she was crying. Then she threw her other arm about him so unexpectedly that it sent him staggering wildly off the path. He crashed through the underbrush until he reached a tree against which he could support himself. He grinned happily.

"Alex," she sobbed. "Take me back to our place. Say it again to me there and I'll love you forever and ever."

He found it hard to breathe. She had both her arms about his neck. Her tears ran down his cheeks. He carried her into the clearing and there, still holding her in his arms, sank down under the elm, and when her sobbing had subsided, he repeated his words.

Fifteen

IT WAS good to lie here beside her, with her breath warm on his cheek and sleep coming slow upon him. He smiled. Tonight, she had told him, if one sat by the window one could see the full moon through the frosted pane. He had drawn up the small sofa. Wrapped in a warm blanket now, holding her to him, he listened as she told him what she saw frozen there.

Laughter downstairs, then silence. Her mother was regaling a late visitor. He heard his name. She was still talking about it. Enough for her to say that the children had spent their honeymoon in the States, but of course she said more, for how could she resist the temptation to speak again of the thirty-five guests who had come to the wedding, and the English president of an insurance company and his wife? Such friendly people. You should see how they enjoyed themselves. "Say, I feel right at home here with you folks," he had said. Wasn't that nice?

And the bride — ah, the bride — and the gifts which had covered two fully extended dining-room tables, and the pictures in the local papers.

"An office man, my son-in-law. So young, and a manager already. Maybe I mentioned it? They spent their honeymoon in the States."

So in the parlour downstairs. And in the front room on Selkirk Avenue — a good housewife she will make, the girl my son married. Such a beauty. A good girl, not like one of them chipsies to think of nothing except a good time and how to spend money. Who would have imagined such a thing? In my arms I held her when she was a baby. They played together when they were children. I told you they went to Minneapolis in the States for their honeymoon?

The voices downstairs grew suddenly loud. The front door opened and closed. Alex sighed. His breathing deepened.

"Alex."

"Yes."

"I'm sorry I spoke like that."

He opened one eye. What was it she had said?

"It's just that sometimes I feel as though I'm not a wife at all," she whispered. "I have to come upstairs to see your brushes on the dresser, and your ties, to make sure. Then I go down again and Momma is making supper like always and won't let me do anything to help. Sometimes I wonder how the days pass. I can't believe it's only a month since we came back. I clean our room and then I sew for a while or unpack our wedding presents and look at them and then I wrap them again and wait for you.

"Momma gets mad whenever I tell her I wish we had our own place already," she continued. "But I don't care. I'd give anything for a house of our own, even for a little room where we could live alone."

Her voice grew tremulous.

"I thought after we were married everything would be different. But even Poppa treats me just the same. Sometimes I feel just like crying."

Like crying, he repeated to himself. But why? She had every reason to be happy here. From morning till night she could do as she pleased. She had not even to lift her little finger. Her mother looked after everything. As for himself, he was perfectly content. They had all the privacy they wanted. This room was their own; no one ever disturbed them. He came home at night to find her fresh and smiling, his mother-in-law greeting him, his every wish anticipated. What was wrong, then?

Probably nothing at all, he thought indulgently. She would get over it. Young wives were like that. And besides, to move now meant that they would have to spend almost all their savings.

He shifted uncomfortably. Although his aunt had paid their train fare to Minneapolis, the amount of money he had had to spend still frightened him.

No. When he built — in a few years — it would be in River Heights. The money they saved by living here would help pay for their new home.

In River Heights, he thought. His eyelids drooped. He saw Eric's home, gleaming white in the sunlight. Not once in all this time had he returned to it, because of the ache it might bring, for fear of finding his childhood vision of it crumbling under what might unfold before eyes that had become too knowing. Not until his own home was built would he revisit Eric's.

He fell into a light sleep. A familiar night terror seized him. He would waken sometimes in the dark with everything he had accomplished looming before him still to be achieved. Or in half sleep a kindred fear would steal over him, a feeling he could not shake off, that as in childhood no good fortune could come to him, it seemed, but that it must be followed by something calamitous; something that, brought into being by his very success, threatened now to extinguish it. And this had nothing to do with any concern lest he misjudge or forget or make any error in his business dealings, and for this very reason, that it remained unnameable, grew all the more fearful, a thing to be allayed only by the knowledge of money safely and securely stored away.

He wondered if she would understand if he tried to tell her. He could trust her. But how could he bring himself to speak of it, to admit this shameful weakness?

He stirred as she shifted her head on his shoulder. Suppose he were to spend his savings on a new home, and then suddenly get sick?

"I've never been sick in my life," he scoffed.

All right, but just supposing. . . . The Agency might collapse, in that event. Had he considered that?

"Yes."

In that case they would need every cent they could lay their hands on, wouldn't they?

"Yes. But I'm not going to spend anything," he moaned. "Anyway, I've never . . ."

Never been sick? What about Mary, then?

"I've heard about women's complaints," he whimpered.

All right, then. Even if she didn't get sick . . . suppose something else were to happen. Just supposing, now, that . . .

"But I'm not spending anything," he cried, and blinking up at the moon through the silvered pane he felt his wife's hand cool on his cheek.

"You must have been dreaming, Alex." She drew him down to her breast.

He breathed in the fragrance of her body, grown familiar now. This was the breath of home. Perhaps some day, he thought, he would be able to tell her of his fears, shameful as they were; tell her what he could admit to no other human being.

She would understand. He remembered the many ways in which she tried to please him, the countless things she had done for his comfort. And all she wanted was a place of her own, even a room. Was that too much to ask for?

He opened his eyes. "Mary," he said. "Listen. I've got an idea. I think we'll be able to manage."

"Alex! Oh, I hope we move soon."

The sudden movement of her body was a torment and a delight. He seized her and pressed his mouth to hers.

"We'll be alone," she whispered. "The way young married people should be. And I'll be able to cook. I'll make my own drapes and do all the things I always wanted to do. And when I feel like playing the piano, that's what I'll do."

"A piano?" Alex repeated. "Mary, for God's sake!"

Her laughter frightened him. This was the way it happened; one thing led to another. First she wanted a room, then a house. Now it was a piano. Next would come a . . .

"Alex. I meant the piano downstairs. Poppa told me we

could take it with us when we moved. Oh, I've never been so happy. Let's move soon, soon as we can."

"I'd like to live in a new house," she continued. "Sometimes when I go with you into those old, empty houses I think that all the people who ever lived in them are still there, watching and listening. The night we went to look at that house on College Avenue, while you were down in the cellar with the light, I was so frightened I couldn't even call you. I remembered the old lady who used to live there, and all the time I was standing in the hall the wind was blowing, and the branches of the trees were creaking, and I thought I could hear her crying and scratching with her nails against the walls, as if she were trying to get back in again where all her memories were. I couldn't live in such a house."

"But she's dead," Alex objected. "She's been dead for nearly six months."

"I know."

"Well, maybe we can move into a new one. I've been thinking. Now listen, Mary. I've got it all worked out. Next Friday when we visit Auntie, when you're alone in the kitchen with her and she asks you how things are, you tell her everything's fine, like you always do, but just sort of sigh and say you wished I didn't have to work late in the office so many nights.

"And she'll say: 'Well, that's how things are, my child.' Or else: 'You're lucky you've got a husband who doesn't have to break his back all day while he's working.' Yah, that's what she'll say."

"And you'll say, 'I know, Auntie. It's only that I don't see Alex very much, that's all.'

"And she'll say, 'My child, thank God business is so good your husband has work to do.'

"And you'll say, 'Auntie, of course I'm glad business is good, but if Alex could only stay home after supper.' And then wait for a while because by then she'll be suspicious. She won't know what you're getting at, see, but she'll figure you're going to ask her for money. And when she finds out that that's not what you want, she'll act almost human and you'll have a better chance of getting what you want."

"But Alex."

"Now, just a minute, Mary. Just listen. Now where was I? Yes. After a while, you'll say, 'Auntie, you know if Alex could only work at home after supper it wouldn't be so bad. Lots of real-estate men in the North End have offices in their living-rooms where people can call on them at night. If we had our own place we could do that too. But we can't afford a home of our own yet, not even to rent.'

"And she'll say, 'But my dear child, your husband is earning thirty-five dollars a week.'

"And then you'll smile at her and say, 'Yes, Auntie. But it's hard for young married people. We have to furnish a whole house. And Alex doesn't like to buy anything until we've got the money. He says we mustn't get into debt.'

"She'll like that. Then you'll say, as if you just thought of it, 'Auntie, why can't you let us have one of those new houses of yours on Mountain Avenue that Poppa and Alex are building. Just until we've got a little more . . .' "

"Alex!"

It was unnecessary for her to say more. The tone of her voice was enough. She was going to refuse. But why? He looked down at her in bewilderment.

"You don't want to ask her, do you?"

"I can't, Alex. Please don't ask me to. I can't," she repeated. "If I liked her it would be different. But I hate her. She's the only person I know that I hate. I don't mind asking favours of people I like. But she used to beat your uncle when he got drunk. I know she did. And the only reason he drank was because of her. And why does she have to tell him, and when we're there too, that he's such a terrible business man? Can't she see what she's doing to him?"

She shook her head. "You know I don't like her. How can you ask me to smile at her, then, and beg her for a favour? It's wrong."

"I don't understand," he said. "It'd save us nearly four hundred dollars a year. I'd ask her myself if I thought it would do any good, but she'd get suspicious the minute I opened my mouth. She's drawing nearly six hundred dollars a month out of the Agency and who do you think earns that money? Your husband, that's who. She even begrudges me my salary. I had to fight for nearly every cent of it. Anything we get out of her is coming to us, believe me. She won't be doing us any favour.

"And it's such a little thing," he went on. "I wouldn't ask you to do anything I wouldn't do. All day at the office I have to smile at people I don't like. It doesn't mean anything."

He stopped suddenly. What was he doing? He was involving his wife in the same kind of situation that almost daily had to be faced or devised in the office. Not that there was anything wrong in what he did there. The rules were the same, for him as well as for the people he dealt with; the consequences of betraying ignorance or weakness worked both ways. It was hard, but it was fair.

Yes. But what he loved in her was her forthrightness, her very inability to do these things — and loved her even more because she was untouched by what he must of necessity do, because she was innocent not only of this but of all that had been ugly and painful in his life. He wanted her to remain as she was, so that there would be this one thing he could hold to that was beyond the strain and turmoil of career, beyond daily fear and ache, yes, and even daily triumph.

He stared up at the ceiling, across at the silvered pane. A gust of wind rattled the window.

And this anxiety he'd felt, about spending his savings. What did it mean but that he lacked faith not only in himself, but in the very things which he professed to believe? Business had never been better. What could happen? He was still young and well on the way to achieving everything he had always wanted. His thoughts veered, upwelled with the sudden full realization of how far he had come. An immeasurable distance separated him from that boy on Henry Avenue.

He smiled and clasped his wife in his arms.

"Mary," he said. "Tomorrow we'll go out and look for a little house."

Sixteen

OUTWARDLY, just another day. The office boy with the mail; a few bills, a few advertisements, a cheque for commission earned. A quick glance at the real-estate section in the morning papers. Kostanuik on the telephone.

He raised the blind and looked out. An ordinary day.

But up there beyond Portage and Main, in the glass-and-steel heights, a man by the name of Brown had raised his little finger; nothing more was required, no greater effort was needed, since the affair which had prompted him to act was barely worthy of his notice. But one result was that a certain Davidson had come tumbling down.

His descent, although he was a small man, a mere building contractor, in fact, had not passed unnoticed. In various small establishments throughout the city there was jubilation.

The man who had strained at the lever which had raised Brown's finger, which had toppled Davidson from his perch, was a certain Williams, one of Brown's minor executives. And Williams had a friend called Lawson. Sunday mornings they played golf; Sunday nights, sometimes, they got drunk. Sometimes they took a flyer on the market together. And Lawson knew a small contractor, an agent of his in the North End.

Alex returned to his desk. If it had not been for Lawson, he might never have heard, might never have got a chance at this contract.

The thought of how he had suspected Lawson, watching

204

him every time they met for a sign, a tell-tale phrase, or even a smile that might reveal the prejudice he harboured, shamed him. And what was worse, since he had not found a vestige of prejudice against foreigners in this man, was that he had actually come to believe that Lawson was in some indefinable way inferior to those who harboured such feelings — as though the mere fact of Lawson's friendship with someone forcign-born was a flaw in his character, an indication of weakness. And he had had the same thought about Lawson's friends.

But they had become his friends too. He smiled to himself. Somehow he had always expected that this feverish need to be accepted by the English would be fulfilled in a great and sudden friendship. Instead, it had come so imperceptibly, week by week, that he had scarcely been aware it was happening.

He looked up and groaned as the door opened; the inevitable North-Ender. But this one — a carry-over from Nagy's time — in spite of his greasy windbreaker and patched, baggy trousers, had money. He was a small man, with an enormous drooping moustache into which he had thrust the stem of a battered pipe so short that the bowl sent its fumes directly into his nostrils.

It was four months at least since he had first appeared, and ever since then, every few weeks or so, he had reappeared; and every interview had been a nightmare. Time meant nothing to Herr Kruger. He could sit for hours, stolidly puffing at his pipe. A grunt signified that he agreed or disagreed, one never knew which; that was one device. The other, quite as effective, was a simulated incapacity to understand what was being said. When he did speak, it was in fits and starts, in a hoarse creaking whisper, impartially contradicting both himself and his opponent.

It seemed impossible that this man should have earned enough even to keep himself alive. And yet he had made a small fortune during the war, buying and selling horses.

Alex nodded affably. "I didn't think you were coming back, Herr Kruger." He spoke German.

Herr Kruger grunted, lowered himself into a chair, and poked a thick dirty finger into the bowl of his pipe.

"You've come to sign the papers?" Alex continued.

"It troubles me how long will it last," Herr Kruger said finally.

Alex blinked. "What?"

"The building I would build, what else?"

"Let me show you something," Alex said. "You see that picture of a building, up there on the wall? Twelve years old, and still in first-class condition. I look after it for a sick man who is in the States. Thirty thousand dollars, he paid for it. Today he could sell it for forty thousand. That's what . . ."

"So who has forty thousand dollars?" Herr Kruger asked.

Right now, Alex reflected, Lawson and Ingram and Grainger and the rest of his friends were probably sitting at their desks engaged in honest-to-God business affairs while he sat here slowly going mad with this peasant. What I ought to do, he thought, is kick him the hell out of here.

"So how long?" Herr Kruger asked.

Alex considered his answer. If he said fifty years, he would probably be asked the price of one that would last twenty-five; if he said twenty-five, he would likely be told that that wasn't long enough.

"About forty years," he said.

"That's all?"

"Well, damn it, I don't mean it would fall apart after that. The walls and foundation would still be good. You'd have to make minor repairs, of course."

"A sad thing," — Herr Kruger shook his head; his eyes narrowed — "a man with such a property should be so sick. What does his doctor say?"

Alex lit a cigarette. There was some outward evidence that Herr Kruger was thinking. In a few minutes, he would have something else to object to. He sat back and waited. When was he going to get out of this hole and away from all this nonsense?

Wasting his time here. . . . In his desk was a copy of the

estimate he had submitted to Williams — the interior of a six-storey office building to be completely stripped and renovated. The cost of rebuilding and decorating the executive offices on the top floor alone would come to more than Kruger's whole block. And Williams had made it clear that the man who got the job could reasonably expect to handle Brown's work in the future.

He looked up. Herr Kruger had removed his pipe. "So a twenty-year building," Kruger asked. "That would cost half?"

"Look, Herr Kruger, I'm a busy man. I can't . . . Okay. Listen. I'm just going to say this once. If you paid one hundred and fifty dollars for a horse, would ho be twice as good as a seventy-five-dollar one? You might have to spend an extra seventy-five on the cheaper one just to keep him on his feet. So you've lost money, because while he was sick he wasn't ploughing or whatever the hell you use him for. Is that right?"

Herr Kruger smiled slyly.

"All right, then," Alex went on. "Do I build for you or not?"

The phone rang. Mrs. Gregory. If Mr. Hunter was still sure that he could get thirty-eight hundred dollars for the house, then her husband was willing to sell.

Good. He would be down tonight. Seven o'clock was fine.

The door opened. A portly little man entered the office, observed that Alex was busy, and turned to go.

Alex leaped to his feet. They exchanged a few words over the counter. The man paid, took his receipt, and left.

Alex watched him go. If only there were more like him. It was two years since he had bought that house, and in all that time there had been not a word of complaint, not a single payment missed.

Herr Kruger came out. "So next week I will come back and we will talk . . ."

Alex turned on him furiously. "You tell me yes or no today," he said. "Four months, just talk, talk, talk! You've seen every contractor in town already. I'm too busy to waste any more time on you."

"Waste! Who likes to waste? I would build. But a forty-year building . . . What? You are unfriendly? I will build . . ."

"Build, hell! You don't want to build. You just want to talk — " He stopped and smiled. "You know, this talk costs you even more than it costs me. You're losing money every day. Thousands of dollars, it'll come to, by the end of the year." His smile widened at the effect he had produced.

Kruger's pipe began to wobble. "Losing money? How, losing money? In the bank . . ."

"How much does the bank pay you? Peanuts. Listen. People need houses so bad we sell every one we build even before it's finished. Four months you've been talking. By now the building would be finished, you understand? People would be paying you rent. Nearly two hundred and fifty dollars a month."

The door opened and closed. A young man, cap in hand, stood behind the counter gate, smiling happily. "Hullo, Mr. Hunter."

"Hullo."

He ushered Kruger into the second office, returned to his own, and motioned to the young man to enter.

"You got money?" he asked.

The man nodded, still smiling. "Got job," he said, extending three five-dollar bills.

Alex ignored them. "Next time you no pay rent, I kick you out pretty damn fast. Four times I call for rent — every time you say next time."

"No more trouble with rent," the man said. "Got job now."

Alex opened the ledger. "Two months' rent," he said. 'Fifteen dollars. Two lawyer's letters, three dollars each — six dollars. You owe twenty-one dollars."

The man wiped his face with his cap. He placed the money on the desk.

Alex swept it to the floor. "Twenty-one dollars," he shouted, crashing his fist on the desk.

The man flushed He stooped down nevertheless and picked up the bills. "You no yell at me," he cried suddenly. "I move. God damn, this is free country . . ."

"For seven and a half dollars rent," Alex said, "where you get house big enough for six kids, huh?

"You want I should call lawyer, maybe," he continued. "By God when lawyer finish with you, you pay plenty. . . . You got lawyer's letters, no?"

The man nodded.

Alex lit a cigarette. Those letters, strictly speaking, had not come from a lawyer at all; he had simply bought three form-letters along with some stationery from a law student.

One word from Williams, he thought, and these cheap tricks would be behind him. In his own office there would be no need of them.

"All right," he said. "Lawyer charge me six dollars, I charge you six dollars. You pay!"

"No got six dollars."

"How much you got?"

The man rose. "Money is for feed kids," he said.

"How much money you got? How much?" Alex repeated.

"Got five dollars."

Alex drummed his fingers on the ledger.

"All right," he said finally. "Five dollars. I lose one dollar."

The twenty dollars changed hands.

For an instant their eyes met, and in that instant Alex grew frightened. Suddenly and unexpectedly a wave of pity came over him. And this was not the first time in his business dealings that he had felt it. Something soft within him that he had tried again and again to crush. He had never felt it so strongly. From my blood, he thought wildly. Where else? Not from my head. He had heard about such things. His father's blood in his veins, carrying this weakness — his father's lifelong concern for other people, handed on to his son. A crazy superstition, he cried to himself, but without conviction because he knew now what he was going to do and knew too that he could not stop himself.

A cold sweat came over him. He held out the five-dollar bill. The man looked at him as though he were mad.

Alex rose to his feet. "Take the God-damn thing," he yelled. "Take it and get the hell out of here."

The man took the money and fled. When he had gone, Alex dropped back into his chair. "A hell of a fine business man you are," he whispered hoarsely. "Next thing you'll be bawling on their shoulders."

A weakness, he had called it. Perhaps some day on the verge of some decisive business deal it would reappear and take possession of him. The thought terrified him. It came always when he least expected it. And until he had destroyed it, he would never be able to handle deals the way Nagy had done, without any feeling at all, without pity and without the hatred that now came over him.

He glanced at the door. If Nagy had been here and had overheard, he would never have been able to face him.

"And it's not the money," he said fiercely. "What's five bucks? But by God next time he falls behind in his rent I'll kick him the hell out so fast he won't know what hit him. I'll . . ."

With a start he remembered that Kruger was still waiting. Forcing a smile to his lips he got up and called him back into his office.

"Well?" Alex asked.

"I will come tomorrow . . ."

"Tomorrow I'm busy. Next day too. . . . Two hundred and fifty dollars a month," Alex exclaimed. "A thousand dollars you've lost already. Can you afford to lose all that money? Think about it. Two hundred and fifty dollars for the rest of your life."

Herr Kruger began to tremble.

Now, Alex thought. It's now or not at all. Taking out the contract, long since drawn up, he held it out to him.

"You sign here," he said, offering him his pen.

Kruger accepted it, lowered his finger-tips to the contract, drew them back as though they had been scorched, squirmed, pulled his chair a fraction of an inch away from the desk, and finally looked up at Alex plaintively.

"I'm sick," he said — "a sick man."

"Write your name down, Herr Kruger."

Kruger took a deep breath and signed.

Alex settled himself in his chair, and wiped his forehead. Four months' work. "Now, if you'll just give me a cheque," he said, "we'll start building."

Kruger began to moan.

Inwardly, Alex joined him. North End business.

Half an hour later, alone in the office, he lit a cigarette and sat back to catch his breath. Why didn't it mean anything? He ought to be celebrating. His first big contract. . . .

He stared at the cheque. When was he going to get out of here?

On an impulse he got up and walked into his uncle's office, to the mirror there, and looked at himself soberly and intently for a long time, searching his features for some sign of weakness. He found none, but as he looked at himself he remembered how it always started, always in the same way, with what seemed such a harmless thing — that mild and simple wonder about the feelings of the person he was dealing with.

His eyebrows rose. Was that it? Was it as simple as that? He gazed at himself thoughtfully, looking into his own eyes. "In the blood!" he snorted. All he had to do was . . . "I'll squash it," he said. "I'll squash it dead."

He returned to his desk.

At ten o'clock his uncle arrived, waved to him, and sailed majestically by. A few minutes later an old woman in a black shawl, the very image of his grandmother, came into the office and looked about her timidly.

This one, thank God, was probably for his uncle.

"You speak German?" He waved her to a chair.

She nodded, seated herself, and folded her hands in her lap. "Mr. Nagy is not here any more?"

"No, he has gone. What can I do for you?"

She began to cry. She and her husband had expected in a few years to apply for old-age pension. But her neighbours and her two sons, who were good boys in spite of everything that had happened, worried her and kept after her day after day; if she and her husband took this pension, they told her, the Government would take the house away after she and her husband were dead.

Alex nodded. An old story. But why was she telling him all this?

All they owned was this house, she explained. She had taken in washing to help pay for it. She began to sway back and forth in her chair, wiping her eyes with the corner of her shawl. Not knowing what to do, she had gone to a lawyer who had made the house over to the two boys.

Now they were homeless, she and her husband. Two old people with no place to lay their heads. Their sons were selling the house. Every night there was quarrelling; her husband was no match for them. She covered her face with her hands and wept.

"Some day they will understand," she said. "When it's too late. . . . Some day your mother's love you'll understand, when you bury her. Millionaires, they would be. Gentlemen with soft fingers. To make business they would sell the roof over our heads."

"I'll let you talk to the manager," Alex said.

He found his uncle with his feet on the desk, reading the paper.

"There's a woman outside," he said. "I wonder if you'd like to see her."

His uncle adjusted his tie.

"She's an old woman."

"They're never too old, my boy."

Alex beckoned to her. "This is our manager, Mr. Daffner," he said. "He'll look after you."

"So you're in trouble, little mother," Onkel Janos boomed. "Well, you've come to the right place, let me tell you. Here we eat troubles and grow fat. Now sit down and tell me — George!"

The office boy appeared.

"Two coffees, George. You drink coffee, little mother? Good."

"I'm going out for a while," Alex said. "I don't know when I'll be back. I'll call you."

His uncle beamed. Few things pleased him more than to be left in charge of the office.

On the street, Alex turned south. First the building permit for Kruger's block; and on the way, bank his cheque. Then arrangements for an electric line to the construction shack. They would have to rent a power saw. And then? Then to College Avenue to see how Kostanuik was getting along. They would have to hire an extra crew to start digging next week. Tonight, call on the Gregorys. Since they lived at the other end of town he could safely pocket the commission. He paused. Tonight he had promised to take Mary to a show. Clara Bow, her favourite actress, was on at the Palace; the last night. But he'd be through with the Gregorys by about eight — plenty of time.

He walked on. It's going to be all right, he thought. He had Lawson to talk for him, and in addition he had a decisive advantage over most of his competitors. The fact that he managed and did not own the Agency meant that he could cut his profits to the bone — even take a small loss, if necessary. It made no difference to him; his salary was assured. He smiled as he continued on his way.

When he returned to the office, it was to find a plump, rosy little matron on the bench waiting for him. At her side was a freckled boy of about fourteen, staring at him through heavy horn-rimmed glasses.

Frau Spiegelknecht. Almost a year ago he had tried to interest her in buying a house. Her husband, he recalled, had created something of a stir a few months back by winning a chess tournament. Her eldest son was a hockey player. When one of them wasn't in the newspaper, the other was. The house she rented belonged to Nagy.

He greeted her effusively as he led her into his office. How was her husband? So! Was that a fact? And her son? Ah! How proud she must be — the envy of every wife and mother in the country.

A few more minutes of this, and then: "Well," he said, "so much for pleasure. Now what brings you here, Frau Spiegelknecht?"

When he heard, he felt a wild desire to tear his hair. What kind of people were these? Certainly, he had never seen their like in the North End before.

And yet it was in keeping with what was happening all around. Peasants going into real-estate, druggists selling hardware, shipping-room clerks playing the market, women bobbing their hair, people spending money like water. And he no better than the rest — his savings gone; up to his ears in debt. First the furniture in the bedroom and the kitchen; then the living-room. Now it was a washing-machine. Where would it end?

He looked across at Frau Spiegelknecht. An ordinary little housewife — and yet so hell-bent on notoriety.

Her son had constructed a model of the Provincial House, out of toothpicks. Would Mr. Hunter consider displaying it in his window? Fortunately, she had turned to her son as she finished making her request, combing his hair back with her fingers. When she looked at Alex again, he had recovered.

"Did you make it all by yourself?" he asked the boy.

"Every toot'pick, Mr. Hunter," she cried. "Anna liddle kewpie doll he painted gold for the top. You know wot he said wen he finished, Mr. Hunter? 'I'm gonna be famous, Ma. Just like Pa and Albert.' Isn't that nice?"

The boy squirmed. "Aw, Ma . . ."

"Ach, my liddle heart," she said, and clasped him to her bosom. "Famous he wants to be like his father and his brother! Here ——"

She opened her handbag. "A pitcher we took."

Alex eyed it thoughtfully. It couldn't do any harm. As a matter of fact, it might even be a good idea. It would certainly attract attention.

"Just a minute," he said, and going to a cupboard under the counter he returned with a bag of raspberry drops.

"Say thank you," Frau Spiegelknecht admonished.

"Tanks."

"And when are you going to let me build you a house, Frau Spiegelknecht?" Alex asked, " — a home you can live in while you're still young enough to enjoy it?"

"A spring chicken I am, maybe?" she laughed heartily. Her cheeks were like two ripe apples.

"You're still a young woman, Frau Spiegelknecht."

"So how do I have a son twenty years old awready?"

Alex shrugged his shoulders. "You adopted him."

He appraised her coolly while she laughed. "You'd pay no more a month than you're paying now," he continued. "I'd make you a special price."

"Ach, you say that to everybody."

"I'm serious. It would be good business for me. Everybody in town knows the Spiegelknechts. And think how nice it would be to have your own home — all the cupboards you want, a modern kitchen, hardwood floors. Why don't you let me call some evening and talk to you and your husband?"

She nodded absently."I'll tell him,"she said. "Maybe. . . . So now wot about the parliament building for the window?"

"On one condition."

"Yaah," the boy leered. "We gotta buy a house first."

Alex patted him perhaps a little too ardently on the head. "I'll need a photograph of your husband with a chessboard," he said, "and one of your son with a hockey-stick. And then a picture of this young man here. I'll have them mounted and put them in the window together with the model. How's that?"

Frau Spiegelknecht clasped her hands. "Wonderful!" she exclaimed. "Everybody will see . . ."

"And your new home," Alex began, and sensed that his timing was wrong. He was allowing her to slip through his fingers; and what was worse, it didn't seem to matter.

"I'll talk to my husband," she said.

When she had gone, he turned to the window.

Brown, he thought. Just Brown.

Once he had seen him in the lobby of the hotel — had passed so close he could easily have reached out his hand and touched him. A big man, towering above those around him;

a man whose affairs in the business life of the city were so diverse and far-reaching they were fabulous. Interests in mining, trucking and real-estate; manufacturer, stockbroker. He had but to nod, to smile in one's direction, and if one had the intelligence to understand such a gesture and the wit to exploit it, one's position in life would be forever changed.

He sighed. Even if he got that contract he would still be only on the outermost fringe of Brown's affairs, in an orbit far removed from the centre, from the man himself. Even Williams, the man he would be dealing with, saw Brown no more than half a dozen times a year. But what was he complaining about? One more step and he would be on his way. What was there to stop him after he got that first contract? Nothing at all. . . . Nothing.

Seventeen

BENEATH the glare of the reflector, the lines running to the lower extremity of her jaw looked like two dark, ancient gullies; her mouth a cavern which, having opened, now puckered itself to be kissed. A shudder came over him as he kissed her. He escorted her to his desk, and as he drew up a chair for her, glanced at his uncle moving silently across the office.

He looked, Alex thought, like a young and portly millionaire out slumming for the evening. On the street beside him, she must have appeared to passers-by to be his grandmother.

Alex seated himself beside her, reached for the balance-sheet, and discovered her eyes fastened upon his uncle, who, having sat down at a small table, now drew a package of cards from his pocket and began to lay them out for solitaire.

When she turned away it was to squint and scowl at the sheet of paper he had placed before her. Then she opened her handbag and withdrew what seemed to be an old mothball. She popped it into her mouth and began to crush it vigorously between her teeth, pointing to the balance-sheet the while.

At best, these occasions were tedious and fatiguing. Any expenditure might haphazardly become the subject of long and acrimonious debate. Tonight she seemed amiable enough and yet, through the set smile of her face, the impatient desire to be done, he sensed that she was holding something back.

They had finished when the blow fell. Quite unexpectedly she reached for the receipt book.

"What about Mrs. Segal?" she asked.

"She hasn't paid yet," Alex said. "I told you about her last month. I'll be seeing her again tomorrow."

"I met her today at the market," his aunt continued. "She was sick last week and sent one of her boarders with the money."

He blinked as she prodded him with a pencil. "Well," she said. Her voice rose. "What have you got to say for yourself?"

"But for God's sake! You can see it hasn't been entered."

She smiled grimly. "Yes. I can see that."

He had nothing to fear in this case, but at the thought of what might so easily have occurred he began to tremble. What could have happened? He would certainly have remembered if he had received the money. There were only two possible explanations. Either the boarder had kept it, or . . . There was only one other explanation. He glanced at his uncle; one look at him, and the whole thing was childishly and transparently clear. Onkel Janos looked at him imploringly.

But how was it that she had not so much as mentioned what she suspected, even to her husband? Perhaps she thought that Onkel Janos might warn him.

What was even more perplexing was that it had not occurred to her that her husband might have received the money. But from the very first, Alex reflected, she had felt that her nephew was swindling her. It was for this reason, in spite of all his protestations, that she had never put her other properties in his hands, and that she had replaced Nagy's lawyer with her own. He smiled; as though this had had any effect. . . .

"You think it's a joke maybe?" his aunt cried. "To sit and laugh. Easy enough to steal from an old woman, you think; to cheat her when she trusts you.

"You're a thief," she screamed, "and if not for your wife the police would be here tonight."

It seemed inconceivable, he thought, that he should ever have enjoyed these rows with her. And yet, only too distinctly, he remembered baiting her, leading her on, laughing at her while she fumed and raved. In the end, he had always been able to vindicate himself in such a way that even she could understand. Tonight — perhaps it was just the way he felt. Had Williams forgotten him? — Tonight he was afraid that some day she might stumble across something, something he would be unable to explain. It could happen easily enough.

He looked across at his uncle and turned sadly away. It was going to be unpleasant, and yet what else could he do? He would have to tell her. God, how stupid she was!

"Auntie," he said. "Listen . . ."

"Yes, Auntie," she mimicked. "You know how to say 'Auntie.' To think of all I've done for you! Don't laugh. Once you didn't laugh. You came, begging me I should buy the Agency and make that old fool a president."

She turned to her husband. "To look under girls' skirts, that you can do, but under your own nose to see what's going on — that's too much to expect."

"And now." A triumphant leer spread across her face as she confronted Alex. "This time I caught you. Now give me the money."

Like an old mud-coloured toad, he thought.

"From now on," she continued, "no more tricks you'll play. Tomorrow my lawyer sends a bookkeeper here to make sure nobody steals again."

Alex leaped to his feet. He had let it go too far. "So you still think I took that money. Do you really think I'd be such a damn fool?" he shouted. "Answer me."

"I won't be spoken to in this way."

"Oh yes you will. . . . My God! Do you know that if I wanted to cheat you, neither you nor all your bookkeepers nor your lawyers could stop me? This is my business. Don't you understand? There are a thousand ways I could swindle you. . . . Listen to me. I haven't taken so much as a two-cent stamp since I've come here. And all the thanks I get for being honest and for running around fifteen and eighteen hours a day for you is to be called a crook and be threatened with the police. Not that I expect anything else. But supposing one day I made a mistake or forgot something. What would happen? You'd get another one of those crazy notions, and I'd be out of a job."

"So. First you're innocent," she mocked. "Now you just forgot the money wasn't yours. You just put it in your pocket by mistake."

"Stupid to the end," he answered. "Haven't you guessed yet?" He looked intently across at his uncle for a moment, then watched her as she sat straining forward, clutching her handbag, her chin out-thrust, her features still twisted in the sneer that had accompanied her last words; frozen as though in a monstrous tableau but for the quivering of the muscles in her withered neck.

He turned again from her to his uncle, who winked at him before glancing nervously at his wife.

"I don't know how I could have forgotten," Onkel Janos said. "The money must still be in my grey striped suit." He nodded. "I think that's what I was wearing that day." He dealt himself a card, returned it to the deck without looking at it, and turned back to his wife. "I think you owe Alex an apology, Kathie. After all, it . . ."

He got no further. In three strides she was upon him.

"So you forgot!" she screamed, and raised her handbag. It struck him a glancing blow on the side of the head, slipped from her hand, and scattered its contents across the table and the floor. He gathered them silently and returned them to her handbag.

"You forgot," she repeated. "You sat there and let me humiliate myself while you played cards."

She swept them from his hand. "A president — an office manager, he calls himself, and forgets what any snot-nosed office boy could remember."

"For God's sake, enough already," he said. "Can't a man forget without causing all this uproar?"

"Hah!" she crowed. "A man, maybe, but not a business man. And you are neither. You are a fool, do you hear? A fool."

"All right. So now I'm a fool. Only stop screaming. I've heard enough."

"Enough," she said tauntingly. "It means nothing to you that you're a failure. I've spent thousands in this business trying to put you on your feet. And how do you show your gratitude?"

He rose slowly, turning his head from side to side, like a huge, helpless animal, Alex thought.

But no. He was mistaken. He nodded eagerly as his uncle reached for his cane, and as he raised it, there flashed before Alex's eyes the picture of it descending and breaking across her skull.

In fantasy he had already seized what the outcome of her death made available, had passed fiercely beyond it, when he heard the cane crash against the table.

His uncle brushed past him. The door slammed.

Alex watched in silence as his aunt bent down to pick up the silver knob-end of the cane. Her coat and skirt billowed out upon the floor so that, as she rose in the half light beyond the cone of the reflector, his mind flooded with the recollection of the female demons in old Hungarian peasant tales. The feeling grew that he was staring at some such creature now, half woman, half monster, rising not from the floor, but from the depths below.

He drew back, unable to tear his eyes from her haggard face, from the loose moist lips endlessly forming his uncle's name.

With a final shudder, she thrust the short knobbed end of the cane into her handbag and walked stiffly to the door.

"That — that bookkeeper," he said.

She paused. "Yes, that bookkeeper." She opened the door. "I hope this teaches you a lesson," she continued. "The next time you feel like playing tricks, just remember. I can always call him when I need him."

She walked out, leaving him standing there, open-mouthed, looking around him as though for the first time with unglazed eyes, with a new and hateful clarity. This belonged to her; it was stupid, but he had never really accepted the fact. It was hers. He was only a clerk here.

"That's all you are," he said. "Just a poor bloody clerk."

But he had prospects. . . .

As though those thousands of others behind a thousand counters, daily chanting the legends of exchange, had not something to dream about too.

Still, he was different. He had plans of some day opening his own establishment.

He laughed. The pipe-dream of every second clerk from Selkirk to the end of Portage.

You're different, all right, he thought. The day her lawyer gets his bookkeeper in here, you're on the way out. That's all he's been waiting for. . . . In what way are you different?

He looked around him. His eyes lighted on the calendar. A red-letter day in the life of A. Hunter — April 3, 1929. A day to remember.

He switched off the light, drew up the blind, and sat down. What other prospects had he? Three months, and not a word from Williams. And Lawson? Lawson had other things to think about. He spent more time at his stockbroker's than in his office.

In the sudden roar of traffic as the lights changed and the windows rattled, it seemed to Alex that he was borne back; through the whisper of the years he heard the laughter inside the red fence.

How would it have gone with him, he wondered, if he had stayed with the gang? A few times, walking home late at night, he had seen them, looking sleek and prosperous; they were their own masters, their affairs grown until one could no longer dismiss them as mere crooks or gangsters. An intense nostalgia came over him; but then he remembered what had happened later. There came back to him the headlines in the papers, and the pictures; the killings; Hank still in jail; and Buggsy dead, sprawled under a truck in a welter of broken bottles on the highway.

Alex got up. He felt tired and empty. As he reached for his hat, the telephone rang.

Mary, most likely, wondering what was keeping him. He raised the receiver.

It was his aunt. The colour drained from his face. With her hysterical cry still in his ears he ran out, caught a cab, and sat straining forward on the edge of the seat, urging the driver on.

Another sordid little story from the North End, he thought; the kind of story they would smile at in the South End. Of course they would smile, or turn from it with disgust, as they read their morning papers. Woman stabs husband. Was that what she had done?

He shivered. The newspapers! If word of this got out, it might ruin him. Would Williams even consider doing business with such people? A man spent the best part of his life straining and sweating — but don't think of that. Maybe it isn't so bad. Maybe it can be kept out of the papers. Get hold of yourself now.

Suddenly it struck him that this was his uncle who was hurt, who might be in pain or even dead.

You remember, he asked himself savagely, your uncle? — Onkel Janos. You finally remembered him, after you had thought of everything else.

A sob broke from his throat. Images of his uncle rose before him — at the station on that first day, so eagerly greeting his new life; the wonder of him in the barber shop on that same day, so instantly responding to his young nephew's affection; and at the party, and on silent streets, confiding in his uncle, telling him what was in his heart and loving him as he loved no other person but Mary, or at least professing to love him. . . . His lips trembled.

The car drew to a stop. He paid the driver. The house was silent, the front door unlocked.

He walked in. She stood in the centre of the room staring with wide, vacant eyes across at her husband who lay on the sofa, his face swollen, his lips and his eyelids blistered, a handkerchief in his hand which he was slowly tearing to pieces. He moaned, and lay still.

The house was filled with the odour of home-made soap, so there was no need to ask what had happened.

No one moved, not for a long time. And it was as though the whole scene beneath the pitiless glare of the chandelier took on the aspect of a picture in a newspaper, printed in some remote and long-forgotten time; as though on that faded, yellowing print they would remain forever fixed, a figure in the dim background with one arm feebly upheld in protest, and in the centre a young man with convulsed features, his hands around the throat of an old woman whose body hung limp within his grasp.

It seemed to him that it was only in response to his uncle's repeated cries that he had finally released her.

She fell, and the room was still again. The story she told reminded him of two characters in a comic strip. She had gone through the pockets of her husband's suit looking for money and, not finding any, had thrown a pot at him. Now he lay groaning on the sofa.

Afterward, Alex remembered, he had laughed. How many jokes were there about that? Only the pot had happened to be filled with lye. And she had gone through the pockets of the wrong suit.

His uncle's features swam into view, the cheeks swollen, the eyes hidden beneath puffed-out lids. Tears came into his own.

But his mind had already leaped ahead to what he must do to avert a scandal. He ran into the hall. First the doctor; then to the summer kitchen, from which he dragged a step-ladder. He threw it on its side. There was some lye left in the pot on the stove; he sprayed the wall with it and then, turning to his aunt, who had been following him around as though she were in a trance, took her by the shoulders and, shaking her, told her what she must say. It was an accident. She was washing the walls with the lye left over from the soap. Her husband was holding the ladder. . . . Did she understand? The ladder had slipped.

He stopped abruptly. She was obviously in no condition to talk at all. As he helped her to a chair, her knees gave way.

An hour later on the porch, after the doctor had intimated

that he was willing to accept his story of what had happened, Alex looked back through the window under the drawn blind.

She was kneeling before her husband, his hand pressed to her lips. She had him now, the way she had always wanted him, helpless in her hands. He was all hers now. He would carry those scars for the rest of his life.

This was the Pirate Uncle, the kind of man Alex had wanted his father to be; like other men, but above them in the qualities they most admired. His uncle was before him now, standing as on that day against the sky with his shovel upheld, laughing in the consciousness of his strength, or perhaps simply because the sun was shining.

Alex staggered down the steps and out into the street. He discovered that his cheeks were wet. He dried them and looked up. As a child he had known that there was malevolence up there if there was anything. And yet it not mere malevolence; it was more refined. Only people like his uncle, the harmless, the innocent and the foolish, were ever stricken. But then those who struck them down — were not they in turn the instruments of that malevolence? He denied this, and the answer he was groping for collapsed into a muddle.

There was nothing up there. And besides, it was not only the foolish and the innocent who were threatened; people like himself too could be struck down — could be ruined. He stopped. The answer he sought lay within himself. Must he admit that he was not blameless, that in fact he shared her guilt? Let him say it then, out loud if need be, and take the horror of it to himself so that he could finally accept what he had felt from the beginning.

And yet, what had he done to justify this monstrous accusation? If he were to blame himself, he could with equal justice blame his parents for having brought his uncle over here. They had meant well, and so had he. It was one's intentions that mattered, and the only person who was guilty on these grounds was that demon he had married. She had disfigured him so that no other woman would ever look at him again.

The image of his uncle came back to him; his eyes opening for an instant, filled with an animal resignation to the pain.

Alex walked on. In unguarded moments, he knew, it would come back. But the knowledge was old in him that in time such things faded. He continued on his way.

Eighteen

TWO GIRLS passed by arm-in-arm, skirts swirling as they stopped before the display in the window. A young man followed, then a newsboy.

Alex reached for a clean sheet of paper, lowered his pen to it, and suddenly sprang to the window, peering out from the far edge.

It couldn't be Rudolph, he thought. It was only someone who resembled him. His brother would have looked in, would surely have stopped, if only for a moment.

He returned to his desk. How long was it since he had last seen them? He could no longer remember. But if it was Rudolph, he should at least have waved to him.

He picked up his pen, lowered it, and on an impulse reached for the telephone. His mother answered.

"Hullo, Ma, it's me."

Her voice drew him back to the kitchen on Henry Avenue, damp and squalid, the clothes drying overhead, the odour of rotting wood under the sink, the cracks in the window stuffed with old papers . . . his mother sitting there alone on a winter night by the stove, wrapped in an old shawl, her head bowed, her hands red and chapped, sitting there cutting down a pair of his father's trousers for him. He felt a lump in his throat.

"Nothing's wrong, Ma," he said.

"You're not ashamed? How did you know we're not all six feet under the ground awready?"

"I'm sorry, Ma. I've been . . ."

"You've been busy. Awright. Your mother said to herself she won't bother you any more."

"Ma! I said I was sorry. Honest-to-God. I've been busy. I'm working day and night — something big. From now on I'll phone you every week, I promise. We'll come over this Sunday to visit."

"Awright. But if you know how much I worry about you. If not for Mary I wouldn't even know you're alive."

"Is Ruddy there?" Alex asked.

His mother sighed. "Downstairs," she said. "He sits and talks. I tell him to go out, even with girls if he wants. On'y he should get out of the house once and stop reading. You know wot I did?"

A low, sad murmur reached him. Was she laughing? When had he last heard his mother laugh, he wondered.

"Last Sunday," she continued, "I invited Mrs. Melanchuck's girl to visit. Rosie. You know her? The dark one. She's the youngest. Such a nice girl . . . a nice family. I took her to the front room where your brother sits reading and went to the kitchen. So wot do you think happened?

"Nothing. He sat and she sat. So when it was enough awready I called her in the kitchen. Poor girl. Wot can I do?"

"So nothing's changed," Alex said. "That's good. And what are they talking about downstairs?"

"They say the world's coming to an end." She sighed. "And with such prices I have to pay for everything, I can believe it."

Alex smiled. "And why is the world coming to an end?"

"Ach! Don't ask, Alex. Last week a book. Tonight the newspapers. Next week something else."

Suddenly she began to cry.

"What's the matter?" he asked impatiently. "Have I said something. . ."

"Awright to sit and laugh," she sobbed. "And what does your uncle do? Nobody cares. All day to stay in that house and never go out, like an animal in a cage. Ach, my God, I told him; I begged him — Janos, don't marry her. Nothing good will come of it. . . . When I go to see him, it's like a knife in my heart. He sits and drinks and looks at the window."

— At the drawn blinds, Alex thought. The blinds were always drawn there, the grass and the weeds grown tall in the yard, shadowed in late twilight; the way it would always appear to him now. The kind of house that small boys in the neighbourhood would grow afraid of, and at night, passing by on their way to the corner store, would cross the street to avoid — the haunted house. In time they would come to believe the stories they heard. And they would be right. It was like a tomb. Dark, so that his uncle might move around without his glasses; his wife had reasons of her own to remain in darkness.

"A wonderful accident for her," his mother went on. "You remember they visited us once and Mrs. Segal's daughter made a few jokes with him. Your uncle couldn't look at her, his wife turned pale already. . . . Your uncle says nothing, but I'm sure she pushed that ladder, maybe something even worse. Who uses such strong lye for washing walls?"

"So you think she did it because she was jealous?"

"Wot else? Who . . ."

"But it was an accident," Alex broke in. "The way I told you, Ma. Believe me."

"Awright, I believe you. But she knows wot she did when she married him. A poisoned old stick she is. I can't cry any more I cried so much. Sometimes I think it was better we never brought him to this country."

"I visit him every week, Ma."

"You're a good boy, Alex. I'm sorry I was cross."

"I'll have to go now," he said. "I'm still at the office."

He sat quietly at his desk after she had hung up. I did everything I could to make him happy here, he thought. I couldn't have done any more.

He looked up as the office boy, freshly washed and scrubbed, emerging as though from nowhere, presented himself before him.

"Kin I — can I go now?" A look of hungry anticipation spread over his face.

Alex nodded. "I'm depending on you to do a good job," he said. "Work the way I showed you. Don't use the lawnmower when you cut beside the sidewalk. Use the shears. And when you're through, Mrs. Hunter will give you your supper. Will you like that?"

The boy flushed with pleasure.

Alex handed him two car tickets. "And here's your thirty-five cents," he said. He smiled at the boy's eagerness to be off. "One more thing," he added. "Don't go yelling and whooping around while you're working. Remember. You're in a high-class neighbourhood, even if you are in the North End."

"I'll remember."

A little wild, Alex thought, but bright and hard-working and loyal. The ten dollars he had given him for night-school was money well spent. He would take him along when he opened his own office.

"Have you got a comb?" he asked.

The boy shook his head.

"Buy one," Alex said, and taking out his own, began combing his hair for him.

"You like it out there?" he asked.

The boy sighed. "I never seen so many trees in my life," he said. "Except in a park."

Alex's hand faltered. He placed it lightly on the boy's head.

"Take this comb," he said softly. "And when you get your pay this week you'll find a little surprise there. . . . But from now on I want to see a change in your appearance," he went on. "You understand?"

"Yes, Mr. Hunter."

Alex watched him as he ran out of the office, running it seemed to him out of his own childhood and into that of Sandor Hunyadi, in a few minutes to be sitting on the edge of his seat in a streetcar moving to the South End, where . . . where the people lived in a park the whole year round. Wasn't that how it had struck him? In a little while he would be seeing Eric and his mother again and lie on the back lawn and watch the clouds sail by.

Did she ever think of him? Surely she who laughed so easily would at least smile when she remembered. Surely across this great, sad distance, that one small ugliness would have faded or at least lost itself in the not unpleasant memories she must also have of him.

He turned to the window, caught sight of his reflection there, and smiled. "Some clerk," he murmured. "Yeah, some clerk."

It was true, he differed but slightly even now from the obscure crowd behind their counters and desks. But that slight difference was decisive. He had succeeded and they had not, and anything else one might say was irrelevant. It was here, in this contract, in black and white. That vast curlicue at the bottom, if one looked at it long enough, spelled Brown. He repeated it aloud and, at the open enunciation of this name so crushingly anonymous, burst into laughter. Turning to catch one more glimpse of himself, he settled down to work.

Once he looked up in mild astonishment that he should be dealing with such enormous sums so casually. This time next year, he reflected, he would be in his own office.

He worked on until it grew dark. Then he reached for the evening paper. What was it his mother had said? That the world was coming to an end. The news had finally seeped down. He opened the paper angrily. What right had they to discuss such matters? The best thing they could do was stick to — to tables that weren't there, and leave business affairs to people who understood something of what they were talking about.

He found the financial section, read a few lines, and laughed. His father and his cronies would be disappointed tonight.

There had been a rally, and what was more, the Chairman of the National City Bank had expressed the opinion that the recent decline in the market had actually been a healthy reaction.

Alex's eyes widened. The first day of the disturbance, feeling somewhat uneasy, he had mentioned it to Williams.

And this, almost word for word, was what Williams had told him.

Lawson, of course, had a different opinion, but that was to be expected; the loss he had taken was evidently a heavy one. . . . Alex pursed his lips in disapproval. Lawson had no business meddling with things he didn't understand. The whole thing had been simply a gamble.

Last week's papers were stacked behind him. He leafed through them, staring hypnotically at the incomprehensible vastness of the figures that were involved. How could one grasp the full meaning of a loss of two, three billion dollars? He opened Tuesday's paper and a feeling of pride came over him. There might be uncertainty and fear down in the streets, but up there in the towers were cool-eyed men who had not only the resources but the courage and the faith to fight back. The losses had run into billions, but billions had shrewdly been thrown in to avert a collapse.

He refolded the paper and left the office.

A block from home he caught the faint odour of flowers in the late summer twilight. The lights from the windows fell warmly on lawns and hedges. Here and there a distant neighbour nodded as he passed. From the schoolyard at the far end of the street came the sound of children's voices. At this hour the illusion was strong that this small, secluded neighbourhood was more than an island, that the order, the cleanliness and the quiet summer murmur were not confined merely to this and two adjacent blocks where the howling chaos of the North End pressed in on them, but extended far and decently beyond.

The odour of food reached his nostrils. He walked on quickly.

"Bad day for some of our friends downtown, eh?"

Alex looked up. His neighbour Schmidt, the druggist, suddenly loomed large and white in his shirt sleeves from behind his hedge.

"Guess it was pretty bad, at that," Alex conceded. "But on the whole a healthy reaction, don't you think?"

"Healthy!" Schmidt exclaimed.

"You're not . . ." Alex faltered. "You haven't been playing . . ."

"Thank God, no! And you?"

Alex shook his head fervently.

"But healthy!" Schmidt repeated. "With two, three billion dollars gone down the drain?"

He leaned over. "Tell you something, Hunter," he said in a low voice. "Things been going too good for too long. People buying like crazy. Salesman told me today . . ."

"But for God's sake," Alex broke in. "Listen to me, Schmidt. If people like us go around talking like this, what's the public going to do? They'll stop buying, that's what. They look to us for leadership in times like these. Tomorrow your customers and mine'll come in and ask us what we think. What are you going to tell them? It's the end of the world? You'll cut your own throat."

"Well, maybe you're right," the druggist admitted. He clutched Alex's arm. "But two, three billion dollars lost! Maybe more!"

"Listen," Alex said. "Maybe you'll laugh, but I think a man should have more confidence. Sure, two, three billions have been lost, but nearly that much has been thrown back in, and the men who are willing to risk that kind of money know what they're doing, believe me."

The druggist sighed. "Anyway," he concluded, "I'm glad I'm out of it."

Alex walked on, his head bowed. A man needed faith, he thought. Even confidence was not enough. But how could one say such a thing without being laughed at? And yet if this was lacking and if there were others like Schmidt — and there probably were — how long would any of them stay in business? Their very fears would create the situation they were trying to avoid. Take his own business, for example. He trusted Brown, and the building-supply houses in turn trusted him. So far scarcely any money at all had changed hands. The whole thing was a chain of faith that extended all the way down to the twenty-one men he was employing, who knew they could trust him for their wages, and through them back and up to the merchants who had given them credit, and beyond the merchants, the distributors and the manufacturers, to the banks and to people like Brown. . . .

He had reached home. His wife was on the porch, fresh and smiling, her lips parting as she opened the screen door for him. He kissed her. For a moment she hung in his arms; then he felt her stiffen and draw away. She raised her hands to his cheeks and looked anxiously into his eyes.

Her concern moved him. "Nothing," he assured her. "Just business."

She linked her arm in his as they walked into the kitchen. "George did a wonderful job today," she said. "I don't know what I'd have done without him. After he finished the lawn, he helped me clear out the basement. . . ."

As she continued, a feeling of affection for the boy came over him. He knew why. But it was not merely because he was reminded of his own childhood. It was more than that. He was training this boy in the same way that Nagy had trained him, in the same way that later he would train his own son, and there was a sense of fulfilment in this, a feeling of continuity transcending his everyday business cares, that was deeply gratifying.

He looked across at his wife and saw her suddenly in a new light. She would be the mother not only of his son but of the man who would some day succeed him in the business he founded. They had not planned to have a child until after the establishment of his own business, until he was certain of its success. But of course it would succeed, and that small office in which he made his start would some day, together with its founder, take on in the eyes of those who came after him the aspect of a legend; they would look back with wonder and respect at his modest beginnings.

After supper, while Mary did some ironing, he sat in an old easy chair beside the ironing-board and tried to visualize the men who would succeed him.

He looked up as she began to sing to herself. His eyes closed. He breathed in the fragrance of the freshly ironed clothes. His head nodded. To succeed, then, he must have someone to succeed him. A successful man was one who had a successor. He laughed to himself. A successor. But in half fantasy, half dream, the word seemed to take on a deep and profound significance. He had only to speak it and he could accomplish what he willed.

He fell asleep and dreamed that he was in a deep canyon. And in the wall of rock stood a bronze door, which when he had spoken the word, opened to him. He walked to the threshold and gazed down at a scene of indescribable confusion. Men ran aimlessly about, trying to accomplish a thing. But none knew how. Then he cried out this word and the thing they had tried to do was done.

He opened his eyes and, not yet fully awake, heard the sound of his voice ringing in his ears. He leaped to his feet.

The kitchen was in darkness. He stumbled to the door and looked up at the sky.

"A successor," he said.

He had considered it a matter of faith, a positive act in the face of uncertainty, an assurance that what he built would endure. He had considered all things but that which now revealed itself to him. He wanted a son, but for no reason that he could think of at all. He laughed at the simplicity of this. It seemed beautifully appropriate that it should be so, with none of the dark and tortuous reasoning that usually accompanied his expression of a need.

He ran lightly down the steps. The garden lay in darkness.

"Alex, I'm here," she called.

He saw her then, holding out her arms to him as he approached. There was an elusive cool fragrance of the nicotianas in the air.

He placed his lips to her ear. She raised her head and a glad cry like a brief illumination shattered the dark stillness of the garden.

Nineteen

N OT UNTIL noon the next day as he left the office did it
occur to him that the strange mood which had possessed
him all morning had come from a dream, the same dream all
night long, infinitely unfolding itself under a multitude of
disguises.

In playful harmony with himself he repeated the two words,
so appropriately related, that had come to him the night
before. They had entered again and again into his dream.

He smiled indulgently. We'll be living in the South End by
the time he's born, he thought. He'll have English friends and
go to school with the kids who'll run this town some day. He'll
know them by their first names, the same way they'll know
him. I'll give him the best of everything. And as soon as he's
old enough he'll start working in the office. Just little after-
school jobs at first, so he won't get tired.

He saw his son sitting beside him at his desk, the two of
them in the quiet of the evening, bowed over the ledger, the
boy wide-eyed and grave, listening while his father explained.

Abruptly the image he had evoked, as though taking on a
life of its own, transformed itself. He saw his son and his wife
together at the piano. The boy seemed infinitely happier there.

Music, Alex moaned. Music! By God, I'll beat the living
daylights out of him.

I'll have to tell her. — Listen, Mary. I know you want the
best for him. But music will make him soft and he's got to be

236

hard, because out there that's the way things are. The men he'll be up against are hard.

Suddenly he recalled how sympathetically, on his last visit home, she had listened to his father's inevitable declamation. His father had given her a book to read, and promised her another. Alex saw what would happen. He would have to contend, not only with her, but with his father too. They would try to steal his son from him. He would have to win her over. — Mary, listen. Books are even worse than music. They'll fill his head with crazy ways of living and make him wonder if things couldn't be different. They'll ask questions they can't answer and confuse him and make him dissatisfied. But he's got to believe in himself and in the way things are, and be happy in his work. It's not such a crime to be ignorant. It's worse to be a failure.

A feeling of tenderness, of affectionate pride and solicitude, surged through him at the prospect of thus discussing his son's future with her, for while doing so it seemed to him that she was smiling in agreement. But now it occurred to him that she might protest.

"All right, then," he shouted. "If I hear any more I'll throw that damned piano out of the window and burn every book I find in the house."

He found himself staring into a pair of tired anonymous eyes that momentarily shone, almost gratefully, he felt, for the brief entertainment he had provided.

He flushed furiously and entered a café. I sometimes wonder what's the matter with me, he thought. What am I worrying about? All I have to do is tell her. She'll understand.

He shook his head doubtfully, but then as though cast up by some indwelling presence which his dream had stirred to life, there came over him a feeling of tranquil assurance that all would come to pass as he had planned it, that all would be well, not only in his home but in the office too, and in those distant business centres where at this very moment such a tragic upheaval was taking place.

He looked about him, as he seated himself, at the malodorous, greasy hole-in-the-wall whose only virtue lay in the understanding he had reached with its proprietor. Between twelve and twelve-fifteen, the end place at the counter nearest the window was his. The privilege of sitting here had to be paid for, but it gave him an unobstructed view of the front door of the Agency. He had only to nod, to place his order: a ham sandwich, a cup of coffee, and apple pie. For the next few minutes he bolted his food, his eyes moving mechanically from the office door to the office window.

A streetcar passed; a truck lumbered by. The pots and pans in the kitchen rattled, and the counter shook. Alex turned his head; by long-established habit he glanced absently at the shelves vibrating behind the counter, at the dust motes there, leaping up as though suddenly and collectively repelled by their dark and grimy dwelling-place. As though in a weird and frenzied ritual, they strained upward to the sad light of a yellow bulb suspended form the ceiling — until, outside, an alien light changed colour. Then the café grew still; the ritual came to an end and slowly and reluctantly its participants descended to the obscurity of the shadows from which they had come.

But not all. Miraculously a few had torn themselves loose, to soar and wheel in their new-found freedom until they were lost to sight.

Alex laughed quietly to himself. Unknowingly he nodded his head. For several years now he had observed this little ceremony and yet not once in all this time had he become fully conscious of what he had seen. But upon every such occasion, the thought formed itself that there was some hidden and joyful thing in this dance of the dust motes which one day would burst into meaning for him. It had already passed from his mind when he turned back to the window. As he did so he became aware of a sudden commotion at the far end of the counter.

He leaned back. The usual noon-hour crowd: two truck-drivers, a milkman, a few freight-yard workers. He frowned at their presumption. His face darkened as he listened. In spite of the uproar they were causing, they were evidently in agreement.

The whole thing was a frame-up. Those billions the papers were talking about weren't lost at all, they were just changing pockets. The trouble was that those double-dealing brokers and bankers had noticed there was too much money floating around. "Too much foldin' money left in our pockets after the bills is paid. They seen that. . . . You God-damned betcha they seen. They gotta eye for such things — a nose too — smell a buck a mile off. Yeah, they sure as hell been smellin' them bucks in our pockets. On'y guys gonna lose anything is you'n me. That's the way they figured her. . . . Oughta take an' run 'em outa the country."

Alex leaped to his feet. He saw himself standing before them, rending their stupid little arguments into shreds, presenting the truth to them, forcing them in spite of themselves to admit they were wrong.

But the impulse to speak died. If they were talking like this, here on Main Street, what were they doing in the heart of the North End? Probably rubbing their hands in the mistaken hope that their dismal croakings were about to be realized. They would be talking, talking, of course — not as stupidly as these animals here, but more subtly doing the same thing, spreading the alarm that the world was coming to an end.

The proprietor was expounding now. — Just a buncha crooks! Had they heard about that broker up-town? Throwing himself out of a window because his records weren't in order. Wasn't the public entitled to know about such things? Of course they were. But would newspapers print it? You could bet your last dollar . . .

Alex threw a twenty-five-cent piece on the counter and walked out. Just like Schmidt and probably dozens of others. Calling themselves business men — with not a shred of the responsibility or the dignity or the guts. My God, couldn't they see what they were doing?

As he hurried across the road he saw the office boy standing behind the window waving to him with one hand, while he held the other to his ear. Alex ran into the office and picked up the telephone.

With an effort he recalled the voice — Anderson, an office-supplies salesman. He shifted impatiently but could find no opening in the torrent of congeniality that issued from the receiver. It was obvious that Anderson wanted a loan.

Alex's jaws snapped shut suddenly. And then, "For *what*?" he shouted. "For —"

An uncontrollable fury seized him. To admit it, without any shame! This man and his kind were responsible for what was happening; meddling with things they knew nothing about. Trying to get rich quick. The men on top knew what they were doing. But how could they do it in the face of this mob of clerks, salesmen, housewives, elevator men — yes, and even business men, who should have known better? Messing around — as soon as things looked a little unfavourable, as soon as they lost a dollar or so, they became panic-stricken and in their thousands brought this calamity down — not only upon themselves but upon innocent people.

"The answer is no," he shouted into the mouthpiece. "And I hope you lose your God-damned shirt and everything you own. It serves you right. You should have stuck to horse-racing."

He hung up.

"Things must be worse than I thought," he said. The tremor in his voice frightened him. Until now, he had thought of this disturbance as occurring on some distant border of his own affairs and likely to affect him, if at all, only indirectly and in the vague future. But now for the first time — no, not the first time. It had been there all along. He had suppressed it.

All right, then, what was he afraid of? That Brown might. . . . He had only to voice it to prove to himself that his fears were preposterous. And yet if Brown . . . But Williams had assured them there was nothing to worry about. Yes, but what else could Williams have said?

I'll call Lawson first, he thought; Lawson will know. He lifted the receiver and dialled.

There was no answer.

"I'm crazy to let it worry me like this," he said, and dialled again. He heard the telephone ringing at the other end. It remained unanswered.

But this was a business line. It was the middle of the day. Lawson had four people working in the office. Alex rose to his feet.

There was something reassuring in the crowds on the street, the flow of traffic, the everyday sight, behind the shop windows, of people buying and selling. He hurried on nevertheless. He was breathless when he arrived.

The elevator man rose from his stool. "Afternoon Mr. Hunter."

Alex nodded absently. Some time passed before he realized that the elevator was still on the ground floor. He looked up sharply.

The elevator man shifted. "Ain't no use going upstairs," he said. "Ain't har'ly anybody up there."

"Is Mr. Lawson in? — For God's sake, man, what's wrong?"

"He's downstairs in the boiler room."

"The boiler room!" Alex stared at him. "Take me down," he said.

The elevator descended. The door opened. "Over there," said the elevator man, pointing.

The boiler room was only a few yards away, down a dark corridor. Alex walked in.

Below an arrangement of prisms, set in the pavement above, he saw a group of men, their features shadowed, sitting in a semicircle watching his approach with unwavering eyes.

As he stood before them, it seemed to him that they moved in a weird unison, but it was only the shadow of someone passing on the pavement overhead. The footsteps echoed loudly and were immediately followed by others.

Alex lowered his head. The men before him were sitting on stuffed burlap bags, he noticed, and upon peering more closely he saw that these were filled to overflowing with discarded invoices and letters, soiled with damp and dust, and faded at the edges. A violent shudder went through him. It was as though the remains of an ancient, long-forgotten way of life lay mouldering here, consigned to this forlorn oblivion by the world above that had long since passed it by.

The room darkened again, the shadows moved slowly over the prisms, the dirty twilight deepened, and in the blessed dark denial of reality the fear within him stilled and in its place there crept a brief jubilation that he had resisted the temptation these men had yielded to.

When the room brightened, he noticed that a bottle had appeared. It passed silently from hand to hand. Alex saw Lawson and faltered as he moved toward him, filled with sudden pity at the sight of his haggard features. Lawson blinked as he approached, and waved him away.

"Jim, it's me. It's gonna be all right. Listen, Jim." He seized Lawson's hand and gripped it in his own, and found himself unable to continue.

"Smug bastard, aincha?" Lawson was looking directly at him. "Too God-damned smart to take a little flyer with the boys."

He wiped his lips with the back of his hand, surveying Alex the while with a bleary-eyed bewilderment that gave way suddenly to a look of such open malice that Alex drew still further from him.

"Yah," Lawson said. "Too smart . . ." He looked at Alex slyly. Suddenly he burst into loud laughter. "'At's the best yet," he cried, and, turning to his neighbour, pointed to Alex and continued weekly, "Guy thinks he's smart. Too smart to take a little flyer. Works for Brown."

The man beside him turned slowly. "For Brown," he repeated, and shaking his head, looked up with an expression of such infinite compassion on his face that for a moment Alex grasped Lawson's shoulder to support himself.

Lawson tore his hand away. "You smug bastard," he shouted. "You gonna lose your pants anyway. Brown closed his doors an hour ago."

Alex heard him laughing as he fled. His laughter rang in the furthermost corner of the room, and seemed to lie in wait for him in the empty corridor beyond; long after he had stopped knocking and ringing at the elevator door and had run upstairs he could still hear it.

He pressed on, staring desperately into the faces of people passing by for evidence of panic, for a reflection of the disaster he feared had taken place. If it had . . . But it's not true. It can't be true. It's a joke Lawson played. Suddenly through his fear, a pathetic, a childish exultation rose in him and was gone.

He was drunk and mad at me, he thought, but he never called me a foreigner. . . . He ran across the street. Tonight he'll phone me and say he's sorry.

It couldn't happen. If it did, I'm finished. I'm innocent, even he had to admit I'm innocent. Doesn't that count? But they'll have their jobs left and I'll have nothing. It's not fair. . . .

He stopped and looked at Brown's name cut deep in the granite above him. In a few minutes I'll know, he thought; and now nothing was left but to enter, to open the door and press on in spite of the loud threatening crowd in the vast hall, through the feel and odour and taste of fear, past the two policemen, to the real-estate division, to stand there while the tumult faded and the last desperate barrier he had erected gave way and the world was only a cold wet doorknob in his hand.

The door opened and Williams appeared. He sped by, turned, and came back. He said something, and when he was finished there was nothing left. Williams' hand fell briefly on his shoulder and then he was gone.

If only he had not involved himself so deeply! If only . . .

For God's sake, he rebuked himself. That doesn't matter now. Can't you understand? You're finished if you don't start thinking.

I need help, he thought. But who could help him now? His aunt? He knew better than to ask her. Had the Agency been his, or the houses he had built remained on the Agency's books, he might have managed. But the titles were in her name.

He considered her lawyer, Kesler; and many business acquaintances. He considered mortgaging Kostanuik's home; it was not enough. If Nagy . . .

At the thought of Nagy he hurried on. Nagy, even if he refused to help him, might at least be able to tell him what to do. Kynanski, the old man's lawyer, would have his address.

A quarter of an hour later he walked into Kynanski's office.

Kynanski remained seated as he entered. "An honour," he said, and waved him to a chair. "What can I do for you?"

"I was thinking of going to visit the old man," Alex said, "I wondered if you had his address."

"His address? Certainly. But it won't do you much good. He's been dead these past two months."

"Dead!" Alex cried.

Kynanski reached for a blueprint that lay across his bookcase and unrolled it. "Take a look at this," he said. "Nagy's pleasure-dome. Stately, eh?"

"A church," Alex shrieked. "My God! He's left all that money to build a church."

Kynanski raised his eyebrows. "A church on the shore of the Alph? Is it possible," he asked, "that you could have spent so many years with the late lamented and still not have understood him?"

Alex covered his face with his hands.

"This, my friend," Kynanski continued, "is a cemetery piece, a mausoleum. Solid marble, every inch of it. To what period would you say this little monstrosity belongs?"

He held out his cigarette case. "Restrain your grief," he said. "There, that's better."

"Kynanski," Alex asked softly. "Who's building it?"

Kynanski lowered his cigarette. As the smoke issued from his mouth, he drew it back into his nostrils.

"I am," he said.

"How — how much did he leave to build it with?"

Kynanski winked solemnly. "Seventy-two thousand dollars," he said.

Alex clutched his arm.

"Kynanski," he pleaded. "You haven't got a contractor. Let me build it for you. I'll be frank with you. I need the job.

I need it bad. Kynanski, listen to me. We understand each other. I'll do it cheap, dirt cheap. We'll use marble facing on concrete. I know where we can get those stone birds and angels for nearly nothing. For old time's sake, Kynanski! We've known each other for a long time —"

He stopped at the cool smile on Kynanski's face.

"Alex. You don't seem to understand," he said. "This is the work of a lifetime; I'm devoting the rest of my life to this job. Would you be prepared to do that?"

Twenty

ALEX SAT by the window, rolling himself a cigarette, pinching off the ends, and gathering the tobacco shreds which had fallen on the ledge. He struck a match and looked expectantly up and down the silent, empty street. From somewhere in the North End, across the tracks, came the sound of church bells. Every Sunday at this hour he heard them, always the same sad clarity, tolling the end of yet another week. The match flamed and burned down. He struck another and lit his cigarette.

Across the way his neighbour sat in his window in an undershirt that bore the greasy imprint of his suspenders. He sat there, fat and complacent, assiduously picking his teeth, holding the toothpick out an arm's length now and again to examine what he had extracted. A fool, but the only man in the block who had a job. It was depressing to think of him.

Alex got up. Tomorrow there would at least be something to do. He could make the rounds again looking for a job. He sat down at the kitchen table and leafed through the newspaper. It contained the usual listings: men wanted to sell magazine subscriptions, kitchen utensils; a boy with a bicycle; the same barber-college ads.

He moved restlessly through the two rooms of the dwelling. Downstairs a radio blared. The windows rattled.

He returned to the kitchen. It was dirty with an ancient grime that nothing could remove. The sight and smell of it was sickeningly familiar. This was what he was going to leave behind him. This was where the great dreams led. It seemed impossible, he thought, that they had already lived here for two years. His son had been born here — here in this —

As he walked out he saw himself in the mirror on the cupboard door. Mary would be back in an hour or so.

"I'd better shave," he said, and opening the cupboard for his razor found himself looking directly into the cold quick eyes of a long-snouted rat. It was fat and sleek. Its flanks suddenly twitched.

He slammed the door shut. I'll have to get a rat-trap, he thought. But the relief office paid only in coupons, and the store he dealt with didn't stock them. He would have to apply for one at the relief office. He foresaw what would happen. First the clerk at the counter, with his supercilious grin. The twelve-dollar-a-week bastard! What did he have to grin about? Then the second clerk, passing him on eventually to the third, the senior one. Weeks would pass.

"We can't sleep any more because they're crawling around the bedroom," he said.

As though they cared whether he slept or not.

"We can't even keep food around," he continued.

But did they have so much food they could afford to keep it lying around?

"Listen," he said, and his voice rose. "We can't even leave the kid alone any more. Yesterday my wife went to see what he was crying about and found a rat sitting on his chest."

That'll get the sons-of-bitches, he thought. "You understand?" he shouted, and grabbed the chief clerk by the lapels. "I want a rat-trap and by God I'm gonna get one."

He shook him so that his teeth rattled. "I'll write to the papers about this," he threatened. "I'll call the mayor. God damn it, all I'm asking for is a rat-trap. It's not enough my wife and kid can't get enough to eat, any more. It's not bad enough you lock us up in this lousy hole. Now you won't even give us a rat-trap. I won't stand for it, I tell you." He drew himself erect. "Maybe you think you're just dealing with another tramp. You're mistaken, let me tell you. You're dealing with a man who owned his own business once. I have influential friends. . . . I'll get that rat-trap," he yelled, "or I'll tear this whole damn dump apart."

He stopped abruptly, gazed at himself in the mirror, and pressed his hands to his face. What was the matter with him?

He felt the stubble of his beard. He remembered he was going to shave, and raised his hand to the cupboard door. His hand hung there. He wet his lips, tore the door open, and jerked his head aside.

The rat landed on his shoulder, squealed, and ran down his back. He heard it drop to the floor, saw it scurrying into the next room. He stood there shaking, still feeling the cold snout where it had brushed against his cheek.

"I'll kill him," he shouted.

From the landing he got a small shovel and a broom. He walked softly into the bedroom, stuffed his jacket and a sweater in the crack under the door, and looked around him cautiously; under the crib, behind the clothes basket and the chest of drawers, and then under the bed. In the corner against the baseboard, two gleaming eyes looked alertly into his. It was up on its hind legs squealing.

He swore at it in a thick stream of obscenity. The shovel was in his right hand, in his left the broom which he now thrust into the corner.

"Blind him," he shouted. "Blind the son-of-a-bitch! Smash him!"

A grey streak lanced toward him.

Alex leaped to his feet. "I'll smash your guts out," he yelled, and suddenly it was on the broom handle. He swung the shovel and caught it with a blow that sent wave upon wave of sheer ecstasy surging through him. His mouth watered.

The rat struck the wall and dropped. It lay twisted on the floor, its head bent back as though watching to see what he would do. He raised the shovel and brought it down flat. There was a squeal. He raised the shovel and brought it down again and again until the thing on the floor was a pulp.

He wiped his forehead, dropped into a chair, and sat looking at it. When he got up his knees shook so that he could scarcely stand. He shovelled the thing that was on the floor on to a newspaper. Then he washed the floor where it had been and carried it downstairs to the garbage heap.

He recalled that while it was under the bed it had crossed its forelegs as though in prayer. The thought of returning to the room where he had killed it filled him with sudden abhorrence.

"I shouldn't have done that," he said, and crossed the back yard to the railway embankment beside the fruit sheds.

He lay down in his accustomed place in the weeds and looked into the shadowed undergrowth. The sun was warm on his body. An ant scurried by, full of enterprise and purpose. He watched it enviously. Everything and everyone, it seemed to him, had something to do, had some place in the scheme of things; only he was idle and alone and unrelated to the world around him — unrelated except through the relief office, he thought bitterly.

He knew this was untrue, that there were thousands such as he, but singling himself out in this way and tormenting himself with the thought of all those who were occupied gave him pleasure.

Even his father had managed to keep his business going — if one could call it a business. Distant friends and acquaintances who were working passed through his mind. Some of the men he had met through Lawson, and Lawson himself who, although on a reduced scale, was still doing sufficient business to stay open. Kostanuik, working at twenty-five cents an hour but at least keeping himself and his wife alive.

Even that clodhopper across the street had found himself a job, while he . . . For two and a half years now he had been out of work.

A feeling of such desperate hopelessness came over him that tears came into his eyes. He turned and saw a small brown beetle making its way along a leaf. The leaf gave way and the beetle fell to the ground, dropping on its back and waving its legs frantically. He watched it, absently at first, then with growing interest and at last with compassion, with a clear and terrible understanding of its plight. A strange feeling came over him. It seemed to him that if he helped it to get to its feet again, he too would somehow be helped. He scoffed at the feeling but obeyed its injunction nevertheless. It took but a flick of his finger.

The thought of being compensated for what he had done extended itself. He wondered whether he had forfeited his reward by killing that other animal. But if a reward were possible, by whom would it be granted? Was there a presence interested enough? Perhaps this being, if it did exist, acted upon motives as inexplicable and capricious as his own. Maybe that explained what had happened to him. Maybe it was only a bigger finger, raised not to help but to harm, flicked unwittingly or out of boredom or curiosity.

He shook his head. It would help if one could believe, he thought, or fool oneself into believing, the way his uncle did.

But at the thought of his uncle, a thin smile came to his lips. His uncle had come to terms with a god who seemed unusually light-hearted, almost frivolous. And yet with his aid he had somehow gathered the scattered remains of his life and made a fresh beginning. It was good to think of him. His old, familiar gusto, his flair for living, had returned, had in fact reappeared within a few months after he had left his wife. It was more sobering to think that he had also found himself a job — in a neighbourhood theatre. Assistant manager, he called himself. He was also the caretaker.

He remembered the last night he had seen him, standing in the subdued light of the lobby, dressed in a braided uniform, taking tickets. His moustache covered the worst of his scars. The rest were barely visible. He joked and laughed, and the customers coming in laughed too, perhaps at his accent, perhaps at his gestures; but ah, my God, the naïve, loud splendour of him as he stood there, his eyes flashing, his great voice booming, the flanges of his nostrils quivering, and all in passionate enjoyment of what? Merely of living, of being with people and talking to them.

Afterwards, he had accompanied him home, to his basement room a block or so from the theatre.

"I want you to meet somebody," Onkel Janos said.

They paused for a moment on the walk, gazing into the

window on whose ledge, in a milk bottle, stood a spray of late lilac. Beyond it, intermittently as the curtains fluttered, Alex saw a worn rug, a bed with a patchwork quilt, a card-table with a chequered tablecloth on it. A woman sat there, a slender dark-eyed woman smiling to herself as she toyed with a wine glass.

Alex faltered as his uncle moved on. Onkel Janos turned. "You disapprove?" he asked.

"No. But not tonight. Some other time." His voice was heavy with envy and longing for the friendly warmth of that basement room, for the untroubled way of life it represented, carefree and happy and yet secure.

"You don't think I have the right?" his uncle asked, grabbing him by the arm. "For three months I lived in that room alone. You know what that means? Every night fighting with myself, like Jacob with the Angel. To go back to that unhappy old woman or to stay here and try to make a new life for myself.

"For three months alone, my soul in anguish. Then one night in that dark room I said to myself: 'Is sin such an ugly word for what you have done?' And when I said this I understood. I fell on my knees and cried like a baby. Everything became clear to me.

"Don't you see?" he cried. "She released me with God's aid when she disfigured me. You understand? Only through suffering could I pay for what I had done and deserve the right to be a man again. And my suffering was over. She freed me. I bear my atonement on my face and because of this I am whole again."

He looked up. "They have made God too sober," he said reflectively. "I am sure on the eighth day He laughed. And why not? He could see what we were going to do to Him."

"Ach!" He laughed and clapped Alex on the shoulder. "Cheer up, my boy. God gives you the right to laugh." He paused. "You know," he continued, "I must confess that in those three months I didn't have enough ardour in my loins to take the chill off a flea." He burst into laughter again.

Alex looked at him in consternation. Had he really said that? How was it possible for him to say such a thing?

"Well." His uncle held out his hand. "Come and see us soon," he said.

Alex turned. The weeds around him swam into view. "With God's aid," he repeated. Very convenient. And yet supposing it were true? "You better watch yourself," he snorted, "or you'll turn into a regular holy roller."

He raised himself and looked thoughtfully at the weeds yellowing in the sun, and there rose before him the high, lush weeds in the red fence and those in the lanes off Henry Avenue; the swaying stalks on the river bank; and unexpectedly an image he tried too late to obliterate: the weeds in the garden of Eric's home.

He should never have gone back. But he had been selling baskets that day and, tired and depressed, had found himself only a few blocks away. He saw it again, empty and deserted, its windows like dark empty eyes through which the spirit had fled, gaping with the vacancy of death; the garden in the back choked with weeds grown strong and tall with the life they drew from the flowers rotting below.

He had returned to find peace, to recapture the untroubled flow of life he had known here. Nothing came of his attempts to bring it back. He remembered, but without any feeling. It didn't matter, he told himself.

He heard the church bells again. That stain on the front-room floor would be dry by now, he thought, and got up and returned home to his place by the window.

Across the way his neighbour had started on his first bottle of beer. His wife had joined him. They would sit there drinking until bed-time. Their lights would stay on all night. Their blinds were never drawn. He looked away in disgust.

The Androychuks' radio downstairs was silent now. They were quarrelling.

The rays of the setting sun fell in warm gold on the mouldering houses. And up and down the street, on benches and upturned boxes, on curbstones and at other windows sat men like himself, waiting. He saw himself growing old and still believing that some distant tomorrow would release him from this window where he sat as though transfixed between the living and the dead.

Sometime next week he would have to go out and sell a few more of those wickerwork baskets. He would have to sell at least two, he thought, and dreamed of how in later life he would look back to that eventful morning on which he had sold them, to the eighty cents he had earned, which paid for the stationery and stamps and newspapers that enabled him to find a job.

He stood before a desk on the other side of which a white-haired old man nodded sympathetically. He had evoked the image of this man so often and from a need so deep that he had scarcely to speak more than a few words and the old man was on his feet holding out his hand to him to signify that he had been given the job.

He could see it so clearly, feel the urgency and the onrush of business affairs, hear the typewriters outside his office and the telephone ringing, see the work on his desk.

Now he was returning home with the news. Mary would be in the kitchen feeding the baby. No word would pass between them. She would understand, and everything would be as it had been.

He sat back and closed his eyes and, for as long as he was able, held the conviction that it was true. All he wanted was a job. Was that too much to ask for?

The front stairs creaked. Mary was back? He opened the door, and his heart sank. His parents and his brother were on the landing, smiling as though they were uncertain of their reception. They were all carrying parcels.

This was what he had become then, an object of their charity. He saw himself as he must appear to them. He saw the expression in their eyes — not only of charity but of pity.

His mother turned her cheek to him. He kissed her.

"So you won't come to us, we must come to you," she said.

"Mohammed and the mountain," Rudolph grinned.

His father shifted his parcel. Alex shook hands with him solemnly.

"Come in," he said. "I'm sorry Mary's not at home. She's at her mother's."

When they had filed past him into the bedroom, he ran into the kitchen for chairs. His mother followed him.

"I brought you some sauerkraut," she began. "We made too much last year."

How could she have changed so, he wondered, her face so familiar and yet so sadly altered.

She moved about, from the table to the window, and back to the table again, avoiding his eyes.

So there was a purpose in this visit. The effort she was making to disguise her feelings was transparent. She had never been able to dissimulate or to hold back what was on her mind.

He nodded as she closed the door.

"It's not right you don't come to us, Alex," she said. "We worry about you. How is he living? we ask. How is the baby; and his wife? Is everything awright with them?"

"We're all right, Ma."

"Please to listen to me, Alex. Your father and me talked. We want to see our grandchild sometimes and talk to our son. Don't be angry. We want you and your family should come to live with us — on'y so we should see you once in a while."

The anxious look had given way to a smile. The strangeness had gone from her face. Her eyes were still the same, he thought, still young, her affection for him rising from their sad depths. She was taking his silence for agreement. She would never know how she had hurt him.

He shook his head. "I couldn't do that," he said. "Don't you understand, Ma? Tell Pa I said thanks."

"But Alex!"

"It's no use, Ma."

"But it's not like we're strangers, Alex. Your own flesh and blood. To make a liddle visit with your family. It's such a terrible thing?"

She held out her hand to him. "Do this for me," she pleaded. "If not for you and your wife, then for the baby."

"I can't talk about it any more, Ma." He opened the door.

Rudolph was in the centre of the room rolling himself a cigarette, his father on the bed thumbing a book. Their eyes searched his, then shifted to his mother who had come in behind him. He sensed that she was shaking her head.

Rudolph looked disappointed. What his father felt, it was difficult to guess. His moustache, Alex noticed, had turned grey; otherwise he was the same, giving one the impression that he was present and yet not present, that he lent himself reluctantly and with an effort of will to what was happening around him.

Alex arranged the chairs. They seated themselves and looked at one another in a silence that swelled and pulsed, ringing in his ears like the sound of their voices out of his childhood, as strange and distant as they themselves had become.

"You know something, Alex?" His brother drew himself upright and struck a mock-heroic pose. What he was trying to do was pathetically obvious.

"I'm working with Pa," Rudolph announced. "Clocks and watches repaired. I take 'em apart. Pa puts 'em together again. Eh, Pa?"

His father nodded indulgently.

"You should work as much as you talk," his mother sighed.

"Ah, Ma. How can Pa tell me if we don't talk?"

A familiar feeling this — to be shut out of their lives. And yet had he not brought it upon himself? Perhaps he had. But sometimes it seemed to him that the choice had been made without his consent.

They had grown silent again. They were waiting for him to speak.

"It sure is good to see you all again," he said. "You look swell."

His mother raised her handkerchief to her eyes. "You look like a ghost," she said. "Worrying yourself to pieces. Is it such a disgrace you haven't got a job? Millions of people are the same."

"Ma's right, Alex," Rudolph interrupted. "Why don't you

just take it easy? Things aren't normal. It isn't your fault the Agency ..."

"No? Then whose fault is it? Sunspots maybe, Jews, Eastern bankers, freight rates? I've heard 'em all. Things won't go back to normal until buyers and sellers — " He stopped abruptly. They had had an argument about this the last time he had visited them and he had no desire to get into another. But his father was already waving his pipe at him.

"Buyers and sellers," he began. "The new gods. An abomination."

Alex controlled himself with difficulty. "And what's wrong with buying and selling?"

"Nothing," his father answered in German. "In its place, nothing at all. A simple and necessary thing. But only a small thing in a man's life — not his whole existence — not an end in itself — not a way of life or a source of one's beliefs. And this is what it has become. A tragic joke, to make a religion of it."

His voice rose in anger. "Day and night one is deafened with the shriek of this new priesthood. Only one word on their lips: Buy! Nothing else is sacred to them. A sad miracle they would perform; to turn man into an animal with only a mouth to fill. And every decent thing in life smirched to satisfy the appetite of this animal. And all this done, they tell us, with the noblest motives. Peddling is their highest aspiration.

"Don't you see?" he cried. "This is spiritual death. Where is there room here for what is good and beautiful, for time to re-formulate the eternal questions, for study of man's conduct? A savage who worships a tree lives a richer life."

There was more, but Alex no longer heard it. The same old argument, he thought wearily. His father was simply carrying on where he had left off last time.

In the end, he reflected, it came back to only one thing. Both buyers and sellers had lost faith, and until that faith returned the crisis would continue.

This way of life his father condemned had taken him to the very threshold of everything he had hoped to achieve. But how could he explain, how tell his father that without it there was nothing left to him? He had started with nothing at all but the belief that this could be accomplished, and if he had not succeeded the fault lay with him and not with what he believed in.

His father sat back and lit his pipe.

"I'll be all right," Alex said. "There's nothing wrong with me a job won't fix. As a matter of fact I've got a good lead I'll be following up tomorrow."

He recalled too late that he had given them this same assurance, and in almost identical terms, the last time he had seen them. Yet his mother's face brightened at his words. She turned with an expression of triumphant vindication to his father and from the look that passed between them he felt certain that they had recently discussed his chances of getting a job. His father had probably taken the position that he would be unsuccessful, but whether that barely perceptible movement of his shoulders was a concession that he might have been wrong, or whether it was an indication that he remembered, it was not possible to say.

Alex glanced at his brother, on whose cheeks the colour ebbed and flowed. Rudolph remembered, then. Alex lowered his head. That his brother should blush for him!

"That's wonderful, Alex," his mother exclaimed. "An office job? Why didn't you tell us?"

"It's still too early to talk about it, Ma."

She returned to her knitting. He watched her needles cross and thrust, and smiled sadly to himself. He had disappointed her. He wondered why he had always denied her the happiness of acknowledging her affection. As far back as he could remember they had been strangers. When they came together it was to ally themselves on some domestic issue or other against his father, and when the issue was settled they separated and were strangers again.

She looked more familiar now. To see her like this, with her lips faintly moving, carried him back. He had just returned from school. He could hear the kitchen door banging behind him. He felt a sudden desire to throw himself on his knees before her and bury his head in her lap.

"Alex. Your mother has already spoken to you about coming . . ."

"Yes, Pa." Couldn't they see that they weren't helping at all? He was tired. All he wanted was to be left alone.

He turned to the window and, to his heartfelt relief, saw Mary on the pavement below, pushing the baby-carriage to the front steps. He waved to her.

"I'll just be gone a minute," he said. "Mary's here."

He ran downstairs.

She stood on the walk smiling, not at him, he realized, but in recollection, as though she were still enwrapped in her music, as though she had veiled herself against her return. He resented it, and yet he was glad that for at least one afternoon a week she should be able to get out of the house and back to her piano. She had cried like a child when they took it away. It had been impossible to get it into the house, since both the stairway and the window were too narrow. Unfortunately, he had been unable to find any other place to live. The rent here was only six dollars a month.

"How's everything at home?" he asked.

"Oh, all right."

He kissed her, then told her that his family was upstairs. Her hands fell to her sides. She surveyed him angrily.

"Just look at you," she cried. "What will they think of me? I left a clean shirt for you on the bed. You said you'd shave. And last night I pressed your grey pants for you."

She paused. "We'll need coffee," she said. "I'll take baby upstairs and you go to the store."

The foot of the carriage, he noticed as he left her, was filled with bundles wrapped in tea-towels.

When he returned, it was to find them all in the bedroom, clucking and cooing at the baby. No one paid any attention to him. On the kitchen table he found a clean shirt laid out.

After he had shaved and changed, he stood by the window for a while. The view of the fruit sheds, however, bleak and dismal and overwhelmingly real, threatened to destroy the satisfaction he was deriving from his misery. He returned to the bedroom where he found his father dandling the baby on his knee.

"A fine boy, Alex," he exclaimed. "Ach. Hoho!"

He rocked with laughter. The baby had caught his moustache.

In spite of himself, Alex smiled.

"Pull, pull," his father continued. "Yes, pull, little man. How else can you learn? Ach, what a wonderful world awaits you!"

He turned to Alex again. "What do you think, Alex? They say he looks like . . ."

"Like Onkel Janos," Rudolph broke in. "He's got the same nose."

A shriek of disagreement rose from the two women, a peal of laughter from his father.

"Well, Alex?"

"I think he just looks like himself," Alex murmured.

"A sensible answer." His father nodded approvingly. "Obviously this child is unique. You think I'm prejudiced?"

He looked up at them and smiled. "But every child is unique. Therein lies the promise and the wonder. Ah, what these eyes will see! He will have thoughts no man ever had before."

Alex looked on proudly. It was good to see them together and happy like this. If only he could join them, sit there on the floor beside his brother and Mary, and laugh — just forget everything and laugh. He remained where he was, silent and aloof, yet smiling at his father's delight, his mother's final successful attempt to lure the child from him.

The time passed quickly and more pleasantly than he had expected. They left shortly after they had had coffee.

On the porch, his father drew him aside.

"You can see how much it would mean to your mother to have you with us," he said quietly. "Why don't you think about it, Alex? Don't let pride stand in your way. No man is independent. You'd make your mother very happy, my boy, and me too — I admit it freely."

For some minutes Alex could not bring himself to speak. How long ago it seemed since his father had spoken to him in this tone! It required so little effort to recall, it might have been only yesterday that he had been walking down Henry Avenue with him. It had never occurred to him then that the words he so resentfully dismissed had been kindly and patiently spoken.

He thought of his own son. And suddenly he recalled the great future which his father had once planned for him and, standing there, he understood for the first time how deeply disappointed his father must have been. And yet not a word of this had ever passed his lips. Or ever would.

"I'm sorry, Pa, I can't."

But he smiled, and his father looking at him, with uncertainty at first, then with eyes brightening, paused as he turned to go and smiled too, as Alex had not seen him smile since he was a boy.

When his father had gone, Alex went upstairs and in his accustomed place sat down with his son on his knee and stared out of the window.

He shifted the child on his lap and, as he did so, his son raised his head and suddenly it was as though Alex were seeing him for the first time. He looked into his eyes, so widely and innocently open to his gaze that it shamed him to look so deeply into another human being. Yet he was filled too with a gladness such as he had rarely known, because in those mild depths, it seemed to him, were all those things, miraculously alive, which he had suppressed in himself; stifled for the sake of what he had almost felt within his grasp, out there, over his son's head, out and beyond in the grey desolation.

Tears came to his eyes. He wiped them away and looked at his son and smiled and wept.

Afterword

BY NEIL BISSOONDATH

The great immigrant dream is just an unwary step or two away from the worst immigrant nightmare.

An integral part of the dream, as vital as material success, is acceptance by the society into which the immigrant has inserted himself: the urge to belong to a family while retaining individuality, the need to make one's personal way through an accepted and accepting framework. The nightmare is when that family takes over, absorbing, smothering: assimilation into the group to the point of effacement.

Swallowed whole.

Mouths are everywhere in John Marlyn's *Under the Ribs of Death*, and they are almost always striking. At Mary's birthday party, for instance, Mrs. Kostanuik screams when her "liddle walnut table" is accidentally smashed, her mouth "a black anguished hole." Later, as Mr. Crawford (whose "full-fleshed red lips" make Sandor shiver) prays with his hand heavy on Sandor's head, Sandor "stared at his vest that gaped where a button was missing – the dark aperture opening and closing to the rise and fall of his laboured breath, a sad, black mouth. . . . " Two deep furrows run vertically down Fraulein Kleinholtz's chin, the space between the furrows reminding Sandor of "a trap door, hinged at the bottom and likely to spring open at any moment to expose a gullet that would swallow him wholly." Later, after the stock market collapse, Sandor (now Alex) finds Lawson drinking in the boiler room, swallowed as it were by the building in which he had made his lost fortune.

In the novel, as in life, mouths sting with their words and delight with their smiles. They enrage, embarrass, scare. They offer passion and threat, they welcome and they devour. Sandor wants Mrs. Creighton "to smile at him the way she was now smiling at her son, to accept him. . . . " When Sandor/Alex is drunkenly told off by Lawson, he takes comfort from the fact that "he never called me a foreigner. . . . " Even as his business evaporates, this urge to belong, to be accepted, offers a curious but vital comfort.

Displacement, the absence of belonging and the search for it, is a major feature of the twentieth century. And Canada, haven to so many, is inevitably a major part of that story. It is curious to what extent our country has been formed from the flotsam and jetsam of upheaval, and yet how little the experiences of the displaced have shaped the development of the country. It is as if the social cataclysms that have sent us so many of our citizens have failed to inform us, have led instead to a curious narrowing of vision. Not, then, a grand political sophistication, but the house, the car, the clothes, the material comfort. It is as if, instead of taking a deep breath of the twentieth century, we have taken but a timid little puff at it before turning our backs on its horrors.

Maybe, in part, it's that we have been formed by people whose past seems devoid of possibility. Sandor's contempt for his father's philosophical obsessions comes from his sense that a collapsed past can lead to what he perceives to be endless babble, an ephemeral prison of the mind. We seem, like Sandor, wary of the past, contemptuous of it, and are eager to embrace only the possibilities of the future. It is an emotionally profound, if intellectually superficial, response to the travails of the century. It is what makes us a country younger than our years, unsure of ourselves – "Who are we?" we keep on asking, even though the answer is self-evident – and seeking ourselves in the opinions of others.

In Sandor Hunyadi, we have not just an immigrant determined to succeed but also someone fleeing the stereotype that is the immigrant's lot – the stereotype which our policy of multiculturalism would later seek to institutionalize. It is important to realize, though, that Sandor does not reject his Hungarian heritage; his delight in the party for Onkel Janos – the food, the drink, the dance, the music by the Nemeth twins with their "pink tongues flickering in the dark caverns of their mouths" – makes that clear. Sandor simply recognizes that his parents' past is not – indeed, *cannot* be – his own. If he changes his name, it is because he recognizes the imperatives of his situation and looks not to the past but to the future, informed but unhindered by his knowledge of what has come before. "Alex Hunter" may be a radical step, but it is not terribly unusual. It merely signals the depth of his wish to belong.

So the question – and it is an open one – remains: Is Sandor devoured by his desires and the seductions of the society he longs to fit into? Is the future he seeks for himself the immigrant dream or the immigrant nightmare unrecognized in his headstrong rush?

The answer is equivocal: Yes and no – and in that is the best answer to immigrant success. For not to be swallowed at all is to remain marginalized; and to be swallowed completely is to disappear. But it is not a truth that belongs solely to the immigrant; and, in this, *Under the Ribs of Death* firmly establishes itself as a vital and enduring work, asking questions and exploring issues that are as old as humankind – and as new as tomorrow morning.

BY JOHN MARLYN

FICTION
Under the Ribs of Death (1957)
Putzi, I Love You, You Little Square (1981)